NIGHT HUNT

by
Mara Rostov

G. P. PUTNAM'S SONS
New York

Library of Congress Cataloging in Publication Data

Rostov, Mara.
  Night hunt.
  I. Title.
PZ4.R839Ni 1979   [PS3568.08493]   813'.5'4   78-24034
ISBN 0-399-12311-3

To Lieutenant Colonel Robert S. Barmettler, USAF, 18613A (Ret.), who outran the hunters, thereby giving me the idea for the story, I wish to make grateful acknowledgment.

To my brother, Robbie.

Nothing except a battle lost can be half so melancholy as a battle won.

—Duke of Wellington

NIGHT HUNT

1

The General in charge of the briefing listened to Dietrich question the survival teams for a while and then daydreamed himself back to the preceding afternoon's golf game. It was a stupid sport. He did not believe in it; perhaps he would just quietly quit playing. And it was humiliating— having to pretend that he didn't see that surreptitiously grinning caddy, when all along he wanted to wrap a club around his neck. That would certainly improve his smirk.

He gazed away toward the next green and was startled by the filled auditorium before him, realizing abruptly that the men were leaning forward slightly, listening with rapt and profound attention. He looked over his shoulder at the rows of men seated on folding chairs on the stage with him. Downstage right, Dietrich had stopped talking altogether. The German's expression had changed; his subtle disciplined arrogance with which the General was familiar had vanished and his face was as blank as a ham except for the scar—a zigzag of lightning running from above the left eyebrow over the bridge of his nose and fading into the lines under his right eye. The General had always been interested in the scar but thought it bad taste to ask about it since it was probably from the war, even though the war was seventeen years behind them and the Germans were part of the Western Allied Team. Dietrich was a good man; in the U.S. Army, he would have progressed beyond a leaf Colonel's rank even as young as he was. The General estimated Dietrich to be about forty, give or take a couple of years.

The silence in the auditorium continued. What the hell was holding things up? The General tried to catch Dietrich's eye. Was the briefing over? He saw the German Colonel study a sheet of paper. "Would you repeat your name, please?"

Across the stage from the General, an American with a black 1890's mustache was facing Dietrich.

"Knight."

Dietrich seemed to hesitate uncertainly. The General, watching, understood the man's indecision. Colonel Knight was one of those outrages the peacetime army had to put up with because he had made something of a name for himself in the war when he was just a kid. If it were up to the General, he'd have Knight mustered out in short order, him and that insufferable comedian's prop mustache. The mustache was not the only affront; it was no secret that Knight had his uniforms custom-made in Wiesbaden. He smoked half-dollar cigars in a holder, and only this last year acquired a vintage Rolls convertible in which he cruised around the base as though he were sailing.

The General stared at him now with stern envious disapproval. How the devil did Knight get in on this? Just like him to show off and volunteer, when he must have known NATO wanted younger, inexperienced men for the games. Well, maybe it would turn out all right. Dietrich obviously hated

12

him on sight, as any good crackerjack officer would, and this might just be the thing to get Knight's ass in the wringer.

"Colonel Knight, your résumé."

"With SAC. Survival exercises in the Sierra Nevadas of California and once in the desert in New Mexico."

"And supplies?"

"The usual, a knife, something of a map, a compass, flashlight, a diet of porcupine."

"Porkpine?"

"*Stachelschwein.*"

"Ah . . . yes. How many days?"

"Five to seven."

"And how soon were you caught?"

"I wasn't caught."

"Never?"

"No."

"You realize that this will not be in primitive areas only. You will be facing both large and small towns in an enemy country over which you have been shot down. Of course, there are some mountains and farms and the Rhine, but all this area is dense with people and you will be obliged to remain in uniform or you would theoretically be shot as a spy. That is all part of the rules.

"Everyone will be looking for you, not only the seven hundred members of the hunter-capture groups you see here, but also the local police, the parks and forestry people; and for that matter the whole German Army will keep its eye open for the survival teams, and except for a few partisans, you will face a hostile population. I can assure you, the public, which is ignorant of these games, would find it strange to see a downed unidentifiable airman at their doors, so you can expect no aid there. In fact, quite the opposite, as you will discover.

"Then, of course, there are the laws. By the rules of these games, you cannot break the laws. The theft of a vehicle or the illegal entry of a home ... anything of this nature, would mean disqualification."

The General thought that the note of triumph in Dietrich's voice was a bit much, as though Knight had already been caught. In fact, from the odds, it did sound pretty much like a foregone conclusion.

"So there you have it. One hundred miles in ten days, from Wiesbaden to Aachen. You will have no money and you must forage off the land. The hunter-capture teams of three or four men will come in jeeps; the local police, of course, have their motorcycles, but you, Colonel, will walk."

"I don't mind."

There was the slightest motion in the audience as though the seven hundred men making up the hunter-capture groups as well as the eighty-four members of the two-man survival teams on the stage had all suddenly held their breath at the very same time.

"I assure you, Colonel," began Dietrich with deliberate slowness, "you cannot count on luck this time."

"I have never counted on luck."

Dietrich smiled. "Very commendable, but you will be caught."

"No, I won't be caught." Knight spoke with stunning casualness, as though he were turning down a proffered plate of which he had had enough.

Again the held-breath aura hung palpitating over the huge room. The General sensed it and briefly suffered a ridiculous hallucination: he saw Dietrich and Knight in one of those old films depicting an eighteenth-century duel in which the two men were in the act of firing at each other. The time was the usual dawn on the knoll of a hill, where the seconds, still holding the pistol cases, stood in black capes on the sidelines. There seemed to be some mists drifting among the nearby trees where two black horse-drawn cabs stood waiting.

Dietrich's manner was malignly mild. "Who is your team member?"

14

"Captain Tyler."

A tall young officer with a clean-cut look of a college freshman stood up. Dietrich's glance barely brushed him, his attention returning to the sheet of paper still in his hand. Now, that was the Dietrich the General recognized. The audience was breathing again.

"Colonel Knight, this will be a night drop."

The proximity of the identically pronounced words threw the German off momentarily. A swell of suppressed laughter billowed faintly from the audience, flattening out instantly as Dietrich continued, this time addressing the hunter-capture teams. "I shall present the hunter-capture team who captures the American Colonel each with a bottle of Dom Pérignon."

A marvelous vibration of surprised murmurs and whispers ran through the auditorium. All eyes fell upon Knight, who was still standing.

"Thank you, Colonel," said the American, "and I shall give a *magnum* of Dom Pérignon to each member of the hunter-capture team who captures me."

A deep silence paralyzed the room; then a mighty roar, a hoarse thunder of cheering rose from the men, filling the hall with a tight, breathless implosion. The General could see Dietrich full-face, but Knight only in profile, and it came to him that the two Colonels might as well be alone in the room, so singular was their detachment from the surroundings. They were remarkably matched, neither much more than forty, Knight perhaps a little younger, of equal height and similar build, although Dietrich was clean-shaven, light-haired, and carried himself better.

The General glanced again at Dietrich: the German's face held an expression of concentrated absorption as if he had stopped looking at Knight altogether, in fact as if he were trying to see beyond Knight or see something directly behind him. He wavered slightly, not from some faltering or trembling but as though he were trying to get a clearer view of that event taking place behind the American Colonel, who

15

was still standing, still looking indolent and a little bored.

The General watched Knight's hands slip into his pockets in a loose easy manner that was particularly annoying. The man took nothing seriously, and now here was some damn fool challenge that was going to turn the NATO games into a circus. That was the trouble with peacetime: it made men careless and irresponsible.

On the other hand, Knight would get caught quickly and become a laughingstock, which would fix his wagon for a while. Still, it wasn't going to look good if the American team got caught before they got out of their parachute harnesses, and from the looks of the way this thing was shaping up, all the other survival teams, even the Dagos and Turks, might as well hitchhike on the open highways. No one was going to give a damn about them after this. Well, Dietrich started the whole business and he could bloody well finish it. He could have ignored Knight's mustache; everyone else had for the last eighteen months. The General wondered if Dietrich knew about Knight's D-day exploits.

2

FROM the very beginning, Knight knew that the challenge had been returned for the most stupid of reasons—vanity. And worse, he had allowed it to happen in one of those unthinking moments when he was actually concentrating on something else. He could not even grace his action with the old Greek *hubris* and lay it off to love of country or loyalty to the outfit or even something as elegant as a fatal flaw in his nature. It was all small-minded vanity. What he had been really giving his best thoughts to, when Dietrich was asking the survival teams about their experience, was a fantasy in which he was able to pull a tablecloth from under a fully set service for eight without budging as much as a single delicately balanced butter knife.

He had tucked that happy vision of himself in perfect performance safely away since childhood, when an itinerant magician of sorts had come through the small town in which his family lived, and performed this extraordinary trick with flawless skill, leaving the audience clapping wildly and buzzing with admiring delight. Unfortunately, Knight never learned to perform the trick, but what he did learn from the ratty-suited magician was a certain manner, an aura of nonchalance directed toward doing the impossible—with ease. From the time he was eight, he began to practice this expression of cool indifference, this blasé inattention and cynicism toward danger which had endangered his life ever since.

And now here he was involved in one of those ego tugs for which he was not only too old but which, in the end, would prove nothing that he hadn't already proved before. However, he rather regretted not having found out more about Dietrich when he had the time and opportunity, not that he believed the man was any real danger to him, but there was an expression of such agitated hatred in the German's face at the briefing that he should have done some serious checking.

He thought of Dietrich staring at that scar every morning of his life. "Poor sonofabitch."

"Who?" Tyler, crouching next to him in the dim plane, wanted to know.

"Dietrich."

"Yeah, since when?"

Knight laughed. "Have a little compassion. As a glorious victor, you can afford it."

"Listen, Colonel, all that Kraut wants to do is bring us in hog-tied; and he is going to move boulders to do it."

"Not you. Just me."

"That's true. What is it with him, anyway? What's he got against you?"

"Would you believe that I don't know?"

"Maybe he's bored."

"The Dietrichs of the world don't get bored. They're so full of themselves all the time, they keep constant court."

"So where do you fit in?"

"Who knows with guys like that. Maybe I insult him by

18

not behaving like a conqueror. He could stand it if I hated his guts, but he knows I don't give a damn; and that reduces everything he is to nothing. So what the hell—he's got to play soldier and try and catch me or it's all a pile of crap."

"Is it?"

"Is what?"

"Is it all a pile of crap?"

"Listen, Tyler, when you asked me to sign up too, I was ready for a change of scenery. I like this country. I was going to take a pleasant ten-day walk, sort of like a backpacking trip in the California foothills, a bit of climbing, some meandering down little-used country lanes, sleeping in cozy barns. Walk, eat, ride, enjoy. And it would have been fine, but maybe Dietrich understood that's all I wanted and it got to him. He had to turn it into a big deal or else it's a pile of crap heaped on him. Dietrich's like a bureaucrat: if you don't act out your life in triplicate for him, he gets anxious about who he is or what he's supposed to do. Those sticklers for form only cut their throats on designated days of the week. They're all a pain in the ass."

3

THE darkness yawned up at Knight as the static jerked him out of his free fall, and as always, he was fourteen and hanging onto the huge four-pronged hay-clutching jack-fork that swung from a fast racing track at the top of the steamy barn where the cow smell—a crotchy musk, female smell, faintly rancid and sweet at the same time—stung the lining in his nose. He heard the fork snap above him, the prongs swinging wildly as he let go, tumbling twenty feet into the stack of new hay, which obliterated the animal smell instantly. He rolled furiously away as he heard the fork rush past his head and plunge, prong down, into the stack near him. In the center of his right palm, the jagged depression where two years before the fork had stabbed through his hand, tingled and itched electrically. He had hidden the wound to keep The Old Man from knowing about riding the fork which he and his brother, Hugo, had secretly done for three years now, elated by the thrill of swinging crazily up off the hay wagon and riding the sixty feet into the barn, and there to drop to the piling hay below. It was the closest thing to flying. The only problem beside being found out was that the fork's catch was worn and sometimes, after it dropped the load, it plunged down after it in a seeming gesture to retrieve what it had given up.

The Old Man would crap hop toads if he knew they were riding the fork, and he would certainly blame them for loosening the catch with the extra weight. The Old Man didn't believe that it was worn out; he never believed anything wore out. Half the farm was held together with baling wire, and still The Old Man blamed them for improper use of the equipment. "You don't use it right. You learn to use it and it works good." Knight, hearing the voice upon the wind, laughed and was joined by another laughter, old, familiar, followed by the mimicked words, *"You betcha, kid, you learn use it and it works good."*

Knight called into the darkness, "Hugo, Hugo." Briefly his brother's face, a sliver of light, laughing, sardonic, with hard bitter eye points, flew past him, fading into the stars as leaves nettled against his face and he flexed his legs for the bouncing earth somewhere beneath him. Suddenly the shroud lines and canopy fell down over him, and the earth stopped moving. With a jerk the harness dug into his groin.

He rolled into the parachute, releasing the harness as he moved, his brain reaching into the dark to touch his ankles, his shins, his knees. Number five hundred and fifty-one and all was well. He no longer worried in advance about broken bones; and the terror of being impaled on spires and poles finally left him after he deliberately and stubbornly decided long ago that death would be instantaneous if he ever met that fate. It was being dragged by the wind that absorbed all his attention. He had seen an experienced trooper dragged by sudden gusts; after two miles the man had no face. His body was pulp in the harness.

He rolled up the nylon and gathered the shroud lines and

harness into a ball. By starlight he made out the dark bushes into which he had landed and the paler spots that were open spaces of grass, mirror-silver under the lidless stars. He dug deep into the mold under the shrubs and buried the chute, covering the spot with leaves and bending branches down over it.

His watch hands glowed one-fifty-two. Moonrise was at three. He tunneled his hands in front of his mouth and owl-hooted faintly, waited, and hooted again, louder this time—a long sustained night-bird sound, mournful and eerie, that he thought carried back a faint echo, but not an answer.

Tyler couldn't be more than a mile away. Knight had gone out only seconds before his partner, so he had to be in the general area. He gave the signal again. Nothing. They had agreed not to use their flashlights. Knight knew that he had read Dietrich correctly: that bastard wanted to catch him the first day, the first morning. By dawn the mountains would be crawling with troops. He was convinced men were already deployed over the whole Taunus range since midnight, waiting for the drop. He checked his compass. In his mind he saw the memorized map: to the south was the bend in the great Rhine, and the strip of land called the Rheingau in whose villages he had tasted some of the loveliest wines in the world. On just such a night as this in Erbach in an ancient inn, all gleaming wood and red-and-gold-tapestried hunting scenes, he had sat before an open fire and drunk wine with a plump little tart who liked to sit on his lap and who wore no undergarments.

What a fool he was to volunteer for these peacetime pastimes of "Bang, bang, you're dead," particularly since not volunteering was his most prized credo, but Tyler had conned him. No, that wasn't true, he had *let* Tyler con him into going with him. Cherub-faced, distant relative of a distant president who loved soldiering, who volunteered his ass off, who regretted having missed the war because he was only ten at the time and who idolized Patton and Rommel;

Tyler was incapable of a con job. He had asked Knight to volunteer with him, saying that he really needed the experience. He was the kind of permanent kid that still said "golly" and "gee whiz" although he was almost thirty. And Knight had agreed in that same unthinking, unconsidering way that had marred his whole life with absurd and senseless situations. "But only to make sure you don't get lost, kid."

But that wasn't all of it, either. A rumor had floated down to him from headquarters that a German officer had made a comment about Knight at one of the war game's planning sessions, something about the American who had "luck like one of his whores." At the briefing, when Dietrich made the statement about not counting on luck, Knight had studied the German carefully, waiting for something to click in his memory, some moment in the years behind him when he might have seen the man before. But he could not place him, and when the exercises began later that same night, all he had been able to find out about Dietrich was that the man had fought on the Russian front, that he was either forty-two or forty-three years old and that the only thing he took as seriously as himself was the military.

Knight moved along the edge of the woods, watching the star-pale places for suspicious shadows. Twice more he owl-hooted and waited for the agreed-upon reply. A whisper of night wind stirred in the trees, but nothing answered him. He kept track of his footsteps to measure the distance he was covering. His plan was to go east, reasoning that Tyler, lighter in weight, would have drifted farther behind him than they had counted on. He moved slowly among the trees, wary of the wayward branch, the pale dead stalks that reached out like fingers of skeletons to tear a man's flesh. Best to move slower and be safe. He knew he was on the southwest side of the Taunus mountains, but on level ground, probably a knoll or an upland meadow. He kept a sharp lookout to his right where the hill fell away. Time and again his eyes chanced upon objects he could not identify, and he would stop until the shape and size of it touched some memory or reasoning that reassured him. He moved to the far edge of the hill and backtracked, gazing down into the ravines.

After a time there was a little fog, misty and pale but not thick enough to conceal the rising moon which suddenly peered heavy-lidded over the shoulders of the trees. It was after three. He paused a long time at the periphery of a grove of black trees and hooted his long fluttering signal. As he waited he adjusted his vision to a row of thin low bushes to his left. They seemed to be of even height, like a hedgerow or a topiary garden, pruned to neat formations. A swell of ground breeze rising off the distant river touched his face. He glanced toward it and saw something balloon up and settle again below the crest of the hill to his left and knew instantly what it was and what the neat rows of shrubbery were. Heedless of the moonstruck open spaces, he began to run, loping at first, then racing wildly until he reached the swelling parachute in the middle of the vineyard. He tore out his flashlight, forgetting all about Dietrich and his phantom troops.

Tyler was still bleeding; death was apparently not instantaneous after all. The grape stave had caught him in the belly just above the groin and he had both hands clutched around it so that he hung balanced like a pinned butterfly, the toes of his boots barely scraping the hard earth, his dead child's face inches above the ground. Cursing with anguish, Knight lifted the young officer off the stake and unsnapped his harness. He folded the chute into a shroud, thinking dumbly of Achilles' shield, and placed Tyler's body on it; then he stumbled away sick and blinded.

"Oh, Hugo, Hugo, I should have told that stupid dumb kid to forget it. Why didn't I do that? Games! Practicing how to die!" He did not realize immediately that he was weeping.

4

In the blue light of predawn, Knight loped steadily toward the river, skirting the edge of two moon-shadowed villages where roosters and dogs were just beginning to awaken. For a time he had run aimlessly, away from Tyler, now only a part of the numerical sum in the "expected accident figure" of which the plans and reports always spoke with such glib, bland, unperturbed acceptance. Then a branch, smelling like Christmas, hit him in the face and he fell back and stopped to take his position. He was headed north. Dietrich would search for him in the north first, in the mountains, because he knew about the Sierra Nevada training. He turned toward the river and only after passing the second village discovered that he was outside Eltville, farther west than he thought but still too far from the partisans to reach them that day, unless he could get a ride. Once he reached the partisans he could sleep his way through this madness while they drove him to Aachen, where he would pack his gear and return to the States, leaving the peace to the military.

The partisans were waiting twenty kilometers away, on the other side of Rüdesheim. If no one were looking for him, he could walk it easily in four or five hours, less if he were really hurrying. But if Dietrich reasoned correctly that he had headed for the towns, all the local police were already alerted and expecting him. No. Daytime travel was out. He would hole up somewhere until nightfall, when his flight suit could be mistaken for a mechanic's jumper.

The smell of the river rose into the morning mist, water, oil, lumber, garbage—and something else, something sweet, familiar, desirable that seduced his senses with a longing older than his memory, older than a time or a place of his past, as if the smell, fecund and female, could touch and rouse his body without his mind's resistance or even its cooperation. He moved noiselessly across a winter garden, vaulted a hedge into another plot of burlap-covered shrubbery, and then a third, a fourth, all as identical to each other as the row of houses fronting them. After the last, he sprinted a street, his bootfalls loud, suspicious, sinister on the lard-slippery cobbles. He slid the last two meters, catching a lamppost to keep himself from falling. How absurd it would be for him to break a leg crossing the street when in five hundred and fifty-one jumps he had not as much as sprained a finger.

More slowly, imagining himself lying helpless in the greasy gutter, he slipped into an alley, where a few cars and small trucks were parked neatly on one side. He checked them for keys. To hell with the rules. To hell with Dietrich. They were all locked.

At the end of the alley, he crossed another street and heard the first voices since Tyler's in the plane, other than those whispering angrily inside his head.

Two men, silhouette cutouts against the river mist, argued at the edge of a white pool.

"The best thing to do is take some out of each of the other cans and make up this one."

"All that work? And for what? I say fill the thing with water. Who's to know?"

"You think they don't know milk from water?"

"No, no, I mean who's to know who filled it with water, or when, or where?"

"The cans are marked, you dummy, you think some inspector can't pinpoint this? No, no. We have to pour a little from the other cans to make up the one we spilled."

"*You spilled.*"

"If you had handled it right, it wouldn't have slipped."

The argument between the two continued for some minutes as they filled the spilled can from the others. Knight, listening from the alley, watched the pool of milk turn gray, seep into the worn timbers, the sweet smell finding its place in time.

He was standing in another dawn, his sockless feet frozen blue in the oversized shoes that by autumn would be too small but which he would still be wearing. At least he could go barefoot in the summer. He glanced at the lead sky. He did not want to think of summer; it was years away. There was still the now of things that he had to deal with. And now it was winter, the earth turned in upon itself like a seedpod, dry and brittle. Outside the door of the milkhouse, the whole earth was a sheet of ice, rainwater frozen upon the already solid and saturated ground that looked swollen, bloated in gray decay.

He was no longer freezing, although the inside of the screened milkhouse with its cement floor was as cold as the silent dead dawn outside. It was the cream that made the difference, the cream that came from the separator in the steady jet and under which he thrust his mouth from time to time and drank with heaving gulps. Even as he drank, he kept his eyes toward the corral for The Old Man, who told him that if he ever caught him stealing cream again he would kill him.

Hugo had laughed when Knight told him what The Old

29

Man had said. "Nicholas, he's not going to kill us. He needs us. Who is going to help him milk forty cows every morning and night if he kills us? Just keep your eye open for him. He's pretty quick with his fists, but he won't kill us."

At twelve, Knight already knew about the fists: six months before when he failed to latch the gate to the pasture securely enough to keep the cows from pushing it open, The Old Man had hit him and broken his jaw. For a week he couldn't eat and the pain kept him awake long periods of the night. Hugo made him suck milk from a tin cup until it filled his cheeks before it could seep through the tooth gaps and down his throat.

"You've got to learn to outrun him. He can't hit you if he can't catch you. And you got to learn when he's coming for you. Look at his mouth; his mouth gets white like he has no lips, just a kind of razor line. And he doesn't say anything, doesn't curse or anything. If you're still not sure, just move out of reach to be safe. There's something else; he sort of lifts his arms away from his side, not far away, but just a little like he was sweating and moving like that would make him dry out. Look for that and the lips disappearing and you can always figure the bastard is getting ready to hit."

Knight gauged the distance between the unloaded milk truck and the two still-arguing men. Stretched from the truck to the water edge of the dock were the milk cans with their warm comforting smell. Knight reasoned that the two workmen would leave for coffee soon, before the barge came to pick up the cans, and in those few minutes, he would be alone with the cans.

But the men did not leave the dock; they sat in the cab of the truck and drank from a thermos, the windows fogging over quickly. Knight slipped to the opposite side of the alley and ran lightly to the back of the truck. He pried open one of the cans, glad for the wide necks, dippered in his cupped hands and drank deeply.

He heard the second truck before he saw it and ran to the edge of the water, lying down on the few feet between the row of cans and the wharf edge. Lights danced up and down as the truck rumbled over the cobbles and pulled up to the dock.

The four men greeted each other, and while they were unloading the second truck, they complained about the weather, their various pains, the surliness of farmers, the night before. The mundane discussion ended abruptly.

"Hey, that was some breakout."

"What breakout?"

"At the Army stockade. Some prisoners stole airmen's uniforms and killed a couple of guards. There's a reward."

"Yeah? How much?"

"They didn't say yet. But the Army is getting circulars with pictures and more information out today. But don't spend the reward already. These guys are dangerous. They got knives."

"The old Army wouldn't have had any of this."

"You're crazy. The old Army was no different."

"No, no, this is different; the ringleader is an American, a real killer. And he speaks good German, they say, so watch who you pick up."

"I never pick anybody up. Today everybody on the road is a troublemaker. Someone to cut your throat."

"I could use a reward . . . new tires for the truck. Maybe a television set for the family."

"You want a television set bad enough to get your throat cut?"

"You forget I can handle a knife pretty good, too. Maybe I do the throat-cutting." He laughed. "Can we bring them in dead or do they have to be breathing?"

"They didn't say, but if they are just hoodlums from the prison I can't see where it would make any difference—not with two guards dead. Maybe we would be doing the military a favor."

The subject changed. "Where the hell is that barge? I got other loads yet."

Knight could sense the men scanning upriver. He leaned

flat against the cans and breathed quietly, deeply.

"We can't wait here all day."

There was a discussion of plans: three of them would go, one would wait for the barge and see to the loading. Knight heard the trucks drive away. He smelled tobacco and raised his head between the cans to see the remaining man sucking furiously on a pipe as the match's flame drew into the palm-sheltered bowl.

Knight rolled over twice and lowered himself off the pier, slicing feet first into the water like a dropped knife.

5

THE barge drew up ten minutes later, and Knight, clinging to the slimy poles under the pier, listened as the bargemen excitedly spoke of four of the escaped soldier convicts who had attempted to stow away but who were discovered and picked up by the military police upstream. "And we got a reward to split, besides being heroes."

There was a booming laugh. "Some heroes we are. Those guys were half froze and one of them had a lame foot and another had a bloody head and kept walking into things."

"We'll split your share if it bothers you too much." More laughter.

After the barge was gone, Knight heard another truck back up to the dock, a door slam, and footsteps sound briefly on the cobbles, then fade away. Someone was whistling, but this, too, faded away with the footfalls. He waited a few minutes, then pulled himself up to look over the pier. A boy of perhaps fourteen was sitting on top of a pile of raw lumber stacked on the truck. They saw each other at once, the boy crying out in surprise and almost falling from his perch. Knight dropped back into the river, dove under water, and moved away from the wharf, the swift current carrying him lightly. When he surfaced, he heard the boy shouting a name, but that voice, too, faded behind him as he let himself be carried effortlessly by the river.

Even as he allowed himself the soft hypnotic pleasure of the embracing stream, he knew that if he did not get out of the water quickly he would soon die in it. At first it had been hideously cold, but now it seemed warm to him and he felt comfortable and sleepy. He swam with long steady strokes to the center of the river, where he struck out hard for the opposite shoreline toward a stand of trees. The weight of his boots held him back and the current dragged him relentlessly downstream. He had a comical vision of swimming as far as Koblenz, where he might hitch a ride up the Mosel to Luxembourg on the back of some giant fish and from there picnic his way through Belgium, walk back across the German border at Aachen, saunter up to the NATO forces meeting five days before he was due and calmly knock Dietrich's brains out.

But there were no giant fish in the Mosel, and there was no way he could swim it upstream. It was certainly too bad that crazy river was running in the wrong direction, because that stupid fact was going to keep him five days further from massacring Dietrich. He wondered if massacring one man had some sort of linguistic error in it. It didn't matter; he decided to massacre him anyway—for Tyler and the four guys with the lame feet and the bloody heads that were captured by a half-dozen bargemen who were now going to get television sets for heroism.

He did not know how far downstream his meandering mind took him, but he finally pulled himself out of the water

34

onto a grassy slope, where he lay panting with pain. When at last he raised his head and adjusted his eyes to the trees before him, he saw through the evergreen branches a white unicorn charging down on him with raised hoofs and screaming mouth.

Knight hurled himself under some shrubbery, grasping at his heaving chest as though he could physically hold his galloping heart still. When he looked back at the spot where he first caught sight of the beast, he saw that it was carved in stone and that it stood on a high pedestal clutched by gangrenous green ivy.

Shivering, he crept through the shrubbery and found himself in a park where mermaids, unicorns, and centaurs on pedestals paraded down both sides of a narrow paved avenue. He moved carefully from one pedestal to the next, listening for human voices, expecting any minute to come upon someone walking toward him from one of the many paths that led through the trees on both sides. It was clear that no vehicles used the road. If this were an estate park, he could count on a gardener's shack, perhaps even something quite large with a stove of some kind.

But the grounds did not turn out to be part of a private garden. The avenue ended at a locked wrought-iron gate inserted between thick, ten-foot-high hedges. Beyond the ornamental grillwork, an amusement park with carrousel, Ferris wheel, and roundabout rides stood deserted in the gray morning.

Knight had no trouble climbing the gate and dropping with ease to the turf on the other side. But the huts housing the machinery for the riding devices were padlocked and windowless.

Knight chose the largest shack, attached to the carrousel, unscrewing the hasp with his survival knife and carefully closing the door so that it still appeared locked from the outside. A piece of grimy canvas covered the carrousel's machinery. It made a fine blanket, light yet warm and waterproof. He removed his flight suit and draped it over the motor, checked his waterproof flashlight, watch, and compass, ate a piece of soggy dried beef from his food pocket, and after rolling up in the piece of canvas, slept at once; his last waking thought was a vision of himself wrapped in a shroud and being buried at sea.

He often thought of his own death, or at least his own burial, watching it serenely from a distance, contemplating the people who were standing around his remains, observing their actions, their expressions, and sometimes even hearing their statements. The Old Man grunted, spat, and walked away. His mother stared at the body with hot, sulfur-colored eyes: "He is not forgiven. The Lord God does not forgive this life. It is sin. It is hell." She held a raised butcher's knife.

Near the open grave, Hugo hung heavily between his crutches, his head dropping forward as if staring into the newly dug hole. Knight wanted to talk to him, tell him to stop grieving, that death wasn't at all bad, but a group of young people came running toward them, all laughing and talking at the same time. He heard their shoes kick at the metal tombstones along the way. *"Not tombstones," said Hugo, "not tombstones."*

Knight awakened and listened to the voices; there were perhaps four or five people, young, laughing, climbing over the ridabouts to the left of the carrousel shack. "Hey, check out the Ferris wheel."

"You expect it to be open? Don't be a dope."

"So check anyway."

Knight, still wrapped in his shroud, peered through a crack in the open door. There were four, two boys and two girls, all about fifteen. One of them was rattling the lock to the Ferris-wheel hut; the others were clambering over the lower seats of the wheel. "Smash it with a rock."

Knight pulled on his flight suit with steady, calm haste,

picked up his boots and the rolled-up tarp, and slipped out of the shack. He ran swiftly, bent over, away from the four youngsters, two of whom he saw already straddling the carrousel animals as he darted behind another pleasure device, a ring of missiles attached by bars to a hub.

At the far end of the park, he found a children's sandlot with huge pieces of piping strewn about. It came to him briefly that a giant plumber had unknowingly dropped them from his pouch. The picture of a seventy-foot man striding along with a swinging pack of plumbing pieces amused him and he swore at himself angrily.

He dashed into an elbow joint, curled up tight with the canvas over him, and lay still. On his wrist the watch gleamed brightly under the tarp. It was eleven and it was Monday; why weren't those damn kids in school? For some time he listened to them talking and roaring with sudden spurts of laughter.

"Hey, look here. It's open. Part of the lock came loose."

"You better not mess with that."

"Who's going to stop me? The island's closed till May. Come on, we'll get it going."

The word "island" pulled Knight up short. Had he, in fact, crossed over to an island, or was that merely the name of this place? Well, it made no difference. He had to cross back to the Taunus side anyway. Rüdesheim was on the other side up near the bend of the river, and the partisans were waiting. The kids would tire of this soon or have to go home. In the back of his head a nagging worry warned him: what if they decided to crawl through the pipes? He answered calmly: he would have enough warning and could run for the hedge and burrow into it and even out the other side and wait under the shrubbery until the brats left.

Within minutes he heard machinery groaning and creaking. Carefully he raised the tarp and peered out of the tunneled opening. The carrousel was moving, but some seconds passed before Knight realized that there was no music, so clearly did he hear the old merry-go-round melodies that came from a certain day in his childhood.

He watched the kids move from animal to animal, riding each for only a few seconds at a time. Lying on the grass near the carrousel was a lumpy sack. Food? Of course, when they tired of the ride, they would eat and leave as swiftly as they came. Knight settled down to wait them out.

"This dumb animal won't go up and down. It only goes around."

"Maybe it's not supposed to."

"Of course it's supposed to; it's a horse."

"Maybe it's sick."

"Poor thing. Let's kill it."

"Good idea. It shouldn't suffer this way."

One of the boys jumped off the platform and took a small pistol from the sack. He jumped back on, and a moment later from a close distance, shot the brightly painted horse in the head. The wood splinters flew in all directions.

"You dope, not so close. We could have been hurt. Come, I'll show you how it's done."

They all jumped from the moving carrousel and walked toward the sandlot, carrying the sack with them, one of them twirling the gun with careless abandon.

The sand was enclosed in a foot-high cement border and behind this the kids dropped to their bellies at the insistence of the one with the gun.

Knight could see them clearly from his plumber's joint, their jeaned legs spread slightly on the sand in front of him. The carrousel was still turning rapidly. "Okay, now before I have to go juice it up again, everybody's got to shoot at least one animal. Aim for the eyes. If you get the eyes, you get extra points. The one who gets the most eyes is the winner."

"What's the prize?" asked one of the girls.

"You *always* have to have a prize. *Winning* is the prize,

you dope. Okay, I'm going to shoot first. Oh, wait, there's another thing, you've got to say what animal you're aiming for. You aim for the lion, you got to hit the lion. If you hit something else, it doesn't count."

"Come on, you're wasting time."

"Okay, okay." The boy raised the gun slowly. "The dolphin." The bullet made a pinging sound.

"You missed, you missed, you missed. You hit the metal bar instead. Ha ha ha. You're not so hot. Give me the gun."

Knight watched in horror, almost screaming out as the boy with the gun turned the weapon's muzzle upon the girl taunting him. "I could shoot you now. I could shoot you right in the mouth—or the eyes, for extra points. How would you like that?"

"That would be cheating because I have no gun to shoot back," she said smugly.

Knight breathed again as the boy handed the girl the gun. The other two watched this exchange with impatience. "Come on, keep it moving."

"The tiger. I will now shoot the tiger." The girl fired, and wood splinters flew from the tiger's flank.

"You shot him in the ass, you dope."

"At least I hit him."

For an hour they shot at the animals, periodically resetting the carrousel and reloading the gun from a box of cartridges they kept in the sack.

A terrible sadness crept into Knight as he watched the children shoot the faces off the lovely creatures. A swan lost its whole head; the unicorn, its exquisite spiraling horn; a vaulting ibex, its bladed hoofs. Memory spoke to him like grief and the weight of the past pushed him into deeper sorrow. Years ago he and Hugo had found a dog abandoned on the highway near the farm. For weeks they fed him and kept him hidden in the hay barn until The Old Man discovered him and bashed the animal's head in with a shovel.

On that day, he and Hugo began to plan their escape from The Old Man.

Knight watched the kids indifferently; they were little thugs, only not so little, and they would grow up to be big thugs and they would breed and raise more little thugs and it would never end. With a tired heart, he looked at the Ferris wheel webbed against a cloud-swollen sky. The world was sick.

He watched the kids take oranges out of the sack and eat them, throwing the rinds near enough to the plumbing culvert so that he caught their sweet, nostalgic smell and hungered for a piece of the fruit with a terrific craving. If he could have reached them, he would have eaten the discarded peels.

"We're running low on ammunition and no one's hit the dolphin yet. He's still got his snoot on him."

"I don't care. I don't want to do this anymore, anyway. It looks like it's going to rain or something. I want to go back to the boat."

"Always the crybaby. The rain can only get you wet. We're going to stay until we've finished, and you're staying too, so shut up. Aim for the dolphin. It's a fish and doesn't belong here, anyway. Knock its snoot off."

Knight crept to the other end of the elbow and again surveyed the distance to the hedge. It was no more than twenty feet, and another one of the cement fittings lay between him and the end of the sandlot. He rolled the canvas up snugly and tied it to his back with the thong from his supply pocket. Then he inched his way out of the culvert and slipped behind the last piece of pipe. From there he moved on his belly, noiselessly in the sand, as the shots, sounding not even very loud, thunked into the animals behind him.

He found the rowboat tied to a small dock. After he cast off, he adjusted the tarp over his head, securing it in front of his chest so that he appeared like any fisherman, mindful of the rain, which could give a man the ague, or worse.

Minutes later, as he rowed past the end of the island, a heavy rain began to fall. He could not hear the gun anymore. He wondered if the kids had finally shot the dolphin.

6

KNIGHT kept the boat to the left bank, reasoning that the hunter-capture teams would still be searching the villages lying in the shadow of the Taunus. Also, if the river police hailed him, there was a good chance he could reach the shore quickly and lose himself in the rain among the vineyards and orchards that were sheltered in mists only a short distance away. After all, the police weren't allowed to shoot him. Perhaps that's what bothered Dietrich. Even if they saw him, a "Bang, bang, I got you!" shout wasn't going to bring him down either. He chuckled at the idea of adults playing the children's game of cops and robbers or cowboys and Indians, which he and Hugo never had the time to play, although they had watched with hot longing other children who were urgently absorbed in these pastimes and who played them with malevolent and chilling seriousness.

If those capture teams wanted to take him, nothing short of a flying tackle was going to bring him down, and there would be a few bloody noses at the bottom of that heap for sure. He was amused that the language of kid's games fit his situation at every turn of his thoughts. Then, he thought of Tyler. And that bargeman's willingness to help the Army rid itself of a liability didn't sound like any kid's game he knew of.

He felt safe for the moment, safe in the rain and safe on the river. It was a good combination. He guessed that the capture teams were sheltering themselves someplace comfortable, and he knew for sure none of them were out slouching around on foot.

He hoped that they found Tyler early. He didn't want to think of the young soldier being rained on. Again he saw the body in his flashlight's beam lying on the folded chute. But as desperately as he tried to recall the details, Knight could not remember having closed Tyler's eyes.

He gazed away at the river rippling in the rain and wished passionately that he could simply float all the way to the sea, past the pulsating cities, the blazing smelters and churning cement plants; through Holland and beyond to the North Sea and from there west to England, and up the Thames to London, where he should have gone to begin with. How stupid for Tyler to die. *"You know, Hugo, it didn't have to be that way. It's all so absurd. I probably could have talked him out of going. I should have talked him out of it. I should have said, 'Listen, Tyler, don't be a jackass. You really want to volunteer for ten days of sore feet and a cold behind?' The problem is, Hugo, he would have said 'Yes.' That's the trouble with these Academy kids, all fire and no sense. Goddamn it, what's the point to it all. This idiotic rehearsing for the next war that can't possibly be won by anybody."*

It was the middle of the afternoon, yet it was getting colder and the rain had a needle sting to it that bit into his face. He ate another piece of beef and drank water collected in a fold of the canvas tarp. The current carried him easily, forcing him to row only when it pulled him toward the faster water in the center. Twice, someone waved to him with that single rise and fall of a hand that speaks for the laconic nature of rivermen. Knight returned the gesture, thinking: They are the same everywhere; not language nor locality nor blood separates them from the brotherhood of their religion; how could they have any other god but their rivers?

Three times he owed his life to a river, but it was not those three distant moments of his past that made him sense his present calm, for those times reminded him only of the madmen whom the rivers had stopped from killing him.

It was the hours which he and Hugo had stolen from The Old Man that brought him now this momentary sense of peace. At the periphery of the farm, there flowed a wide stream which deeply flooded the bottom land every spring but which by late summer was shallow with silver, singing rapids that he and Hugo crossed to reach a small strip of sugar-fine sand beside a deep pool half-concealed by golden willows whose catkins trailed in the water. It was here that they swam and slept whenever The Old Man drove into town believing they were raking and stacking the hay for the wagon to take to the barn. Knight smiled at the soft summer memories. He must have been about thirteen then.

As much as he hated the farm and the long hours of labor and The Old Man, he knew there were no happier hours in his life than those. He did not deceive himself into remembering more hours than there actually were, nor into forgetting the day when they ceased forever and his life seemed to stop, too, with Hugo's long, animal scream that he knew he would hear until the last beat of his heart.

River horns sounded near him in the thickening mists which the rain, gone now, had left behind. He struck out for the right bank; it would not do to pass Rüdesheim in the fog and have to backtrack to reach his partisans. His partisans? True in one sense at least: each survival team had its own group of partisans, whose existence was known to the hunter-capture units, but whose location was not. The "downed airmen" had been given the location of their partisans in sealed orders which they memorized and destroyed before the jump. Knight had examined his packet with great care to make sure someone had not had the opportunity to memorize the information before he did. Tyler had been amused at his suspicions. "You think Dietrich would cheat to that extent?"

"Yes."

"That would be pretty unfair."

"Listen, Tyler, Dietrich's definition of fair is whatever he can get away with."

"What chance have we got, then? Here I was getting ready to dub this whole thing the champagne campaign, but not if the other side has all the advantages."

"We can probably count on the partisans. Plenty of our guys had to count on them during the war, and they made a difference. They'll have vehicles for us and they'll know the best routes. They'll look like ordinary Germans going about their daily business. Crossing the rivers will be tricky because that's where the roadblocks are most effective, but they'll have that figured out, too. All we have to worry about is getting to them."

When he had made that little speech to Tyler, he had believed it himself, but now as he pulled up to a muddy bank below the town, he tried to convince himself that he still believed it. He scuttled the rowboat, crawled into a culvert from which a foot of water fed into the river, and climbed the hill on the other side by way of the gushing brook. The weather had turned bitterly cold since he had left the island.

He hurried now, for the December night would fall early and he still had an hour to go before he reached the clearing in the woods below the monument of Germania where the partisans would be waiting for him. Several times he stopped and checked his map of the area.

Just before he reached the clearing, the first snowflakes

began to filter through the trees. He stood perfectly still in the dense shrubbery and peered into the clearing, taking in every detail: the small darkened mountain house at the far side of the open area with its dormant garden in which a few beanpoles still stood upright and the raggedy leaves of some half-pulled turnips lay limp and blue on the muddy ground.

Something was wrong. There were tire tracks, motorcycle-tire tracks, recently made. Everything was wrong: if the partisans were in the house, a light would be on. And if the partisans had been captured and the hunters were in the house, the light would also be on, to keep him from suspicion, to invite his confidence.

He made his way through the undergrowth to the back of the house, where a cord of firewood was neatly stacked in rows under a shed. Here he waited as night fell and the snow whispered to him, although he knew it was only the sighing branches growing heavy under the fall. He thrust his bare hand out from under the shed; a few minutes later his palm was filled with large dry flakes. It would probably snow most of the night. He wrapped himself in the tarp and lay between two of the wood stacks and listened. No sound came from the house, and the deep silence of the snowstorm all around him in the dark gave him an eerie feeling of aloneness. Still, the weather was to his advantage: wherever those hunters were, they were inside, and warm. Warm! He rose up quickly, smiling to himself, and sniffed the air: cold, cut wood—beech, probably, but no sweet smell of burning logs, no hearth smell, no cozy smoke smell.

The back door to the house was open and as it gave to his touch, Knight was certain that the partisans had been forced to leave and that they had left the door open for him as a sign of some kind. Did the unlatched door mean: use the house—it is safe? He elected to take that meaning and flashed his light around the single large room. Two chairs lay on their sides; pieces of broken coffee mug were stacked on the table; on another table against one wall, marks where a large rectangular object had rested, showed up clearly. A clean mess: that's what this was. There were no signs of serious violence, but certainly someone had been forced to leave. A row of pegs on the wall had no coats hanging from it, yet there was fresh bread in the cupboard, and cheese, a bowl of stewed pears and half a sausage.

Knight ate by the light of his flashlight, wrapping up the leftover cheese in a piece of rough dish towel and stuffing it into his food pocket. He spent some time carefully searching the cabin, not knowing what he was looking for—except answers. If the hunter units had found the partisans and taken them away, they would have left some men behind to await his arrival and capture him. The forestry people or the local police would have picked up the partisans only if they were doing something illegal. Highly unlikely. There was no reason for them to leave of their own accord: their job was as clearly defined as his.

He remembered his last conversation with Tyler. "Barring any accidents, we should rendezvous with the partisans around noon." Barring any accidents! The phrase caught in his throat as he saw Tyler clutching the grape stake that impaled him.

And that planned noon meeting was now twelve hours behind him; and Tyler's death, ten hours behind that. He lay on one of the two cots and hoped again that Tyler had been found quickly. He clearly intended not to sleep, since the uncertainty of the situation made him anxious and watchful, yet toward morning he slept for about an hour and dreamed.

All his life he had had nightmares, grotesquely irrational and terrifying dreams triggered by a single thought or a glimpse of some event that imprinted itself in his mind as clearly as a mirror image.

No one had found Tyler. Weeks had passed since the jump, and Knight was still running through the Taunus forests, always bursting out of the trees into the open at the

48

same vineyard where Tyler lay on his chute. The young officer was in advanced decay: maggots squirmed in his eye pits and filled his open mouth, but the wound in his belly gushed fresh blood continually. As Knight dug the grave beside the body, Tyler metamorphosed into a human foot cut off at the ankle, from which the same bright blood flowed endlessly. Knight rolled the chute around the foot and placed it into the grave, but when he tried to fill in the hole, the dirt piled on his shovel flew away in the wind and turned into a swarm of bees. The faster he shoveled, the faster the bees flew into the sky, until great clouds of them whirled and circled fiercely above him. Hunched on a nearby fence, a buzzard casually picked its teeth.

Knight woke up disoriented and shivering. A wind had risen and was blowing snow against the one small window facing the clearing. He watched it briefly and thought about heating some water for coffee, when he heard the first helicopter.

"The bastards. The bloody bastards!"

He tore about the cabin, cleaning up any evidence that he had been there, snatching up all his gear and stowing it in the various pockets. Last he tied the rolled-up tarp to his back and leaped from the back door to the woodshed. He slipped between the stacks to the far edge, knowing that he had to keep from walking in the snow until he got far enough away from the house to make the hunters believe that he had not been there.

From the shed he reached up and grasped a branch from the nearest tree, pulling himself up into it and climbing from one branch to the next, finally dropping into some bracken from which the snow was being blown by the wind. He crawled underneath it and clawed his way through the forest for several hundred feet until he felt it was safe to move upright under the trees. After another hundred yards he felt he could rest a bit, but not stop. He glanced at his watch as he slowed his pace, moving downhill and westerly. It was at that moment as he zigzagged under some trees that he heard the second helicopter. He knew they couldn't see him under the trees, but he looked up anyway, and in that sudden thrusting back of his head, he hit a snow-covered branch from which a jagged piece of dead wood pierced his right eye.

He ran, then, straight down the hill, screaming in pain, the blood streaming down his face and between the fingers of his hand gripped against the wounded eye. Abruptly he hit a low stone wall with the full force of his body, stumbled over it, and lost all consciousness.

7

"A buzzard does not have teeth."

"What does he say?"

"He says that a vulture does not have teeth."

"A vulture?"

"He uses an American name for a kind of vulture that is a carrion bird. They call them buzzards."

Knight listened to the conversation and tried to orient himself. Two women were speaking, one of them young. He was lying in a narrow bed and his face was bandaged. The pain was low-key: the beginnings of a headache on his right side. The smell of disinfectant was strong, and neither of the women, one on each side of his bed, wore scent. He was definitely out of uniform.

He backtracked to the second helicopter. Something stabbed him in the eye, and he ran down a hill and fell over a wall. And now he was in bed in only his underwear and two women were talking to each other about an American bird, or at least its proper name. At that point he remembered the dream in which he was trying to bury the bleeding foot, while the buzzard sat on the fence and picked its yellow, rat teeth which the younger of the two women denied the bird had. No. That wasn't right. He had denied the teeth.

Knight opened his unbandaged eye. A nun stood on each side of his bed, neither woman appearing at all surprised that he was conscious. "Am I in a hospital?"

"You are in our infirmary. This is a convent." The older woman spoke. Knight thought she had rather cold blue eyes. Her face was deeply lined and the collar of her habit cut stiffly into her neck. "How do you feel?"

"Just fine."

"Are you in pain?"

"No."

"You will be."

"I don't mind. Could you tell me how long I've been here?"

"About seven hours."

"I slept seven hours?"

"You were sedated."

"How did I get here?"

"One of the sisters found you in the lime orchard this morning around eight. It is now three in the afternoon."

"Does anyone else know that I am here?"

The two women exchanged glances. "No, but we know that you have escaped from prison. We are not isolated from the world here. Your picture is in the newspapers, and the radio tells of the prison break. You cannot stay here. You should give yourself up and hope for mercy."

Knight did not believe in hope any more than he believed in luck, and in his whole life he had never even thought of mercy, was even vague about its meaning. "I shall leave at once if you will return my clothes to me."

"No, there is still uncertainty about your eye. It is possible you will be blind, though I cannot be sure: the puncture did not miss the cornea, but the fullest force of it tore into the flesh around the eye. You must not risk infection, which is why you should let the police find you. In a large hospital, they can do more."

"Are you a doctor?"

"I worked twenty-one years in a hospital in Africa. I learned much, but I have no medical degree." She paused. "I have cleaned out the eye and anesthetized it. We have given you antibiotics. The dressing must be changed and kept clean."

Knight felt the bandage gingerly with his fingertips. "I think I'll take my chances with you, lady."

"I am called Mother."

"I'm sorry." Knight reflected briefly on the ambiguity of his statement but let it go.

The older woman nodded. "Sister Adelaide will take care of your needs and bring you food. I suggest that you sleep as much as possible. If the eye looks good tonight, you can leave then."

"Why have you not called the police?"

"We do not judge here."

Knight smiled—were there places in the world where no one judged? "Isn't letting me stay and taking care of my eye a judgment?"

"No. This is our work. Only you can choose to go to the police."

Knight was struck by the curious comedy of the situation. He wondered if he should tell her about the war games. She would probably not believe him—a convict would say anything. Anyway, she would be right in not believing him; there were no war games, there had not been the moment he had offended Dietrich. He must try to figure out Dietrich as soon as he had time to think out his own next moves.

The older woman prepared to leave but turned back to him. "How does it happen that you speak such good German?"

"I spent many years learning it."

Again the woman nodded and turned away.

The young nun took his temperature and checked his pulse. She had large glistening gray eyes that dominated her face.

"Where did you hear about buzzards?"

"I had five years' training in America." She answered him in English but quickly reverted to German.

"Where?"

"In California, at the capital."

"Sacramento?"

"Yes. There is a hospital there run by our order. That is, the nurses are all from our order."

"So you chose America."

"No, I go where I am sent."

"Would you have liked to stay there?"

She shook her head. "It made no difference; I go wherever I can serve."

"Don't you miss the world?"

"I am in the world. I work five days in a nearby hospital. It is a good vantage point of humanity."

"At its worst?"

"Who is to say? Perhaps a prison is the worst." She did not look at him. "You should sleep. But perhaps you are hungry?"

"No."

"You are in pain?"

"No."

"The sedation has worn off and the anesthesia in your eye will be wearing off quickly, too; do not be afraid to show pain. There is no need for you to suffer more than you already have."

"I'll keep it in mind."

She picked up a basin and left the room. Knight watched her go with an unfamiliar regret: here was religion, soft and comforting. He thought of his mother and her mad god.

There was a time, too long ago for him to place accurately, when there had been that same gentleness around him that the young nun brought to the room. He thought of it as a touch, but perhaps it was only a sound, not spoken words but something lovely and profoundly tender, more encompassing than words, more strangely fulfilling. He reached back through the dark years searching for the elusive essence, and for a moment he thought himself near as a faint murmuring floated past him. Something touched his cheek.

"Are you in pain?"

He opened his eye. The young nun was looking at him anxiously.

"Did I sleep?"

"I don't know. When I left you a little while ago you were quite awake, but just now you cried out."

"Did you speak to me?"

"When?"

"When you came back into the room."

"No."

"I thought I heard something."

"I'm sorry I disturbed you; I was humming."

"What . . . what were you humming?"

"Oh, it is only an old song, a kind of lullaby. Mothers do not sing it much nowadays."

"How does it go?"

She flushed with embarrassment and smiled uncertainly, her eyes downlooking, her hands fluttering near her face.

"Please, how does it go?"

She collected herself quickly. "I don't know all the words, only the melody and some of the refrain." She began to hum in a sweet soft contralto, muted and deep in her throat.

"Yes, yes, that's it."

She stopped humming. "You know it?"

"Years ago, I heard it. Perhaps only once, perhaps more. I don't know."

"Your mother sang it to you?"

"I don't know that, either. I cannot remember my mother before she got sick."

"How sad for a child to have a sick mother. And how sad for the poor lady. Was she sick long?"

"Yes. When I was very young, she bore an abnormal child. It was supposed to be twins, but it didn't develop properly. My mother saw it. She was never right after that. She thought God had cursed her."

The nun put her hand over her mouth, cutting off a gasp. Her eyes looked larger than ever, more deeply gray and filled now with pain.

"There were no more children after that, no more life. She began to talk to God, got messages from Him. She was quite mad, of course, and the messages were mad."

The nun's hand had slipped down to the front of her habit; her mouth was slightly open; her head shook slightly.

Knight wanted to tell her that he was not a convict, that he had not killed any guards, that no one had killed any guards; but that he had probably endangered almost a hundred men with his stupid careless vanity. He wondered if Dietrich would have offered that absurd reward to the general public for the capture of the airmen if he were not so dead set on catching him. Would he, in fact, have sent out the report about the breakout and the dead guards?

"Where will you go tonight?" whispered the nun.

"I don't know. I must cross the river." He was amused at the irony. "Actually, I was across the river yesterday, but I had to come back to this side to meet some friends, only my friends were not home, so now I have to cross the river all over again."

"Couldn't you go back to your friends? In time, they will come home."

"No, that's precisely the trouble; they probably won't come home in time." Knight was touched by her concern for him; after all, he was a dangerous killer.

"Are they nearby? Perhaps someone can get a message to them."

Knight stared at her for a long moment. "That's very kind of you, and I want you to know that I shall never forget that. Unfortunately, I think my friends will not be coming home at all. Did you hear a helicopter today?"

"Yes, there were several."

"I think they are watching my friends' house; they are waiting for me to show up there."

"Oh, no, they are after more communists."

"What communists?"

She smiled. "I'm afraid this will amuse you. There were some men in a house near the Niederwald Monument. They wanted some electrical work done and went to town to hire an electrician. But when the man saw all the radio equipment the men had in the house, he went to the police and made a big story about how the woods were filled with communists. So the men in the house were arrested because they had no explanations for what they were doing there with all that equipment and their identification papers were not in order or not complete. I am not sure on that detail, but anyway, everybody is afraid of the communists, just like in America."

Knight started to chuckle, but his eye hurt too much. He put his hand over it and shook with suppressed laughter. Leave it to his partisans to go hire a local electrician and get themselves thrown in the can, the dumb bastards. And by now, that information must have reached the hunters, who were probably just outside the convent tearing up the whole forest looking for him. And his precaution that morning at covering his tracks was backfiring totally. If he had left evidence that he'd been there and gone, the hunters would be gone, too, downriver, probably roadblocking the bridges and searching the barges. Now he would have to get through the lines with the enemy hiding behind every rock. In fact, he was surrounded.

"How far am I from the river?"

"Only about five kilometers if you go back to the Nieder-wald road at the top of the town, then turn left to go past the monument and on down to the river. It is longer if you go north and then go toward Assmannshausen, and also, that way you cut out the Binger Loch, the whole bend of the Rhine where there is much river-traffic control because it is the most difficult for boats. There are bad rapids and reefs. It has one of the few pilot stations of the Rhine. There would be many people there, more than at Assmannshausen, which is only a small town and perhaps no one would look there. . . ."

Knight knew the towns she spoke of, had, in fact, floated past them two years before on a Rhine pleasure cruiser, a gaudy ship crowded with tourists and rich food and noise. After that, he had driven along the shore, preferring the right bank because there were fewer trucks, although fewer accessible castles, also; but then he had learned long ago that castles were more mysterious and fascinating from a distance. Some he had explored up close were composed of a series of empty rooms smelling faintly of mold and strongly of urine.

Knight wanted to ask her how she got to the hospital where she worked, but he felt he had no right to involve the nuns in his escape. They were already involved too much, and if Dietrich knew civilians had helped him he would see it as a form of treason against the State. The more he thought about Dietrich, the more he found himself sensing how the man thought. Yes, during the war, Dietrich would have had the nuns shot. The partisans would have been hanged at once, probably from the town's lampposts.

The old nun came into the room quickly. "There are three Army policemen outside, searching the grounds."

Knight glanced from one frightened woman to the other. "I shall give myself up. You will be in no danger. Do not be afraid."

"We are not afraid for ourselves. You are in danger. They seem to be willing to shoot you without question. They said you were dangerous and safer to the country dead than alive."

Knight knew that this had to be a line to frighten the nuns. "No, no, they will not shoot me. You see, this isn't really real. I mean, this whole thing is a kind of game." He stopped. The fear in the women's eyes was real. And why not? Here he was, a hunted killer that they had found wounded and half-blind in their lime orchard; and outside, three armed men were searching the buildings for him. What was unreal about that?

"Do not be mistaken, young man: they are serious. They said they have been ordered to shoot you on sight."

Knight caught his breath. Dietrich wouldn't dare give such an order!

The Abbess's voice was low, clearly comforting. "They will not come in here," she said. "It is forbidden. Tonight or perhaps tomorrow we will take you to a place from which you can go north." Knight knew then that the Mother Superior had heard his conversation with the young nun. "Sister Adelaide, please prepare the robe."

8

THEY buried him early the following morning.

During the night the two women dressed his eye again while the Abbess gave him instructions. "Once you are out of the box, you will find a molding on one wall; it is a door which will take you from the crypt. Follow only the main corridor. If you leave it, you could get lost and never be found."

"Will I recognize it?"

"Yes. By the bones."

"The bones?"

"Yes. You will understand. It is a long distance and will take you several hours. When you get to the river ..."

"What river?"

"No, it is not the Rhine. Those who know of it call it the River of the Dead, but that is inaccurate: some small blind fish survive in it. The motif carved in the stones of some of our older buildings represents those creatures.

"You will hear the river long before you see it. When you get to it, follow it downstream. There is a narrow ledge. In places it will appear impossible to go on, but it is not impossible. The river will take you to the outside."

Knight stared at her for a long helpless moment before he spoke. "I know that you think I am a murderer, and it is true that as a soldier, I have killed; but you must believe me, I did not kill those guards."

After a pause, she said, "Perhaps for you that is an interesting distinction. For me it is not."

"Then why are you helping me?"

"The police outside ... I do not think you can expect mercy from them. Possibly some others, somewhere else, but not these."

"Will they not be suspicious of a burial out here—just at this time?"

"Probably. All policemen are suspicious, even as you are. But that does not stop us from burying our dead in our own holy ground. They are welcome to watch."

Knight did not believe he would sleep during the hours before dawn, but he did, a deep restful sleep. If he dreamed, he could not remember the dreams. Sister Adelaide gave him a cup of apricot juice to drink after they treated his eye the second time, and reflecting upon that the next morning when she awakened him, he believed that there must have been a sedative of some kind in it.

His flight suit with its bulging zippered pockets hung over the back of a chair, and on the floor beside it were his boots and the rolled-up tarp. He dressed quickly, discovering bandages and a vial of antibiotic tablets in one of his unused pockets. When he was finished, he left the infirmary through a narrow doorway behind a screen. Sister Adelaide was waiting for him in a barren antechamber stunningly different from the modern clinical room he had just left. "You will find everything you need inside the box. Make no attempt to open it for at least two hours, and even then do everything as silently as possible. Should anyone open the coffin before we lower you into the chamber, your body will appear to be heavily bound in the burial shroud. But you will have no difficulty in freeing yourself when the time for it comes."

He followed her into another chamber, larger and less severe than the first, with high arched windows ornamented with Gothic tracery. On a low table in the center of the room lay an open coffin.

"Once you remove the springs, the lid will raise easily. Please wait." She left the room through imposing wooden doors, which she pulled closed behind her.

Knight examined the coffin. It was a plain box of wood with metal bands which reminded him of pictures of pirates' chests half-buried in the sand, only it was much longer. He found the springs and understood at once how they could be removed from the inside to raise the lid. He realized with a curious calm that he was about to get his long-fantasized burial. More interesting to him was the knowledge that he was entrusting it to women, people who he knew were not only beyond his comprehension, but also beyond his respect. He did not know why this was so, but he knew since childhood that the world was run by men and that females were somehow lesser in every way one could think of. He did not believe in the intelligence of women, although they were useful. They were useful to his comforts, but not necessary to it. At thirty-eight, he had slept with perhaps a hundred women, some of them total strangers who took his money and walked out of whatever room he was in without comment. That was the way he preferred it. But a few times he had become involved with women who wanted him to marry them, and these episodes always ended badly when he told them, with no intention whatsoever of hurting them, that he did not believe in marriage but that he would be agreeable to supporting them. Some of them had hit him, which at first

63

he found astonishing; others had wept and screamed and ended up calling him names. He was sorry that they felt as they did, but there was nothing he could do about it.

When the massive doors opened again, three figures in coarse hooded robes which hid their faces entered without speaking. One of them moved noiselessly to the coffin, while the other two held a black garment open to him, motioning him to slip his arms into it. He did this and for the merest moment felt blind panic as he realized the garment was similar to a straitjacket, except that a cowl came up over his face and also covered his head. He breathed easier when he heard the garment being snapped closed down his back. Moments later he felt rope being wrapped around him, but this seemed secure although not excessively tight. For a few minutes he stood thus, straining to hear the motions around him, when abruptly many hands picked him up and raised him off the floor. He felt himself lifted into the box. It did not dawn on him to speak. When he considered this later, he felt it was because the robed figures did not speak, that their silence was a warning to him that they would not answer anything he might ask. He lay quietly, counting slowly. For years, whenever he was in the dark he measured time by counting the seconds of an imaginary clock that ticked away in his head.

Finally the Abbess spoke. "When you are ready to release yourself, press your elbows out to the side; all the knots will slip open. But do not do so until you hear the stone of the crypt returned to its place."

Knight started to thank her, knowing that her face must be very near his, but she stopped him. "Do not speak." There was a pause before she addressed him again. "The weather is with us; it is raining. They like not to get wet, these policemen."

In the dark of his shroud, Knight remembered the woman's deeply lined face and glacier-blue eyes. He marveled at her words; somehow he had always concluded that that information about policemen was his own private piece of knowledge.

She whispered one more thing, "God will show His mercy."

Knight was glad that she could not see his face, since he did not believe in God any more than he did in luck or hope.

Moments later, he heard the lid being closed and fastened, and again he began to count. But only a minute passed before he felt the coffin being gently lifted and carried some distance. He could hear neither footsteps nor voices, but presently he heard the rain fall steadily on the lid. When the box was at rest again, he heard the first male voice since the kid on the island ordered someone to shoot the dolphin.

"Can we help you sisters?"

"The hand that wields the weapon must not touch our hallowed vessel."

Knight recognized the Abbess's voice at once, although it was no longer low and gentle. The voice implied a priestess, a woman huge with authority and command. In his imagination he saw her tower above the hunters with their puny weapons.

"We shall be happy to escort you to the cemetery."

"God escorts us, but you are welcome to join the procession."

Knight heard the wheels of a wagon and the hoofbeats of a single horse. He was being moved again. Then an engine, laboring without haste, mingled with the sound of the horse.

For a long time he heard only the car and the animal and the wagon beyond the rain, but when he had counted as far as seventeen minutes, a moaning chant rose above those sounds and a few minutes after that he could not hear the rain at all, nor the horse or wagon. He was being lifted again. People were walking on a stone floor. Fifty seconds later the coffin was put down, and Knight heard the chant

65

rise and fall steadily. He tried to make out the words, but decided there were no words; the nuns were humming a dirge.

Abruptly that stopped and the Abbess's voice echoed as in a long chamber, "We return this clay to the earth and commend the spirit to God."

Minutes later, Knight believed he heard a winch or a wheel of some kind turning slowly. He felt the coffin being lowered. Fascinated, he forgot to count and was unsure how much time passed before it came to rest.

Some minutes later he thought he heard the machinery again and a strident rasping sound reverberated over him, and for twenty seconds there was silence; then heavy boots stomped loud and hollow above him. Someone was walking on his grave, and it was clearly not the nuns.

He did not wait as Sister Adelaide warned him to, but proceeded, within minutes after the thundering footsteps faded away, to loosen the knotted ropes and the shroud. The bolts holding the springs turned easily, but he took great care in raising the lid.

He sat up and found his flashlight, discovering that concealed under him was the tarp carefully folded. In the spray of light, he saw that the crypt was large enough to hold several coffins the size of his, but there were no others. Eight feet above him, a huge metal lid closed an opening three times the surface size of his coffin, which had come to rest in one corner of the chamber. He climbed out of the box and examined the room. Engraved into the center of the floor was a large ring of eyeless fish swimming after each other forever. The crypt had no other ornamentation except the molding on the wall that the Abbess spoke of.

He had no difficulty moving the panel, but a force, heavy, inert as the stones of the crypt, kept him from passing through the opening. It was a smell, a pungent odor of mold, older than the stones, a smell that lived inside the earth, a smell that the sun never touched and that would have shriveled trees. It was more than death; it had surpassed death as though it were waiting through the centuries in its black space for all life to end—when it could climb out of the ground in the form of blind trolls and starving goblins and take over a dead earth under a cold sun. Knight turned his face away, but his eye streamed as though an acrid gas had been blown into his face. Hurriedly he checked the coffin to make sure he had dropped nothing, forgotten nothing. He thought his head had rested on a small pillow, but it turned out to be pieces of bread wrapped in a canvas bag. He took the shroud and the rope and rolled them inside the tarp, which he tied to his back. Then he closed the coffin and again faced the opening through which the smell bulged like a massive physical presence, swollen and threatening to explode. He fought back nausea and stepped out of the crypt, closing the panel behind him.

Flashing the light ahead of him, he discovered that he was in a narrow low-ceilinged tunnel that sloped sharply downward. Although the stones on which he stood were as smooth as a washed floor, all was dry—the path, walls, ceiling. He must still be underneath the building, possibly a chapel. He crept forward slowly, wary of the descending passageway and the jagged rocks overhead. Twice the tunnel narrowed sharply and opened up again. After half an hour, Knight rested; the odor constricted his throat, and his breathing became labored. Also, his damaged eye throbbed and pulsated with pain. The last time the Abbess had dressed it, she told him that if the eye was to be saved, it would have to be treated and remain bandaged.

Treated! Some chance. With all Germany out looking for him, there was no likelihood that he could get it treated without turning himself in, but that was no longer possible. Tyler's blue eyes filling up with snow denied that possibility forever.

"Dietrich, you bastard," he swore aloud, and was rewarded with a musical echo that floated away in lyrical concentric circles like a pebble-disturbed pool. He hurried on, faster than before, drawn forward by his own ringing voice. Even his whispers echoed back.

Abruptly the tunnel vanished and the light, no longer restricted to its narrow confines, glowed upon a huge chamber whose walls were stacked from floor to ceiling with human skulls. They were arranged in orderly rows as though some master mason had seen to the construction.

Knight swept his light back and forth across the seemingly mortared jawless heads. Some of them had fractures on the frontal bone; others carried jagged gashes and large holes on the tops and sides. He examined one of the damaged skulls closely. It bore a slash across the nasal bone and eye ridge. Something had hit it in the face, not in death, but in life.

He walked to the end of the long chamber and found that it spread out into several narrower passages. But only in one did the walls of skulls continue. He followed it, moving his light back and forth on the path before him like a blind man's white cane.

The pain in his eye became more severe, and he found that he was dizzy and physically ill. Still he walked on, straining to hear the sound of the river of which the Abbess spoke.

Two hours later he stumbled and fell against a low ridge of stones that he had failed to see. He lay still and thought of sleep.

He and Hugo had crossed the river and were lying naked on the sugar sand under the feathery willow, talking. They always talked about the same thing.

"The way I see it," said Hugo, "once we get to be of age, there's no way The Old Man can stop us. He wakes up one morning and we've cleared out."

"But I'm not going to be of age until two years after you."

"Listen, Nicholas, when I go, you go. No way can only one of us go, so don't worry. He'd be so mad, he'd kill the one that was still here. No, it's got to be both of us, at the same time. The way we do it is this: we go downriver, cross over at the rapids, and follow the cow path on the other side. From there we go straight to the railroad bridge where the train almost stops. And from there, well, from there it's the whole world. We move at night and sleep during the day, in barns or out in the open; it makes no difference. By the time he wakes up at four, we'll be halfway out of the state and gone for good."

"Gone for good! How great that sounds." The skull nearest Knight's flashlight nodded and smiled.

"See, that's what we planned. It was 1939 and there were jobs beginning to open up. We thought we would head for Texas, someplace big enough for us to get lost in so he couldn't send the police after us."

The skull nodded sympathetically.

"He was always saying how he was going to get the police to take us to reform school if we didn't do as he said. He said he would tell them we had sold off some of the calves behind his back and stole the money.

"We were dumb to believe him." He sighed and held his head in his hands. After a time, he looked back into the skull's eyepits. "You were in a war, weren't you? All you guys were in a war of some kind. What was it, the Thirty Years' War? You look old enough. Where's the rest of your bones?"

The skull moaned faintly and Knight came to with a loud cry. "What the hell am I doing?" He took out one of the antibiotic pills and swallowed it. "If this goddamn eye gets infected, my brain's going to rot out through my ears. I swear to you, Yorick, if I ever get hold of Dietrich I am going to personally deball the sonofabitch."

The skull moaned again. They were all moaning, a low

muffled moan, soft and muted, but sustained.

"The hell they are." He rose quickly, and with one hand clutching his eye, he half ran toward the sound that became louder around each bend in the cave.

9

THE walls of skulls stopped abruptly long before Knight reached the river. Once he was past those ruined heads, the cave took on a new character: he came upon wet spots that smelled of salt, and once under a low dripping ceiling where he had to stoop to pass, a large shallow pool let off an odor of sulfur and ashes that made him think briefly of the hell his mother used to scream about when he was a child.

His footing on the slippery stones became more precarious as he ran toward the rumbling river, his light leaping ahead of him, a bright dervish dancing over the floors and up the walls that loomed massively, then fell away, only to rise suddenly again in spectral forms that seemed to watch him pass.

When he finally reached the river, he was stunned at the small amount of water: the thunder came from the falls that poured off a ledge into a pool fifty feet below the bank on which he stood. He began at once to follow the narrow path downstream. As the course of the river twisted away from the cataract, the roaring lessened and Knight began to consider his bearings. He was going northwest. He could not gauge the distance he covered because the path was circuitous and he was obliged to slow down periodically to climb over loose rocks. His creeping progress made him anxious. It seemed to him that he had been running longer than a week. The various incidents he had experienced fell into elongated time slots, stretching a few hours into whole days. Aachen no longer seemed a mere hundred miles as the crow flew; from the way things were going it might as well be on the black side of the moon, and he wasn't even across the Rhine.

It seemed to him as he flashed the light into the river from time to time that the water was slowly but steadily decreasing in volume, and after a while the path became a ledge on a sheer rock wall. Looking down upon the water, he occasionally thought of the blind fish and found himself looking for them with that old curiosity that had made him interested in sideshows when he was younger. The bizarre had always fascinated him, yet he felt a curious loathing toward it and an apprehension that gave him bad dreams. The barren water on the even more barren stones seemed unnatural to him, having always pictured rivers with grassy banks, trailing trees or wharfed with gently bobbing boats. There were dangerous rivers, even deadly ones, but lifeless streams such as this were against all nature and made his skin crawl, making him feel a bad anxiety in its presence.

The ledge narrowed until he was forced to drag his feet sideways, his back to the rock wall, arms outstretched, his left hand holding the flashlight with the beam straight down along the stone edging. Occasionally the river narrowed and moved faster; several times it spread itself out, channeling around rock islands. Then abruptly it twisted away from him, his ledge thirty feet above the water taking a sharp turn into another arm of the cave, narrower, steeper. He climbed laboriously, pausing to consider this change. The Abbess had said to follow the river, but there was no way to do it: between him and the branch of the cave that the river took was a straight drop of over forty feet. Below him, jagged rocks stuck up, their bladed edges glistening in his moving light.

He was considering the use of his rope as he scraped slowly forward, moving continually away from the river, when the ledge suddenly widened and a smell as putrid as rotten eggs stuck in his nostrils and throat. He flashed the light as far forward as the turn in the cave allowed and peered into the circles of light. All seemed the same as before. Then he slipped, unaccountably, for he had begun to move with even greater care when the smell first came to him. He slid backward on the ledge and over the side, in the last moment grasping a knob of rock that hooked on the ledge. The flashlight, attached to his wrist with a strap, clattered against the stone and went out.

Knight hung on the piece of rock, aware for the first time that it was covered with a slippery substance on one side. Slowly he pulled himself back upon the ledge, sitting with his feet dangling into the dead black space he knew was in front of him. He shook the flashlight gently and twisted the cap. A pale, fuzzy light shone in his eyes. He turned it on the rock that had stopped his fall. A thick black liquid oozed down one side of it where his arm had gone around it. Knight stared at the congealed mass, convinced for one irrational moment that the stone was melting. Then he turned the light ceilingward and choked back a cry, raising his arm over his face and finally retching when the filthy sleeve of his flight suit touched his mouth. He was sitting in bat guano. Above him, clusters of the little beasts hung sleeping, their heads tightly tucked beneath their folded wings. Ahead of him the ceiling was solid with their slow-breathing mass.

A thousand ghastly stories about bats ran through his mind: they stuck to human hair so that the head had to be

73

shaved to free them; they were diseased with rabies; they sucked blood for food. . . .

He rose slowly and picked his way ahead, the smell burning his eye, the slime shifting under his feet. In his throat the vomit rose and fell with each labored breath.

He did not know how long or how far he walked under the twitching headless bodies. At one point he found himself half-running, his fear no longer rational. When he fell, he pulled himself up slowly. "Idiot! They're only bats, and they're hibernating." But a short time later, the old horrible terrors of his childhood returned, and he was rushing forward again, his boots sinking into the fetid dung, his memory opening into long-forgotten dark places which had taken him years to shut away.

He was running frantically, and a boy was running after him, howling at him. When he glanced back at his pursuer, he saw other boys come out of the bushes and from behind trees, joining the one who was running him to earth. He ran across a street and scrambled through a hole in a wall, cut his hand on some barbed wire, jumped over a deep ditch half-full of shattered bottles and upended sheets of broken glass, and kept running until he reached a grassy bank, from which he plunged into a fast-moving stream. He came up gasping and heard a shout behind him and moments later a scream, a shriek of pain and rage.

The howling stopped or perhaps he only floated out of its range. Where was that, exactly? He could not have been more than seven. Why were they chasing him? What bad thing had he done that made them howl after him like that? And there was a name they kept calling him, a name he could not understand because it was not in any language he knew, but they screamed it derisively. He knew it was something disgusting.

In the cave Knight stopped, held his hand over his throbbing eye, and tried to think of the name the screaming boys had called him. But the memory ended there and the elusive name was only an unintelligible shriek in the dark. He did not remember how he had gotten out of the river, either.

He walked doggedly on, holding the light ahead of him carefully; if the flashlight gave up on him, he was dead. Above him the bats were closer to his head, but again it was some seconds before he realized that the cave was getting smaller, the guano deeper. He pulled his boots through it, held his hand over his nose and mouth, and struggled with consciousness. He'd be damned if he was going to drown in bat shit. Dietrich would love that!

The cave became a narrow tunnel in which Knight had to stoop to avoid hitting the bats. Then suddenly the cave ended. Knight, bent over, failed to see the ceiling drop abruptly, and plunged headfirst into a solid mass of bats. He screamed as they rained all over him, squeaking shrilly, but he flexed his knees and rolled, protecting the wounded eye with both hands, the flashlight dancing crazily before it went out. He felt himself fall on a slippery slide of some kind and thought he had crashed into another cave until he saw the star.

He was lying on his back, still holding his injured eye, and above him was a star. No. He was wrong. There were many stars. It was not another cave. It was the universe, and it was night, and he was alive.

He breathed the good air and waited for his head to clear, even believing that in a moment the pain, too, would fade out of his eye and he would rise up—a well man. But after a few minutes, when the pain still pulsed steadily, he sat up and discovered that he was on the shallow slope of a hill. Off to his left, but clearly distinguishable from the highways on both banks, was the mighty Rhine, and below him was a smaller river entering into it. He knew then that he was looking upon the valley of the Wisper, where the small stream vanished into the great river, for there at the juncture was the town of Lorch with its towering church of Saint Martin visible in the town's lights, and just beyond the town, but not visible, he knew was the ruined castle of Nollig, where he had once gone on a picnic with a pretty girl. He had to remind himself that that was six months—not six years—ago.

He descended into the valley through layers of terraced orchards and vineyards, taking stock of his situation. He had been in the cave all day but had no idea how many miles he had walked, but as that bloody crow could fly it, he was approximately fifteen kilometers from the summit of the Taunus. This realization stopped him cold as he stared at the peaceful scene below him: after two and a half days into the operation, he was less than ten miles from where he began.

10

By the time Knight reached the bank of the Wisper, a biting wind sweeping out of the small river's steep valley chilled him to the marrow. Always in his life, he had hated the winds, feeling singularly helpless in their force. One could predict rain and snow, protect himself from them, but the winds seemed to him to have no pattern, no clear reason for rising when they did. As a child, it was the only weather he truly feared.

But wind or no, he could not stop now: he had to move by night and hide by day. The cave had allowed him to do both, but that meant no sleep until the next morning. No matter, he had gone longer without rest. The trick was to stay alert and outthink Dietrich. One thing was clear, he would not cross the Rhine until he was below Koblenz where the Mosel flowed through the city and entered the greater river. Dietrich would guard the Mosel well and, anyway, there was no point in having to cross two major rivers; there were plenty of minor ones that were going to give him trouble if he wanted to stay dry, and this was now paramount; the weather was bitterly cold. He could not risk getting wet again. Once he crossed the Wisper, there was still the Lahn, which poured into the Rhine on the east side, upstream from Koblenz, but that was a future concern; first, the Wisper.

There was still another reason he wanted to follow the right bank: he knew it better, had spent some time exploring it and felt a familiarity toward it that haunted him in old thoughts and fragments of scenes that came and went in his mind at random moments when he was not even concentrating on that part of his past.

With the wind at his back, he followed the bank of the Wisper to the outskirts of Lorch, one of those German villages with half-timbered houses and a few old architectural Renaissance relics that caused the town always to be described in travel folders as "picturesque little village steeped in old-world charm." It looked exactly like a thousand other German villages described in exactly the same way. What amazed Knight about the tourist description was the writer's condescending implication that the townspeople were discernible characters out of a Grimm Brothers fairy tale. Where, wondered Knight, did the tourists think the Dietrichs of Germany fit into this silly sunny picture?

He stopped under the first bridge over the Wisper and waited, gauging the amount of traffic. It was no longer his airman's uniform that concerned him, since it was black with filth from the cave so that it did finally appear to be a mechanic's greasy coverall: the real worry was his wounded eye; not only was the pain hideous, but the bandage, raggedy and flapping by then, would certainly attract attention to him. He swallowed another of the antibiotic tablets and drank from the river. The water tasted of iron. He wrapped the burial robe and tarp around him and lay on the riverbank under the bridge, waiting for the traffic to subside. The ground was damp, but at least he was out of the wind.

He examined his situation further: he did not have a fever, only pain; he had enough food for a couple of days, and in the morning after he holed up for the day, he would repair the flashlight. He was fifty kilometers from Koblenz and the time was twenty-one hundred hours, and why didn't these Grimm characters go home and go to bed instead of drive around all night?

He contemplated the Rhine between Lorch and Koblenz: it was a massive river, swift and dark with brooding, moss-encrusted castles on the hills and cliffs on both banks. It twisted like an awakening serpent, and Knight knew that Dietrich would search every vessel whether rowboat or barge, tug or pleasure cruiser. So a boat ride was out. Roadblocks precluded stealing a car or taking a surreptitious hitch on the back of a truck. There were, of course, the trains. But Dietrich, too, must be thinking about the trains by now, but perhaps he was thinking about the trains on the other side of the river—and perhaps not. Knight saw himself walking the fifty kilometers to Koblenz. After that, the only real problem would be the crossing. Once on the left bank, he could lose himself on the Eifel plateau with its forsaken moorland, harsh rocky roads, and shrunken trees and, of course, its mean winds. But that was nothing—even a little like the Sierra foothills. It was the crossing of the Rhine that would take some doing. Too bad there was no mined bridge to cross at Remagen. That would be spit in Dietrich's eye.

As the time passed and the cars still rumbled over him, he began to make out the details of the dim underside of the bridge. Not six feet above him was a cable. He followed its course from the pilings near him but lost it in the dark halfway over the water. How German, he thought, to tuck the thing neatly out of the way rather than string it between two poles from one bank to the other.

A child on monkey bars in a playground could have crossed as easily.

On the north bank of the Wisper, he followed a culvert

under the highway and began his ascent toward Nollig castle, whose ruins, according to legend and the girl at the picnic six months back, were haunted by mountain sprites who whimsically favored the knights-errant of earlier times who performed dangerous feats.

"How dangerous?" Knight wanted to know at the time.

"Oh, they fought dragons and trolls and saved ladies who were imprisoned in old towers by vile witches who could cast evil spells."

Knight told her that dragons and trolls were no problem, but witches were unpredictable and he would rather not mess with them.

They joked away the June morning, made love under the trees in the afternoon, and never saw each other again.

Below him the river was alive with traffic; it pulsated with flashing lights and booming signal horns. He listened for sounds from the highway, but heard only the voices whispering in his blood. *"Listen, Nicholas, if there is any way, any way at all, I mean after I am finished here, I'll try to get to wherever you are. Think about that. I'll help when I can, I mean if it's possible."* Hugo's eyes were huge and hot with assurance and certainty and fever.

"Well, at the moment, it's just this bloody eye. It hurts like a bastard, you see, and I swear if I don't watch it I'll be walking backwards. If I can make it to the Lahn during this night, I'll hole up there and cross the Rhine the next night."

Below him a train sped through the town without stopping; Knight saw the bright windows of the dining car flash by, *". . . go straight to the railroad bridge where the train stops, and from there it's, well, from there it's the world. . . ."*

He rose quickly and began to run down the slope toward the Rhine. "Of course, Dietrich, you're going to think of the trains, of the freight trains! The trouble with you, Dietrich, is that you really haven't any class. The freight train! How provincial. How very lumpish and uncivilized of you."

80

That first year after he was away from the farm, when he was still fifteen, he must have hopped three dozen freights, Hugo's voice always clear and loud in the last moment before the speed was too great and the opportunity was taken or lost. *"Do it the way we practiced. If it's too late, forget it. There's always another train."*

At the next station, two kilometers downstream from Lorch, Knight, crouching behind a hedge, waited over an hour for the local to come through. It was past twenty-three hundred hours and the pain from his eye was making him nauseous; still he ate methodically the bread the nuns had packed for him. Briefly he saw the clear, cold eyes of the Abbess when he tried to tell her that it was all a game, that he was in no danger of being shot. He wondered for the first time then what the local police actually believed. What had they been told by the military? He considered the message he would give out to local authorities if he were Dietrich, and knew at once, that the policeman inside the station buying cigarettes, as well as the one he had dodged coming through town, knew him only as an escaped killer. He could actually visualize Dietrich's communique, "Advise local authorities to make every attempt to capture escapees. Shoot only if subject attempts to run." He snickered to himself. "Bang, bang, you're dead."

Minutes later he caught the last car opposite the entry side of the platform, just after it left the station, pulled himself up over the door, and lay flat on the spine of the roof behind a raised vent.

He knew the towns were close together and the train stopped at every station whether there were passengers or not. It was going to be a slow trip to the Lahn.

The road ran alongside the track between him and the river, with trucks rolling on it in steady caravans in both directions. On the opposite bank the same thick, livid blaring procession of smoking diesel and thundering engines roared through the night. On the water, the cacophony of horns and

81

whistles echoed up through the narrow valleys which dropped toward the Rhine gorge. Knight lay spread on the train like a shadow. As long as it was dark and his dirty uniform blended into the roof, he was relatively safe.

He turned the damaged side of his face downward to protect it from the wind, and moved consciously into the pain—long elliptical shapes of intense throbbing that swung outward, returned again into the center of his head, and flew out again, only to return once more.

For a time he tried to think of other things: the pool under the willows in the river in the Central Valley of California where he and Hugo swam, dreamed, slept. But always the image faded into the pain, liquefying and dissolving, siphoning away like something vanishing into quicksand. The pain churned in his head, sucked away his thoughts, leaving only one reality: hang on.

The little villages came and went, marked only by the brief stopping of the train and the jerking spasms that returned it to its slow pleasant crawl along the highway where the trucks were going twice as fast. When he looked toward the right, he saw the dark sleeping hills crowned by ruined castles, their towers and battlements silhouetted insolently against the starry sky. He passed through Kaub, where he knew subterranean slate had been quarried for centuries.

At the Lorelei rock, the train tunneled and Knight clawed to the roof and stretched his body into it. The train's whistle blew stridently, the sound turning the pain in his head white-hot as he willed himself to remain conscious. His mind sought out the old legend: *Not this time, Lorelei, not this time, not under a train. Down in the bottom of the Rhine, deep ... deep where the treasure lay buried. I'll meet you there, but not here, not in the smoke and filth. I'll take your golden body there, embrace it and not even mind dying.*

He wanted to laugh into the pain in his head. "*Listen, rivermen, if the siren is calling you, enticing you to your deaths, make the trip worth something. Don't go for nothing.*"

The train passed below several castles towering high above small towns which clung to the rocky cliffs. He gazed at Kamp-Bornhofen with a smile: a handsome young woman at a bar in this town once told him that Saint Nicholas was the patron saint of rivermen and Kamp-B was the town that honored him. He had come back to it several times, staying at a local inn and visiting the castles nearby. A particular day stood out above the others, an ordinary day, not unusual, not strange: he had merely spent the whole morning on a bench in a park watching some children sail their toy boats.

He was pulled out of his memory abruptly when the train passed over the road and ran next to the river. A few miles later, the highway, now to his right, had a long line of halted traffic. It could be stopped for any number of reasons, he thought calmly: an accident, an intersection, even a brake check. *No, Nicholas, not in Germany. There's not even a speed limit. You can kill yourself as fast as you want.*

A minute later the train reached the spot at the head of the line of halted cars and trucks. Several flashing red lights winked from vehicles at the side of the road. As the train passed the spot, the scene imprinted itself into Knight's line of vision down to the very last minute detail: the gleaming boots of the uniformed men as they peered into the backs of trucks and the trunks of the cars with long probing flashlights and drawn guns, and the insignias on the vehicles at the side of the road that were not police cars but Army jeeps.

Nine kilometers later at Lahnstein on the north side of the river, just past the town itself, he jumped from the moving train, flexed his legs, and rolled down a grassy bank that had patches of snow on it. Across the Rhine was Koblenz, its happy night lights twinkling in the boat-rippled river.

Knight walked some distance back toward the town before he found the culvert that got him to the other side of the highway. He followed the runoff ditch until it disappeared into a thicket in the hillside. From the wooded slope he faced the valley of the Lahn. Below him a road bordered the smaller river and disappeared behind the curve of a hill.

Somewhere near that curve was an old half-timbered house with a barn and a root cellar, a blacksmith's shed with a long tool table and a forge. For years he had had nightmares about that house, until one terrible night when he awakened screaming, he swore to himself that he would never think about it again, never let his mind see it again, and never, never dream of it again.

And now, at three in the morning, as the stars were vanishing behind fast-moving clouds, and the pain in his head was like the roar of a train in a tunnel, he was setting out to find that house, hoping that it might give him just one day of rest.

11

WHEN he left the Rhine and started up the Lahn Valley, Knight was moving east. Dietrich was not going to look for him in the opposite direction from Aachen, so he was safe for a while, at least for the day while he was holed up (a good word for it, he thought) at the farmhouse he was convinced his instincts, if not his memory, would find for him.

He walked carefully around the slope of the hills, circumventing the thickets when possible and staying parallel to the road several hundred feet below him, where the occasional car lights gave him some idea of the terrain. Frequently he stopped to stare hard at darkened houses surrounded by outbuildings and gardens; but each time he moved on, his mind rejecting the shape of the house because the roof was not steep enough or it was too wide or too narrow. Once his heart quickened when the house below him seemed to be the one of his memory, but the barn was different and the blacksmith shed was gone. He walked on. Then slowly he backtracked to look at the house again. The barn was larger than he remembered, the trees in back of the house smaller. He walked closer and saw the root-cellar mound that he knew at once ran along the top of the garden. But many gardens had root cellars adjacent to them. For some time he stared intensely at the three-storied house built against the side of the hill. Above him clouds ran before the stars, covering and uncovering them, giving him brief glimpses of things that were both familiar and alien in turns.

The top floor of the house had two windows set far back into its steep roof. Slowly Knight walked to a point where he was in direct line with the windows; there he turned and looked toward the crest of the hill above him and waited for the starlight to return. A great mass of heavy clouds blotted out everything for a time; then as it thinned and passed by, an escarpment of bare rock rose like a giant's head out of the hill.

Knight breathed deeply. Hugo had been the first to say it looked like a one-eared giant early one evening when they were kneeling on the bed looking at the rock formation. It was winter then, too, and the brooding head gazed down at them darkly through the thin tops of the leafless trees. "And his body is sitting inside the mountain, captive forever, or until someone cracks open the earth and frees him."

"How can we do that?" a five-year-old Nicholas had asked.

"With lightning. When we find out how the lightning works, we'll get it to crack the mountain wide open, and the giant will stand up and stretch and shake off the earth and say, 'To whom do I owe my freedom?'" Hugo spoke these last words deeply in his throat, and they both laughed at the giant's voice. "'Why, to my brother Nicholas and me. We got the lightning to open up the earth.' And the giant will say, 'And what can I do for Nicholas and you?' And we will say, 'We want to climb on your shoulders and go see the world,' and he will say, 'Done. With my twelve-league boots we can walk across all of the Westerwald in a few steps.'"

"How much is twelve leagues?" Nicholas wanted to know.

"Plenty."

"Could we go to Berlin?"

"Easy, but Father says the opportunities are all in America, and we will get the giant to take us there."

"What are opportunities?"

"I'm not sure, but I think they are things that make you rich."

Knight shivered in the predawn night. *Ah, Hugo, my brother, there were some rich days. Do you remember the summers, the warmth, the sun on our skin, the cool water, the soft sand?*

He wanted to weep, to walk into the house and up the stairs to that slope-walled room, climb back into the bed with the thick patched quilt and dream with Hugo about freeing the giant imprisoned in the mountain under their uncle's farm.

He collected himself quickly, knowing that his exhaustion and the pain in his eye, which throbbed continually, was weakening him. As soon as he was hidden in the root cellar, he would rebandage the eye and take another pill.

He moved cautiously down the slope until he was quite near the house. The people who bought the farm from his uncle must have removed the blacksmith shed and added to the barn. The shed had been to the right of the house, and neighbors came from all the other farms in the area to get their horses shod and their axles and wagon wheels fixed. He approximated where the building had stood. Perhaps it had burned down; he hoped it had burned down.

For years the red blazing fire in the forge entered his dreams until he screamed, or usually only dreamed he screamed, and woke up clawing the bedclothes. The nightmares began shortly before he was six. It was almost spring and his Aunt Mary had told him and Hugo that they would soon have another brother, or possibly even a sister. There seemed to be a good deal of uncertainty about that.

Early one morning they woke up in their room on the third floor to great confusion in the house: one floor down, their mother lay moaning in bed. Aunt Mary was talking to her gently. "It's all right. It's coming along fine. You've had two so you know what to expect."

Three hours later, their mother was shrieking, "I am dying! I am dying!" and Aunt Mary was running up and down the stairs with towels and hot water and more sheets, while he and Hugo waited in the little room one floor up and cried and shook with fear.

Then briefly everything was still, and they opened the door and came down the narrow stairs to the hall, just as both women screamed and Mary ran out of the room and down the stairs shouting to their father to come at once.

Hugo and Nicholas went to the open door of their mother's and father's room and looked in. Their mother was crouching up against the headboard like a cornered animal, her eyes mad, her foaming mouth uttering incoherent guttural sounds. Near the foot of the bed in a spreading stain of blood lay a baby twisted grotesquely; out of its mouth, attached by some blue ganglia, grew the head of another child.

Nicholas saw the thing twitch. He began to scream just as his uncle and father reached the top of the stairs and shoved them roughly away from the open door. The two boys gazed at each other in horror and Nicholas vomited against the wall.

A few minutes later their father rushed out of the room and down the stairs carrying a blood-dripping bundle by the bunched-up corners of a sheet. Uncle Albert ran out a moment after that, taking the steps three at a time. The front door slammed twice.

Hugo and Nicholas could hear the men shouting at each other in the yard and ran to the window at the end of the hall just in time to see their father knock Albert down, tear open the furnace door, and in a swinging motion, so that the bundle arced back before it swung down and forward, cast it into the maw of flames.

After that, it seemed to Nicholas the whole world changed completely. For months their mother did not come out of her room at all, but they could hear her through the closed door, talking to God, demanding to know what He wanted of her.

Uncle Albert and Aunt Mary and their father never talked and laughed anymore at the dinner table as they had done before the fatal birth. It seemed that no one ever talked at all. The two men worked silently and did not look at each other, and Aunt Mary frequently wept as she cleaned the house and took care of their mother. Sometimes she would look at the two small boys and shake her head, murmuring, "Poor babies, poor babies."

When Hugo started school, Nicholas was mad with loneliness. He would climb to the top of the mountain, sit on the giant's shoulder, and tell him how bad things were. "They fight all the time now. Today Father hit Uncle Albert and made his nose bleed and Uncle Albert said bad things and Aunt Mary said for them to stop but they didn't. Hugo says we are going to have to go away as soon as Mother gets well, but he doesn't know where we are going to go."

One Sunday late that fall, their mother descended the stairs just as they were all sitting down to the midday meal and announced loudly that God told her they were all going to hell because they killed His son. Aunt Mary tried to get her to go back to bed, but she kicked and struggled and grabbed a butcher knife from the sideboard and slashed the air in front of her and told them to get ready to die.

Aunt Mary pushed Nicholas and Hugo out of the room and closed the door. The two boys listened to their mother screech for a while until someone must have hit her, because she broke off in the middle of a word, the rest of it sounding like she had something stuck in her throat. They carried her back upstairs and a few days later she came down again but this time she was quiet and docile with dead eyes that looked off at nothing. She didn't seem to know who anybody was. Aunt Mary got her to help a little around the house, but mostly she just sat and stared, her hair hanging loose and uncombed around her face.

Nicholas and Hugo began to stay out of the grown-ups' way as much as possible because they all seemed to be angry most of the time. Only Aunt Mary occasionally talked to them, telling them that things would get better in a little while and for them not to worry about what was happening now, but she always began to cry before she said very much. That December there was no Christmas tree.

The following year, when Nicholas went off to school with Hugo, things improved, not at home, but away from home, not so much at school, but on the walk to and from school and the long hours they spent together on the giant's shoulder, planning their journey across the Westerwald to the North Sea and from there out into the world.

Late that year Uncle Albert announced abruptly that he intended to sell the farm. The quarrels became more bitter after this news, but Uncle Albert was adamant: he wanted to leave the farm and get work in a factory. Their father spent days at a time in Koblenz on some business of his own.

The next spring, when Nicholas was eight and Hugo ten, the family got on a train early one morning in Lahnstein, where Uncle Albert and Aunt Mary waved good-bye until a turn in the track blocked Nicholas' vision. For some years he saw Aunt Mary's white handkerchief waving furiously while her other hand covered her sobbing mouth.

The train went all the way to Le Havre, where they got on a ship that took them to Galveston, Texas, where they got on another train which after five days left them in a town in the Great Central Valley of California. There, a friend of Uncle Albert's came in a car and took them to a farm on the

Tuolumne River. Six months after they arrived in America, their mother set fire to the small farmhouse while he and Hugo and their father were doing the evening milking. She burned to death before anyone could reach her. The neighboring people thought it was an accident, but Nicholas and Hugo knew better; she had been talking wildly about burning in hell for months.

After that they lived in a two-room outbuilding originally meant for the storage of seed corn and farm tools. The boys went to school whenever the weather was bad and The Old Man could not find anything for them to do. They ate haphazardly—cornmeal and rice and sometimes black bass that got trapped in the swamp at one of the river-bottom lands after the spring flooding ended and the channel from the swamp to the river dried up. From the farms around them, they stole grapes and peaches and walnuts and survived. Seven years passed before he and Hugo engineered their escape from the farm.

When Nicholas entered military service two years after their escape, he was six feet tall, had no cavities in his teeth, but X rays showed eight broken bones that had never been medically set. When the Army doctors asked him how the bones were broken, he truthfully answered that with the exception of his jaw he could not remember.

Knight decided at first that he would enter the root cellar just before dawn. It would probably be safer to get into while it was still dark, but a more subtle caution made him want to check the farm out in the early light before he climbed down into a hole in the ground from which there was absolutely no escape if someone looked into it. He reasoned also, however, that with the new kitchen appliances, there was an excellent chance that the root cellar was only rarely used. And there was also a good possibility that a lantern would be hanging from a hook on one of the support beams. He thought of Aunt Mary telling him and Hugo to bring up some radishes and to mind the lamp—not to hit their heads on it, since it hung low above the stairs.

He had considered hiding out in the barn but decided against it since the new addition to the building made it unfamiliar to him. If it was a workroom of some kind, someone might be hammering in it all day. He glanced toward it out of casual curiosity and in that exact moment saw, or believed he saw, a frail blur of light that lasted no more than a few seconds.

He dodged behind a tree and waited, peering at the barn steadily from around the curve of wet bark. Had there actually been a light, or was the pain in his head making him see things? He had to consider the possibility that the light was real, and began to pose questions to himself. A match? No. No farmer would light a match in his barn. A lighter? Ridiculous. What kind of farmer owned a lighter? He waited impatiently for some logical, at least reasonable, answer to present itself.

After a time he glanced at his watch and wondered if farmers were getting up later than they used to; it was almost six and the cows lowed fitfully in the barn. Not twenty feet from him, half-concealed by a clump of dried shrubbery that would turn green in the spring and produce enough berries for a half-dozen families, lay the three-foot-high mound of the root cellar. The double doors built into it at a forty-five-degree angle were clearly visible to Knight. If he crawled on all fours and opened only one panel slightly, he could slither down the rough stairs with no one in the house or the barn being any the wiser. Still, he waited.

He did not know when the light in the house went on, but the next time he glanced back toward it, the room he knew was the kitchen had a light burning in it. Moments later a man obviously a farmer walked from the house to the barn, whistling. In all the years he had spent on a farm, Knight could not recall a farmer whistling in the morning. Still, that didn't prove anything. Maybe the guy spent a great night in bed.

The man looked neither to the left nor the right but walked briskly to the barn, his whistling sharp and steady in the bitterly cold December morning. Knight heard his boots crunch through some iced-over puddles. There were still patches of snow on the ground.

After the man entered the barn, Knight crawled to the narrow space between the cellar mound and leggy leafless berry bushes. Again he waited, although he was only a few feet from the door. He noted the patch of snow covering a good portion of the area in front of the root cellar and realized he would have to avoid stepping into it.

For a moment he focused his attention on the door handles, but something far inside his head whispered to him to look back at the remnant of snow. He did. He heard a wise seven-year-old Hugo say to him slyly, "Nicholas, never eat yellow snow."

Yellow snow! On the patch of white was a stain, a citrine stain. What kind of farmer would pee at the front of the door of his own root cellar? No kind. The man at that very moment inside the cellar who must have relieved his bladder sometime before Knight reached the farm was a professional brother of the same bastard that smoked cigarettes in the barn, and neither of them were farmers.

12

OF course, Dietrich would have all the records by now. How stupid of him not to have thought of that. If he were Dietrich, that would be the first thing he would have done: picked up Nicholas Knight's records and searched them for every fragment of information on how the man thought. He would have hunted for patterns, peculiarities, impairments, anything that could give him leads on how Knight would behave under pressure. And then he would have discovered that the subject was born near Lahnstein, Germany, thirty-eight years ago, that he left Germany with his family in 1932, that he joined the Air Force in April of 1941, and that he had participated in D day and was promoted in the field.

As he crept back up through the scrub and scattered trees above the farm, Knight considered those facts. Could Dietrich be so ridiculous as to hate him because of his war record? No. The sonofabitch would admire him for that. He was a soldier through and through; that ramrod neck, the permanently marching walk, the clipped ordered voice was all military.

At the top of the mountain, Knight wedged himself between the two stones that composed the side of the head and the single ear of the giant and watched the farm as he rebandaged his eye and swallowed another of the pills. The day was going to be dark, with heavy snow clouds hanging tumidly over the Lahn Valley. He took the flashlight apart and tightened it. It worked fine. He ate the rest of the nuns' bread and the partisans' cheese and thought of the kitchen in the house below, where he used to watch Aunt Mary slice roast meat on a cutting board. What if he was wrong about the farm and Dietrich didn't know about it? Then he was out in the open, during the day, under a threatening sky, with exhaustion and pain dulling his senses and making him doubt his own judgment—for nothing.

A truck passed on the road below, and Knight watched it with casual interest, following it on down the highway until it was out of sight. But something snagged on his mind, and he reexamined the road again: the truck had slowed down when it neared the narrow drive onto the farm. He telescoped his hands and looked through the fingered tunnel: behind the barren plum trees bordering the road stood a large unmarked van, large enough to hide a jeep in.

"An unmarked van parked beside a highway ... in Germany? Come on, Dietrich, you're not that dumb. Why didn't you paint a bottle of beer on it or a link of sausages, you klutz! Sorry, buddy, for you that's *Klotz*."

Knight started down the other side of the mountain toward the Westerwald with its lovely beech trees, bare now and ghost-trunked in the silent winter. He looked back once more toward the giant, but saw only an outcropping of random rock.

For several hours he walked steadily, skirting occasional clusters of farm buildings and small villages, mindful of the sudden country roads that ran winding through the woods.

He traveled due north, planning to make his westerly move later near the Neuwied Basin where the Rhine Valley suddenly opened up. Dietrich would not look for him where the river was most difficult to cross.

Between two hills, he came upon a raw cut in the land and barely missed being seen by a construction crew which had stopped their freeway work to have lunch. Knight, watching them briefly from the cover of the woods, wished he could walk up to them, talk to them, maybe sit awhile and rest. Perhaps they would offer him some coffee. He tried not to think of coffee, although he was convinced that he could smell its rich dark aroma rising out of the thermos mugs in the men's hands. In lonely desperation he turned and hurried away.

An hour later he passed through a campground fed by a gushing stream that raced around large boulders. He drank deeply, gratefully, and realized that he had ignored his thirst for some hours. There were too many things wrong with him to consciously admit to one more, but he knew that he would have to rest soon. When had he last slept? He thought back to the farm, to Lahnstein, the train, the Nollig citadel, the Wisper, the bats, the skulls, the burial. Of course, before the burial the nuns had kindly drugged him, not once, but twice. He had slept with the taste of apricot juice sweet and luscious on his tongue.

By three o'clock he was hallucinating. Coming over the top of yet another hill, he saw, or believed he saw, a castle cresting the summit of the next rise. It seemed to float, settle, and float again, cloudlike upon the mountain. He held his hand over his damaged eye and squinted with the other. The castle stood still. He had only to descend the present slope, climb the next one, call to the gatekeeper, and ask for a few hours' lodging. He would be happy to pay for this with stories of his adventures, for he could tell of strange things: he had been to the home of the dead and discoursed with soldiers from the Thirty Years' War, touched their fatal wounds and listened to their sad moans. Ah, he had much to tell: a prancing unicorn had died in front of his eyes in the middle of the Rhine, and the enchantress Lorelei had spared him although he had invaded her castle rock on the back of a dragon that belched deadly fumes. All he wanted in return was a few hours' rest and perhaps a cup of wine and a scrap of bread and a little salve for his wounds.

He was already preparing his speech for the gatekeeper when he stumbled up to the crumbling wall of the castle and found that the gate was missing. "Hey, somebody stole your gate." He waited. "If you give me the use—only temporary, mind you—of a trusty steed, I'll go after the varlets for you." Again he waited. Somewhere, water dripped steadily. "You got a leak in the roof? I can fix that, too. I am a handy man to have around the castle." He walked through a courtyard and into a roofless room, where snow lay in the corners.

"Hello. Hello." He climbed stone steps to a second level and entered another chamber, which had half the ceiling intact. "Anybody home?"

At his call, violently fluttering black wings burst out from the overhanging slate tiles and rushed past him. He screamed and dropped to the stone floor, his heart jumping. When he looked up, a half-dozen ravens were flapping above him, their cries wild with outrage. He breathed deeply. "Come on back, I'm not buying the place." The birds soared, circled, wafted downward and settled on a crenellated wall at another level of the castle.

Knight rose slowly, his whole face beating with pain as silver stars danced around his head. He stumbled into another room and then two more, all roofless, all the doorways in line, all the rooms empty and dusky in the failing day. In the final room through which he passed, he turned a corner into a large hall which stretched almost the whole length of one end of the complex; this room, too, opened to the sky. Off it he found the kitchen with its huge oven in which six centuries before someone had baked bread. He smoothed the tarp on the floor of the oven and slid in upon it feetfirst, pulling the burial robe over him. He slept almost at once, as the swollen sky seemed to release a great breath and thick dry snow began to fall.

He awakened during the night and for the merest instant thought he was back in the coffin, but his memory cleared and he checked the time. It was one-thirty, exactly ninety-six hours after he had dropped into the Taunus mountains.

He slid out of the oven. The whole world was white; in the sky a thin cloud drifted across the sleepy eye of the waning moon. From the outer wall of the castle, Knight scanned the area to the north and saw headlights flash briefly and vanish: clearly a bend in a road, and from the amount of traffic it was obviously more than a back-country lane. He headed for it, adjusting his senses to the moonlight and wary of the sound of rushing water. Twice he crossed shallow brooks; on the second one he slipped on the stones and got his feet soaked.

When he reached the highway he was ten kilometers from the Rhine. In the shadows of the trees, he followed the road, knowing that up ahead a railroad bridge crossed the Rhine upriver from Neuwied. And since he had disappointed Dietrich at the farm on the Lahn, the hunters were probably searching the Mosel Valley.

He heard an engine laboring up a grade and began running almost at once. It was a truck and trailer, heavily loaded with cattle. Just as it reached the top of the grade, Knight ran from the snowy bank and caught one of the slats, pulled himself to the top, slipped under the flapping canvas, and crooning softly to the cows, lowered himself among them. He patted their bellies and necks and flanks and whispered continually.

At the bridge over the Rhine at Neuwied they were held up by a roadblock. The man in the truck got out and asked the driver ahead of him what the problem was. He was told about the escaped convicts.

"They haven't caught those guys yet?"

"Not the ringleader, the American."

"Oh, he's out of the country by now."

"No, no; he shot some people in Frankfurt last night."

"No fooling?"

"They never had a chance."

"The bastard."

"They say he's like a mad dog, froths at the mouth and shoots anybody that gets in his way."

The line moved and the driver jumped back in his truck and drove forward slowly. Several times more the line came to a complete halt before the truck reached the roadblock on the river.

A policeman walked up to the cab and flashed his light into it. "Just some cows in back," said the driver. "No killers."

The policeman started to walk toward the back of the truck but the driver called to him. "Hey, is it true that he's a real gangster, one of those killers from America who shoots on sight?"

"That's true."

"I heard he put so many notches in his gun the handle fell off."

The policeman laughed. "That's butt."

"What's butt?"

"You mean the butt fell off. In American 'butt' is gun handle; also means rump. You get it—his rump fell off," said the policeman, roaring.

"What do you mean his rump fell off? What's his rump got to do with a gun handle?"

"It's a joke, stupid. I said 'butt' in American is like rump; so his rump fell off."

"How could his rump fall off?"

"Forget it, you potato." The policeman shook his head in disgust and motioned the driver on with his flashlight.

The cows staggered as the truck lurched forward, and Knight grabbed the slats on the back of the cab and braced his feet against them, terrified that at this most fortuitous of moments both of his feet could easily get crushed.

The truck crossed the Rhine and headed north. When Knight began to think about the policeman's problem with the foreign pun, he laughed aloud. In seconds he was unable to stop laughing. Tears drenched his face, and it was only the pain that forced him to pull himself together and end the hysteria. Calmly, he wished that he could buy the truck driver a drink. "Ah, Dietrich, it wasn't my rump that fell off in the Rhine; it was yours, and all because of an impatient policeman and a potato that couldn't catch on to a small joke."

Knight read the road signs. He was forty-five kilometers from Bonn: no, the capital didn't interest him; he'd seen it. He felt light-headed. Everything seemed just slightly amusing to him. He patted the nose of the cow that was sniffing his filthy uniform.

"No, sweetie, a field of fresh clover I'm not, and I'm truly sorry. I wish I had a pocket full of apples for you. You've all been fine company. You didn't step on my feet once or squeal to the cops, and I'll bet you don't even think that I shot anybody in Frankfurt last night."

He rambled pointlessly in a thick mushy voice until he heard himself, suddenly, coldly, with a kind of abrupt shock. "Good God. I must be ill." He quickly swallowed another of the antibiotic pills, but it stuck in his throat, and in forcing it back up, he vomited a hot thin liquid that only made him retch more.

"All I need is some dry socks. In this whole bloody world, the most underrated of all comforts is dry socks."

Near Brohl, the driver stopped and got out to urinate.

101

"Keep it quiet, girls," he called over his shoulders to the cattle.

Before the truck moved back onto the highway, Knight, already over the side, leaped clear of the lumbering vehicle, dropped to a crouch, and rolled down the snow-covered embankment. He lay still in the darkness of the ditch and felt calm: he had crossed the Rhine, and that was as good as being halfway home.

13

Kₙₖₕₜ slipped away into the snow-covered underbrush at the bottom of the embankment and from there into the narrow band of forest ribboned along the river where the Eifel mountains shove the Rhine into a narrow ravine at Brohl. He circumvented the town, sloshing through old forlorn orchards clinging to the rocky soil in narrow terraces. When he began the long climb up the steep Brohl Valley, he was sweating profusely although it was bitterly cold under the clear sky. He was annoyed with himself: he had slept nine hours in the oven, ridden a truck for some twenty-five kilometers, and here he was exhausted.

At first light he tore a dried, witch-faced apple from a tree and ate it, core and all. He scooped several handfuls of snow into his mouth from the stone walls of the terraces but could not assuage his thirst.

The pain in his eye no longer came in waves; it was a continuous roar that caused him to drop to his knees from time to time and hold his head between his protecting arms until he heard his own voice, loud and angry out of the fire behind his face, "Get up. It's daylight. Move on. A barn. Find a barn."

At the periphery of a mixed forest of oak and beech, with sudden hosts of snow-heavy spruce, he followed a deserted winding road to the edge of a hamlet behind which he climbed to higher ground, carefully scanning each building, hooding his good eye with both hands. Smoke rose from every chimney in clean white threads, dissolving languidly. A good sign: no wind. He looked at his watch and was momentarily stunned when he saw only a blur of several watch faces. He closed his eye, opened it wide, and focused again: it was eight in the morning, Friday, the fourteenth of December.

The farm he chose was farthest from the town and nearest to the top of a hill where the beech forest continued again not far away. If he were seen by anyone, he could reach the woods easily before anyone could raise a cry and bring help from the village. The farmer probably had a gun, some antiquated relic once belonging to his grandfather who hunted deer, fox, and boar with it when such animals still roamed bountifully through the highland heath.

All the buildings, house, barn, and stalls, formed three sides of a square with an interior yard. Behind it, not fifty feet from the winter-barren beech trees, stood yet another building, a smaller barn, set in close to the curve of the hill.

Knight entered the isolated structure easily through a top-hinged door on the high side of the slope, opening to a hayloft. The lower half of the barn was partially stacked with firewood and partitioned from an attached chopping shed by a sliding door. He swallowed another pill, chewed more snow, and settled down into the sweet-smelling hay and waited for sleep. But the pain kept him awake and he thought about Dietrich: he would be getting more desperate as each day passed. By now most of the hunter-capture teams must be in the lake area near Aachen. He imagined Dietrich deploying an arc of men around the eastern side of the city. *Well, they could hold hands if it suited them; there were enough of them for it.*

Whatever possessed the man to let out that rumor about the murders in Frankfurt?

There was no doubt left in Knight's mind that Dietrich wanted him killed. But why? What had he done to Dietrich, or what did the man think he had done to him that he should want him dead? He tossed and burrowed in the hay, pulling the burial robe over him to shut out Dietrich's mean face.

In the dark, he settled into the pain and tried to think of other things, when the door in the lower half of the barn slid open and heavy footsteps sounded on the hard earthen floor. Knight froze, waiting to see if the man would climb the ladder to the loft. But a moment later the sound of chopping and the cracking of wood let Knight breathe more easily. Carefully he peered over the hay to the floor below where the man was splitting pieces of sawed-up logs into firewood under the shed. He worked steadily, carrying armfuls of the wood into the barn from time to time and stacking them on the rows already split.

Knight could easily have left the barn unseen, but he reasoned that the woodsman would go away when he was tired or finished, and then he could sleep for a while, leave at dusk, and rustle up some food. A woman's voice broke into these plans with such timed coincidence that Knight, half-sick and light-headed with hunger, wanted to laugh aloud.

"Come eat it while it is hot."

The chopping stopped and two people entered the barn below. Moments later an aroma, rich with meat and vegetables, made Knight giddy. Again he peered down into the barn: a woman of perhaps thirty, not fat, but big with a solid body, sat on a bench, an open steaming pail beside her, and a loaf of dark bread. The man wiped his forehead and hands with a cloth she gave him and sat beside her. While he ate from the pail with a large spoon and dunked pieces of the bread into the stew, the woman talked. Her voice was low and intimate.

"The hens are laying better with the new feed. We'll keep it up. I'll have four dozen to sell at market tomorrow. We'll offer no geese now, but next market is three days before Christmas and we'll bring out a dozen, and, I think, a half-dozen cocks; not everyone can afford a goose. Tomorrow we can put out a dozen links of the blood sausage and offer a few bushels of potatoes. Everybody will have cabbages and sprouts in the stalls, so we'll bring out only enough for those who always buy from us anyway."

The man nodded to all this and ate steadily, washing down the stew and bread with bottled beer which she held for him.

"I'll offer my embroidered runners tomorrow, too. There won't be much interest in them on the twenty-second, what with everyone more concerned with food for the holiday table. What do you think?"

"Yes, it sounds good. I've got orders for three more loads of wood to be delivered by Wednesday next, and Diehl asked me if I could part with a few sacks of oats. I'll manage a half-dozen; that will still leave us enough.

"What about the children's Christmas?"

"The sweaters and socks are almost finished. They'll be ready. But I'll have to go up to Ahrweiler for the oranges. It wouldn't be Christmas without oranges. The candies are all made and hidden, but I'm sure they know every hiding place. Still, they'll not touch them until we say so."

The man drank the last stew juice from the pail.

"Was it enough?"

"Yes, enough. I don't like leaving any."

"I'll start to bake on Monday. With school out now, Berta can help; she's eager to learn anyway, and she's sensible."

"Did the boys finish cleaning the stalls?"

"Yes, they're working on the henhouse now."

"Good. Good." The man put the pail down, his face glowing. Knight estimated him to be about his own age.

For a few moments they were silent; then the man leaning back with his hand behind his head said softly, "Would you like to?"

"Yes. But close the door; it's cold."

The man got up and slid the door shut while the woman unbuttoned the bodice of her dress so that her pale breasts were bare. She stood with her back to the man, bending her body at the waist and holding onto the bench.

The man had his penis out when Knight glanced back toward him, as he raised the woman's long heavy skirt and several petticoats. He took her from behind, first stroking her full buttocks with both hands as he positioned his penis between her slightly spread legs. Their breath came fast and loud in the cold room, the man twitching in sudden agitation and emitting a low cry, his arms encircling the woman, grasping her breasts as he draped himself over her back and pushed against her in short rhythmical thrusts.

Knight watched them with profound pleasure, finding in their choice of coital positions an appropriateness attuned to the land, the weather, even the hour of the day. He would have died rather than have them know he had seen them, yet their embrace made him want to know them, to see the inside of their house, to see the children they spoke of. He breathed cautiously, quietly, for he had discovered he had an enormous erection.

The couple adjusted their clothing and the woman left, the man returning to his work and staying with it until it was almost dusk. Knight watched him for a time until the sound of the ax blended into the normal world of winter sounds and changing light that filtered through the cracks in the opening to the loft. By midafternoon he was asleep, a condition aided by the draining of his own engorged organ.

He left the barn after dusk and struck out for another farm

farther west on the slope of the hill. The arrangement of house, barn, and stalls around an interior yard was almost identical to the first farm. The full day of sunshine had caused the snow to slide from some of the roofs and pile up around the buildings. Knight crept on all fours under the eaves, listening at each stall for the sound of its occupants. At the henhouse he stopped, dug away the drifted snow until he found the latch to the narrow trapdoors used for cleaning out the henhouse floor.

He took only four eggs, cracking them open on the edge of the roost and swallowing the raw insides on the spot, then crushing the shells and shoving them under the straw in the nests. Twice he gagged, but the eggs stayed down.

Back on the hillside, he moved away from the hamlet and headed due west toward the River Ahr, passing through deserted moors and silent forests and once circling a crater lake whose water, fringed by the white snowbank, looked like a round dark eye under the stars.

Just before morning he stood on a high bluff above the river. Below him a dense thicket and clusters of conifers hid the Ahr from view, but halfway down the steep embankment he intersected a path, snow-covered now, but clearly a path through the brush and basalt outcropping. He followed it cautiously, only to have it end at a narrow clearing on the riverbank.

Knight followed the river upstream where the bottomland widened and an area of marsh covered with thick tall grass spread out for several hundred feet. In time, a railroad or isolated auto bridge would show up and he would get to the other side leisurely.

His main concern now was to cross the Ahr without getting wet. He knew that he lived on the edge of some kind of fever: the pain was constant, and frequently now nausea came upon him unexpectedly and he perspired liberally between bouts of feeling cold and dehydrated.

Some fifty paces into the tall grass, a dark form, low in the

108

reeds, charged toward him and knocked him down. Knight rolled desperately to the side, only to be attacked again by another of the barreling creatures whose gruntings suddenly filled the morning air. Wild boars! He felt a sharp pain in his side, and an ancient instinct forced him up; half-crouching, he began to run toward the river, the hurtling dark forms racing after him. He saw one in his path, just rising, its small, brilliant eyes staring at him over the points of its tusks. He leaped over it as it lifted its head sharply to rip at his flying feet, one tusk gashing the inner side of his left boot. Knight dove into the water, the herd of boars lunging up to the bank, their bristled snouts snarling and snorting after him ferociously.

On the other side of the river, Knight climbed the steep bank and rolled under a stunted spruce. He checked the cuts on his side and foot and discovered they were superficial. But the carrousel tarpaulin and the nuns' burial robe were gone from his back.

14

WHEN he discovered that the roll on his back was missing, Knight ran downstream for some distance, thinking he might yet be able to save the pack, for in a curious way the tarp and the robe had come to mean more to him than merely two pieces of fabric that kept him warm. The animals on the carrousel had died because he broke into the engine shed and stole the tarp. That piece of canvas tied over the machinery had been protective cover for the sleeping animals through the long winter, and he had wrenched it off them, leaving them cold and vulnerable and naked targets for the hunters' gun.

He stopped running when the riverbank disappeared and a perpendicular wall of black slate with the river hurling against it rose before him. He walked slowly back upstream. *And the robe—his own burial shroud—given him at the price of the nuns' fear, at the sacrifice of their convictions, possibly even their safety. . . . All lost in the swift waters of the Ahr because he had become careless.* Why hadn't he examined that intersecting path; certainly the tracks of those dirty boars must have been on it, and even more certainly, he would have known what they were.

He gazed at the cliffs high to his right. He had to climb them to reach the plateau and continue westward if he was going to end this bloody business. At that moment, as he looked up and saw the rising sun touch the rim of the bluffs, the years swept away and a moment of his life reached out and touched him like a living hand laid upon his shoulder.

For weeks he and Hugo crept out of bed at night, crossed the river at the rapids, and practiced catching the freight train that slowed to a crawl at the railroad bridge over the Tuolumne. The snow in the mountains had not yet begun to melt and they had to make their break before the runoff, before the shallow river turned into a roaring flood choked with whole trees, their entire root systems still attached, came crashing across the bottomland, crushing everything in its rush to the valley floor.

They planned their escape for the end of March. Twice a week all that winter the two boys crouched underneath the trestle and waited for the train.

"If it's too fast, forget it. There's always another train. But once you're on, hang on and flatten up against the car, and don't think about anything else except hanging on. It stops just before that junction where the highway comes in, and the train waits for the passenger streamliner to come through. There we can jump off and have plenty of time to find an open boxcar. It's illegal to hop freights, but everybody does it, and all they can do is throw us off." Hugo laughed. "If they throw us off of Southern Pacific, we'll just give our business to another line."

Toward the middle of March the white bull that The Old Man had bought two years before was missing. The boys were sent out to search for him in the rolling oak-dotted pasture on the highland upriver and the swamp in the bottomland, where little pools of black water, inert and rotting in the dry winter of that year, were mirror-silvered with their thin coating of ice.

They came back late in the afternoon, failing to find the prized animal, worth five thousand dollars and the pride of The Old Man's herd.

"Somebody steal him," said The Old Man.

"How could they? No one can get near him," said Hugo. "He's crashed a fence somewhere to get to some cows."

The Old Man looked at each of them slowly. "You get near to him."

"Yeah, well, we fed him for two years and he knows us, so sure he's going to let us get near him."

It was true, the handsome white bull had become a kind of pet for the two boys, and sometimes as they cut or raked hay in the field, the animal with its soft rose eyes came and stood, his head over the pasture fence, waiting for one of them to come stroke his silky neck. The Old Man didn't approve of their petting him and usually yelled at them to quit and get back to work.

"Maybe you steal him." Under the light bulb hanging over the table, The Old Man's eyes were hidden beneath the shadows of his heavy brows. "Tomorrow we look again, and this time we find him or I go to the police."

"That's a good idea. Maybe they know where he is." Hugo stood near the door just in case The Old Man got mean; but as things turned out, they all went to sleep without a fight, and the next day after the morning milking the two boys started out to look for the white bull. They began on the upper side of the pasture, planning to go through the thickets and hollows and along the bluffs of the river.

They found him almost at once: he had wandered down the side of the slope toward the stream, apparently slipped and caught his head in the crotch of a warped tree growing on the sagging face of the bluff. Struggling to free his horns, he had only trapped himself more, and so, hanged—his head twisted backward so that his ruby eyes looked upon his own broken neck.

Hugo touched the blunt nose with his fingertips and looked away toward the river.

The boys returned to the farmyard, where The Old Man was working on the disk harrow, and told him about the bull.

"It's not possible!" he screamed at them, and then, dropping the wrench with which he had been replacing the sharpened disk wheels, ran toward the river, cursing great oaths into the sunny morning air.

"He's going to have a shit fit when he gets back. Now, remember to stay out of reach. Get ready to run when he makes his move," said Hugo, watching the rim of the river bluffs. "He's going to have to take it out on somebody, and we're it."

"How long's he going to stay mad, Hugo?"

"Christ knows. I wish we had beat it the hell out of here before this happened. Poor Rosy, if we only could of gotten to him ... could of helped him. I hope he died quick."

When The Old Man returned, he seemed calm, although his face was pale and he looked at neither of the two boys standing apart waiting to spring and run. He returned to his work on the harrow, slowly reattaching the disk wheels that lay spread around him.

Abruptly he stopped and with a wild scream of rage turned and charged toward Hugo, the massive wrench raised high over his head.

Hugo, expecting the madness, leaped aside and began to run. Nicholas, too, ran, his breath trapped in his throat as he made for the river bottom. Behind him a cry, a sharp terrible animal cry, caused him to stop: Hugo was lying only a few paces from where he had stood when the attack came, and standing over him was The Old Man, the wrench still raised above his head, a look of confusion and indecision on his face.

Nicholas rushed back, scooping up a stone as he ran. But

114

The Old Man had not hit Hugo. Nicholas could not see why Hugo did not jump up and run out of reach. Then he, too, saw the turned-up disk wheel, freshly sharpened that morning. Next to it, Hugo's foot, spouting blood at the ankle, lay with the toes turned away from the knee.

The Old Man washed and bandaged the foot himself as Hugo screamed and passed out.

Nicholas ran to the nearest farm three miles away and told the farmer that his brother was badly hurt. When the neighbor and Nicholas reached the Knights' farm in the man's pickup truck, The Old Man said that it had all been taken care of, that the boy had cut his foot, but was now in bed and sleeping. He thanked the man for his trouble.

All that night Nicholas sat beside Hugo's bed and tried to get him to drink milk, but Hugo only moaned softly and turned his face to the wall. Toward morning, he seemed to sleep for a while before Nicholas and The Old Man went out to do the milking.

After a few days, Hugo seemed to get better; he ate whatever was put before him and used the crutches The Old Man made for him from cottonwood branches, hopping around on one foot while sweat ran down his face.

At night the two boys whispered while The Old Man slept in the other room.

"What did he do about Rosy?"

"He had those tallow people on the edge of town come haul him away. They almost didn't take him because he fought with them over the price of the hide."

In the cold room, the boys listened to The Old Man snore through the wall. "Listen, Nicholas, this old foot of mine is healing up just fine. Now, we got about ten days before the runoff starts, and we can't let anything get in our way. By then I'll be as good as new."

Nicholas listened to Hugo and nodded rapidly. "Right." But later in the night, a great dread came over him as he heard his brother groan deep in his throat.

Nicholas was not in the room when The Old Man changed Hugo's bandages a few days later, but he saw him carry a can of creosote into the house when he went to do it, and that night the room stank of the disinfectant.

"We've got to get him to a doctor," Nicholas said loudly, his despair welling up around him and strangling him with wiry invisible arms.

"No, no. I fixed it today. It's going to be good now. The sheep-dip is a flesh preserver, always used for this in the old country. It works good on animals, so it works on men."

But a few days later, the foot was huge inside the straining bandages, and Hugo moaned day and night and twisted on the bed, raising up on his elbow to look with rapt astonishment at the ham-shaped weight at the end of his leg.

On the last day of the month The Old Man took one look at the foot and swollen blue leg and went into town for a doctor.

Nicholas sat beside Hugo's bed, crying.

Hugo suddenly sat up and spoke clearly, his face bright and rosy-cheeked. "Stop crying, Nicholas, and get the wagon."

"The wagon?"

"The hay wagon. Hitch it to the team—I don't expect you to pull it yourself—and bring it over to the house."

"But the doctor . . ."

"The doctor will cut off my foot," he said matter-of-factly. "And I'm not going to run around with just one foot. Bring the wagon and we'll cross the river just like we planned, only we're going to go in style."

"He's not going to cut off your foot!"

"Yes, he is. Now, are you going to get the wagon or do I have to do it?"

When Nicholas saw his brother start to get up, he rushed to the barn and hitched up the team. When he drove the wagon to the front of the house, Hugo stood in the doorway, dressed, his shoes tied together and slung around his neck.

He leaned on the crutches and hobbled to the wagon, but it was Nicholas who lifted him onto it.

"Now, drive down to the river and take it right on across the rapids."

"But there's no road up the other side. There's only the cow trail."

"We'll go by foot from there. It's not far to the trestle."

"But you can't jump on the train." Nicholas stared with sick horror at the swollen lump that protruded from his brother's split pant leg.

"Yes, I can." He began to laugh. "What do you mean I can't jump on the train? Who taught you?"

Nicholas hesitated and looked again at the bloated, still-bandaged foot that reeked now of corruption. "Maybe the doctor has some medicine that will make it well."

"No. He will cut it off, Nicholas. I don't want him to cut it off. If I have only one foot, I'll be here with The Old Man forever.

"Come on, we have to go now, please. You're the only one that can get me off the farm. If you don't do it, I'll drive the team myself."

"No, I'll do it."

Hugo lay down on the wagon bed with a deep sigh. "Try to miss the bumps."

Nicholas looked back at him once and then drove toward the river. Along the side of the rough road, bees were already on the magenta thistles, and off to his right a cluster of wild pear trees were rich with blooms.

Nicholas drove carefully, talking to the team urgently to take it easy. Hugo did look better. Maybe getting away would make him well, make the foot heal up. Maybe it was worrying about not getting away that had made him worse. And once they were on the other side of the river, he could carry him to a doctor who would make him well without cutting off his foot. They could hitch a ride into town on the highway. And he wouldn't leave him alone with the doctor, but stay with him and make sure that he didn't cut his foot off.

His thinking ran furiously in several directions as Hugo groaned on the back of the wagon. Once he cried out, and Nicholas stopped, but Hugo urged him on. "I'm okay, just a little bump . . . a little un'portant bump. . . ."

It was already late in the afternoon when they reached the river. The horses were reluctant to enter the water. "It's going to be a big bump, Hugo. It's going to hurt you; let me carry you over."

"Cross the river. It's our last chance . . . . Please, Nicholas, for me. . . ." Hugo's face was white now against the dark boards.

Nicholas forced the horses into the stream, and the front end of the wagon dropped off the bank, tilting crazily forward for a few moments before the rear wheels followed. Hugo was silent as the wagon rose and fell in the potholes in the river.

On the opposite shore, it took several jarring attempts to raise the wagon out of the river. Nicholas jumped off after they were on the bank and rushed to the wagon bed. "Hugo, I'm going to carry you from here. We'll get new crutches— real ones—for as long as you need them."

His brother was looking at him with huge eyes. Like his own, they were neither blue nor green, but a deep dark mixture of the two colors. "Listen, Nicholas"—Hugo's voice was thick, and twice he tried to clear his throat before he went on—"we both know what I got now, and it's too late to fix it. . . . You've got to do everything we talked about— learning to fly an airplane and going around the world, and girls . . . lots of girls. . . ." He gave a strained smile. "Get away now and take the train . . . be careful . . . do it like we practiced. Don't look back. Hang on."

"No, I won't go without you." Nicholas climbed on the wagon and held his brother up by the shoulders. "I won't go." He was crying.

118

"You go. If there's any way ... any way at all ... I mean, after I'm finished here, I'll try to get near you. Think about that.... I'll help when I can, I mean, if it's possible." His voice was clear, no longer thick.

Nicholas rocked his brother in his arms. "No, I won't go. You'll get well, you'll see." Hugo's body was hot and heavy, but still he shivered violently.

The failing sun touched the river bluffs with blood and vanished.

Hugo whispered one more thing before he died. "Free the giant."

15

THE Ahr became increasingly wild, with sudden cataracts and tormented trees clutching the thin soil of the cliffs as Knight followed it upstream. He could not risk breaking any bones by trying to climb the long sheer drops spaced between the few stubborn stunted growths. His rope was lost to the Ahr when he lost his pack; he was thoroughly wet, sick, and in pain. The remaining strip of bandage that the nuns gave him was soaked, and the dressing on his head was loose and dirty. He had raised it gingerly after he crawled out of the river, testing his vision in the eye: he had none. His five-day beard itched his neck, and he had to stop himself from digging his fingernails into his skin.

He tried to remember when he had eaten last, and only remembered the four raw eggs after some minutes of reconstructing the night before. It was Saturday morning: market day everywhere. His mind wandered to fat sausages hanging in rows in stalls; creamy, rich cheeses squatting on cutting boards; and fancily packed oranges with their individual wrapping paper curled back so that they looked to him as bright as sunflowers.

He tried to pull his mind away but only ended up zeroing in on thick juicy hamburgers with lettuce and tomato slices and tall chocolate milkshakes that he had to stir to drink. *Cut that out, there are no hamburgers and milkshakes in Germany!*

Yes, there are; back at the base. The base is an island in the middle of Europe where half-pound hamburgers with smooth soft buns and relish and mustard and frosted metal containers full of chocolate milkshakes that you have to eat with a spoon. . . .

He stopped climbing and pulled himself together, cursing steadily. Above him the soil ended and sandstone walls grew straight up, their blind faces high and indifferent above the river below.

An hour later, as he rounded another bend in the river, Knight's wavering vision saw a pattern of giant webs stretched across the gorge. He blinked and held his head between his hands: the trestle fell into focus. He stumbled to it and climbed the triangled trusses to the dark hills lying west of the Ahr as the sun vanished behind massive clouds moving fast and low above him in the rolling wind.

He leaned into the cold air, the pain in his eye throbbing sharply again, his whole body stiff with pain and fatigue as the icy blasts cut through his wet clothing. The color of his uniform was again discernible after crossing the Ahr. Although spotted with dark stains, the sage-blue flight suit was clearly an airman's uniform. He cursed the river, the wind, the wild pigs, Dietrich: *You bastard, you and your bloody rules. I'm disqualified if I break a window! What disqualifies your side? How about those imaginary murders in Frankfurt? Or the two guards in the prison break? Or, for that matter, my murder? All these local cops are carrying real guns. Will my murder disqualify you, ol' buddy?* Knight laughed. *No, no, not you. It's going to be reported as some kind of unfortunate accident, isn't it? Some kind of misunderstanding. A breakdown in communications. Of course, a breakdown in communications: the great euphemism for fuck-ups. Someone's going to shoot me through a breakdown in communications! Well, you bastard, I'm not dead yet. Cold, but not dead.*

Lightning cut zigzags in the clouds, and minutes later the rain fell upon him, a gray canopy moving across the volcanic wave of hills. *What bothers me, Dietrich, is why? What in hell did I do to you? The family that got killed that morning of the invasion was French. If the German officers in that headquarters were buddies of yours—well, that's the whole game, isn't it? You were a thousand miles away on the endless Eastern Front with endless Russians coming at you so you could understand all that without getting excited about it. So what are you mad about? You must know by now that I never made it to the Rhine. I never even made it to Aachen. Isn't that funny? So why aren't you laughing instead of trying to blow my head off?*

Knight plunged on across the rise and fall of hills, staying near the wooded areas as much as possible, but from time to time having to move into an open meadow or swale to reach the next stand of spruce and beech. Here and there, lone larch trees, their needles long fallen, drooped their naked branches toward the earth, their rounded tops seeming to cower under the heavy rain. Twice he came upon scenic roads where painted signs of leaping deer warned of animal crossings.

He knew he had to stop soon and get a few hours' sleep before darkness overtook him. Exhaustion would make him vulnerable to infection, and this he feared above all else. An infection in his eye would kill him off quickly. He had taken another pill after the boar attack, but it had disintegrated in his mouth, its bitter taste making him gag and retch. Now, seven hours later, his mouth was dry, his lips cracked, and he knew he had a fever.

He hurried forward, at times pulling himself to the tops of hills by grasping at mantles of deep ground cover and using it as a tow, moving on it hand over hand when his knees buckled under him and his wet boots became weights attached to his legs. In gullies he splashed across rivulets, indifferent to the water. He chewed absently on roots he tore from the clumps of wild grasses smashed flat in the steady rains.

Twice he discovered he was going in circles, coming across the same stand of birches, their winter skeletons ghostly white in the dead December. He moved then with closer attention to the compass, his progress slower, crawling under barbed-wire fences and across rocky areas with studied, carefully considered motions. The earth tilted, spun, fell on him. Each time he got up, gaped and blinked at the face of the compass, shook it when he found himself moving south or east. He began to suspect that something was wrong with it. He crossed a boulder-filled river and followed it downstream. It had to be going north or northwest; of that he was certain. He knew a few things about the Eifel terrain, but none of it had ever excited him enough to explore the region, any more than he had any interest in exploring the panhandle of Texas.

By midafternoon the wind had died down and the rain fell intermittently—sometimes a waterfall, sometimes only a white mist. Knight stayed near the stream, where there were hiding places in the shrubbery, convinced that a village of some kind would show up soon. Yet when he saw the outer wall of a town, he thought at first it was a natural rock formation. He had mistaken slate outcroppings for castle battlements before, and rushed toward them so often that this gray wall in the gray rain was no more than that to him until he saw the towers rise from the massive ramparts at regularly spaced intervals, too regular for nature. He moved toward it cautiously, stopping in a small wood on a hill opposite the walled town, the rain beating sullenly again on the thickly matted ground. He shaded his eye from the water with both hands and studied the configuration: old half-timbered houses, a church with octagonal towers, a road leading up to the wall, where huge gates stood ajar. He estimated the age of the town: either the twelfth or thirteenth century. All of those old walled towns were built straddling a river. He would have to move around it. If the town followed true to form, there was a dumping ground on one side where he might find something to eat.

A sign on top of one of the old buildings advertising life insurance amused him. Knight grimaced. *How much would my premiums cost, Dietrich? Today that is, not Thursday at high noon when I'm supposed to check in at the base in Aachen. Odd how that name sounds like a scream cut short in the middle—onomatopoetically speaking, that is.*

Did you know, Dietrich, that I once wanted to be an actor? You see, there was this carnival that came through Lahnstein, and my aunt took my brother and me to see it. I must have been eight, maybe only seven, I can't remember. But anyway, there was this magician who pulled a tablecloth from under the dishes of a fully set table without upsetting any of them. You can't imagine how much I wanted to be able to do that. I used to try it with rocks and a blanket on an old tool table. It was funnier than hell: all I ever had after my violent jerk of the blanket was a pile of rocks on the ground and my brother laughing so hard tears would run down his face like he was crying. But he told me not to give up trying to do it, that everybody makes a fool of himself at first when he is just beginning to become an artist.

It would be pleasant, Dietrich, to walk into this picturesque walled town, rent a cozy hotel room, have a hot bath, a delicious dinner, a good cigar; but because of you I have to raid the garbage dump.

He watched smoke on the road leading to the entrance

gate to the town. How curious: a half-dozen covered wagons belching smoke outside a medieval town in the Eifel mountains in Germany in the second half of the twentieth century. He blinked and dodged behind a tree. *Army trucks—parked! Parked? No, unloading.* He began to scan the wall around the town: men in rain ponchos were walking along the battlements. Knight, even hidden as he was, believed he could feel their binoculars on him. His gaze searched the hill to his left: what he had taken to be haystacks and isolated animal shelters were tents, a whole pattern of small tents placed over the hills and across the meadows as far as he could see, all positioned in a kind of random regularity conceived by a military mind trying to fool a civilian.

"Ah, Dietrich," he said aloud, *"you couldn't have ordered this. It's too dumb: a canvas Siegfried line? Ho ho. Is that what's getting to you: this confounded peace with its soft soldiers and bogus bullets; by the way, which kind are you forced to use—those tricky noisemakers? Is that your problem, Dietrich, that the games are exactly that and not a war? Not even very good games—a silly circus or maybe only a fifth-rate sideshow. But you've fixed it, haven't you? Not all the guns are mere sound effects. How about that stuff the local cops are playing the game with? Yeah, how about that?"*

Knight slipped back to the river and began to search for a shrub, but decided upon a juniper branch instead, already partially broken off and hanging over the water. He twisted it from the trunk, and holding onto it, walked into the river.

The current carried the branch swiftly to the center of the stream. Under it, Knight, clutching onto it and mindful of the long needles, brought his face up between the aromatic stems, breathed easily, and floated toward the town.

The stream flowed under the wall near the towered gateway, passed along a street lined with wall-to-wall, half-timbered gabled houses, and entered a little park thick with pines and evergreen shrubbery. Two small children, dressed in yellow slickers and matching peaked rain hats ran along the stream jabbing at a block of wood with a stick.

"I saw it first. It's mine."

"I saw it at the same time you did."

"You did not."

One of the children ran ahead. "I'm going to stop it at the bridge."

Knight watched the other child hit the block of wood, which only caused it to turn over and float toward the center of the stream. At this the second child, too, ran ahead.

Knight raised his head to see the bridge the boy spoke of. It was beyond the park in what was apparently the main part of the town. He could see a steep cobbled street rise to a pink church on the slope of a hill. At the bottom of the street on both corners, restaurants with their red-and-white-striped awnings rolled back were filled with people eating, but no odors except the heavy oil of the juniper needles came to him. On the opposite side, the stalls and tables from the Saturday-morning market stood empty under the dripping canvas canopies, and beyond that, steps led to an ancient public building topped by the incongruous insurance sign.

In front of him was a charming bridge, a perfect little arc of a stone bridge on which the two children waited with their sticks. Knight ducked under the water as he came near them, tasted raw sewage, and came up gagging under the bridge, losing the branch for no more than a moment before his flailing arms grabbed it again toward its thinner end just as the bridge passed above him. He looked up, saw one of the children with his raised stick, and ducked down again, pulled himself forward along the branch, but remaining underwater.

When he could bear it no longer, he pushed his face between the needles, gulped air, and plunged down again. When he came up, he saw the two children running along the bank.

"It is not a man!"

"It is too a man. I saw him."

"It's only a branch in the water."

"I saw him, and he had a thing on his face."

"What kind of a thing?"

"I don't know. He had only one eye." The boy picked up a stone edging the walk and threw it toward the branch. It fell short.

"One eye? A man can't have only one eye."

"He had only one eye!" The boy scooped up another stone and ran with it along the water.

"I suppose it was in the middle of his forehead."

"He had a thing on his forehead." He threw the stone, which again fell short.

Knight edged the branch farther away, but to his horror discovered his feet were touching bottom. The river was getting wider and shallower. He moved back to the center, but still his feet dragged along the bottom. Ahead of him the river divided around the monument of a mounted rider brandishing a sword.

Knight clutched the branch and stayed underwater as it passed near the shore where the two children could look down on him. He was in less than three feet of water. A moment later he breathed up through the needles and saw a hedge pass near him as the water began to move fast again and the bottom slipped suddenly away. He raised his head: he was passing between hedges on both sides of the stream. High above them, a stone wall came into his line of vision just as he heard a cry.

"Mama, Mama, there's a man in the river."

Something snatched the branch from his hands and he dove, the water becoming suddenly black. He struggled to rise to the surface, but there was no surface. His hands scraped against cement: he was inside a tube. Moments later he shot out through the opening, sailed briefly in the open air, and plunged into a deep pool. He swam to the bank and surfaced behind some overhanging grasses. Slowly everything fell into focus: he was outside the town again, his bandage was gone, and high above him on the rampart's walkway, their rifles ready in their hands and faces searching the pool, were a half-dozen policemen.

From his hiding place Knight heard the two-toned braying of a police siren as he watched the men relax their rifles but continue to crane their necks toward the fall of water and the pool in the river beneath it. A seventh man joined them and made a sweeping motion with his hand over the water. A moment later the six men fired their weapons into the pool, shooting back and forth from one side of the riverbank to the other.

Knight clawed and burrowed into the silt under the bank as the shrubbery and grass in front of him were cut to pieces. Something hit his right hand, something small and quick that stung sharply and moved off fast. He jerked his hands up to his face, curled his legs under his chin so that he was in a tight ball, half-buried in the mud. The shooting stopped.

For a long time he remained thus, barely able to breathe. When nothing further happened, he began to count to the clock that ticked in his head. After a few minutes he felt heavy footfalls above him.

"It was nothing; come on, we're wasting our time. The kid said it was a one-eyed man. A one-eyed man! Sure it was—with scales and fins and a tail. How could the kid know what he saw in this rain? It was a branch with a funny shape.

"Kids are always seeing things. Come on, it's nothing; or do you want to throw away more ammo shooting into the water?"

A second person cursed the rain, the Army, the American killer who was probably eating oranges in the sun somewhere in Spain.

The heavy boots tromped away and Knight resumed counting. He became aware again of the old pain in his eye and the new one in his hand, his groaning empty belly and the crushing cold against his chest. Visions of worms burrowing through the mud and snakes gliding silently toward him from the stream made him shiver. His nose was barely out of the water, and above his eyebrows and over his head he wore a thick pack of mud. He saw the men on the rampart continue to watch the pool, occasionally spitting into the water. As darkness fell, only two of the original policemen remained, their hooded ponchos giving them the shape of gnomes in the dim tower light.

When the rain turned to snow, Knight pulled himself free of the mud, sank silently beneath the water, and under cover of the drifting white powder floated away.

16

THERE began now a time of unreality that Knight recognized as such even as he was living it. He was like a man asleep, who was dreaming that he was only dreaming.

In the silent snow, the whole world lost its momentum. Everything was slowing down: the water no longer hurried him along; the snow whorled around him patternless, coming not only from the sky but also from the land, the river, the winter-still trees. He was inside the glass dome of a Christmas-scene paperweight lifted by a random hand which toyed with it absently, tilting the settled world.

At a sweeping bend in the river, the town vanished from Knight's view and after another few minutes he pulled himself upon the shore, which sank ponderously beneath his weight. He fell several times as he slogged his way through the unstable marsh of dead plants, the sick smell of decay wafting up at each step. Abruptly he felt solid ground beneath him and dropped to his knees.

His mind, too, was moving in a slow-motion way that was alien and strange to him: *Do one thing at a time. Protect your eye.* He took the rag in which he had wrapped the partisans' cheese and wound it around his head, covering the injured eye. *Check your hand. Something bit it.* He lit the flashlight between his knees and held his hand close to the light: a raw wound ran diagonally across the back of it. *It's not an animal bite; one of those bloody bullets hit me!* He stared at the shredded skin, the exposed bone. *You'll get yours, Dietrich; you'll get yours!* He sat back on his heels, took out the nuns' soggy piece of bandage, and wrapped it around his hand, his thinking clearer, moving a little faster again, but still de-tached and shadowy. *Can't think about Dietrich now. Only do something stupid. Must get warm, get dry, find food.*

He listened for the river; it was to his right. He thought of the streams that flowed north out of the Eifel plateau into the lowlands, listing them in order as they appeared on the map in his memory. He was under fifty kilometers from Aachen, less than thirty miles, but it was impossible to travel any great distance without light. If Dietrich had men de-ployed all over these hills they would see a light, however faint. He had to stay with the river for a while yet; at least it concealed him from the men in the hills. What he needed was a place to sleep. If he stumbled around in the dark, he could fall into one of the hunter-capture-team camps. No, it was not a good time to travel by night.

He rose to his feet and followed the solid ground like a newly blinded man, his arms ahead of him, his feet reaching out testing each step, his senses listening for the river, sniffing for it. He touched trees, bushes.

Suddenly a light off to his left glimmered briefly, lighting up the myriad snowflakes into a million galaxies, filling the deep open space ahead of him, vanishing at the curve of a hill.

He dropped to the ground, taking in the briefly lighted landscape with hungry eyes. He had heard the car that passed in the snowy road beyond the dark hump of the hill, and he knew there were no major highways in the area. An hour could pass before another car came by on a country lane, or ten hours—and in the meantime he could freeze to death or blunder into the camp of one of the hunter teams tented in the heath.

In the last second before the light vanished, Knight had noted the configuration of the rise beyond which the road passed. Off to the far side of the hill there was a secondary hill, much smaller and rounded into a perfect arc.

It took him ten minutes to get to it with his blind man's walk, but when he stood on it, he knew at once why its shape had the configuration of absolute roundness. He lay flat upon it and reached over the side of the perfect little hill, finding the concrete slots at once.

Like most of the war's bunkers, its entrance was partially choked with debris. He climbed over the rubble and found barely enough room to slip through the remaining space. Inside, he briefly flashed his light around the floor, then began to brush away the rubbish in one corner with his knife. He formed a hollow, pushing the rubble and earth to the side. After he lay down in it, he scraped the loose debris back over him. For a time he shuddered with the cold, but it was the pain that kept him awake. When he finally slept, he dreamed of Hugo.

Nicholas was fifteen when he lifted his dead brother off the hay wagon and carried him to the white sand by the willow pool in the river. With the sun gone, the sky turned dove-gray and the poplars and cottonwoods along the bank shivered in the rising ghost airs off the water, extinguishing the last warmth of the day. A long wavering wedge of wild geese returning to the north honked faintly above him, a sound that was to haunt him down through the years as he ran from the ghosts who were forever just behind him, forever within his hearing, their whispers loud in the dark night that became his life. *Be ready to die . . . Poor Rosy, I hope he died*

quick ... Maybe you steal him ... Cross the river ... Please,
Nicholas, for me ... Don't look back. Hang on. Free the giant.

He was still kneeling on the sand beside Hugo's body when
he saw the headlights of the farm truck joggling on the rim
of the bluffs leading to the river road a mile away. In the
dark he could hear the horses pulling at the wild grass at the
water's edge.

Struggling with bitter regret and despair, he talked fever-
ishly to the dead face near him.

"You promised, Hugo. You said you would get near me ...
if it's possible. You got to make it possible. I don't know
where to go...."

When the truck stopped on the opposite bank, Nicholas
touched his brother's face briefly with his open hand and
then slipped away through the hanging willows and tall
reeds to the path that took him to the trestle.

Later that night, he caught the freight train and rode it for
three days, sleeping on the wood floor that smelled of coffee
and burlap. When he was not sleeping, he talked to Hugo. "I
should of got the doctor before. I should of run and got him
a week ago. I should of. People can live with only one foot.
Remember the man in the sideshow that time we sneaked off
to the carnival: he had no feet, never had any, nor even legs.
He stopped right up where his legs should have started, and
he got around in that little cart specially made for him. We
could of had a special thing made; there are people with
wooden legs....

"It was the ride in the wagon, the bumps on the road and
in the river. I should of made you stay in bed and wait for
the medicine to come, and maybe the doctor wouldn't of had
to cut off your foot at all but just rub something on it to
make it well. Remember those people at the carnival selling
bottles of medicine that made all kinds of things get well?
We could of got some of that to put on it. We could of. *I*
could of."

For three days he watched with burning eyes the world

race past him: orchards in bloom and freshly disked fields and lines of cars waiting at crossroads, and cattle looking up from their grazing. Sometimes children waved from yard fences, shouting to him words lost on the wind.

Each time that the ominous message of the wheels telling him to *goback, goback, goback,* put him to sleep, he dreamed of Hugo. They were at school again, groping through the garbage cans behind the cafeteria. It was recess, and everyone, even the teachers, was out on the playground with their games. He could hear their urgent, inane shouting, *"Red Rover, Red Rover, won't you come over?"*

Nicholas believed he and Hugo were stealing when they took from the garbage cans the remnants of peanut-butter sandwiches and pieces of baloney stuck to mayonnaised bread and bits of yellow cake, and once a miracle: a whole tangerine.

They never ate the food there, but heaped it into one of the crumpled-up brown paper sacks and sneaked under the schoolyard fence to a nearby ditch, where they ate the refuse in voracious, wordless ecstasy, passionately and swiftly, their eyes constantly peering through the weeds toward the schoolyard, where their benefactors played their incomprehensible and meaningless games.

The ball games made some sense if you got to keep the ball when you caught it, but if you had to give it back, then those were as dumb as all the chasing games. *Ally ally ox in free.* What kind of business was that? *And who the hell was Red Rover?*

For two years after Hugo died, Nicholas found jobs on farms, milking, chopping wood, cutting and raking hay, but always after a few weeks he jumped back on the nearest freight train and moved on. The nights that he spent in bunkhouses where hard-eyed grown men looked at him oddly and asked about his family were hours of desperation and wariness: he was afraid to sleep because he knew he talked and screamed in his dreams. In Colorado, someone woke him

135

during one of the nightmares, shaking him by the shoulder and asking with sly humor, "Whatja do, kid, kill somebody?"

He gazed at the man in horror, then settled back on the bunk. "Yes."

The man laughed. "Sure you did, kid; we all did."

By dawn he was standing under a trestle, waiting for yet another train, having heard its wail now for a month as he lay in the dark bunkhouse terrified of his own dreams.

He was sixteen when he reached the Midwest and saw his first naked woman, a tall, bony prostitute with black pubic growth and a head of platinum-blond hair. He did not know that this was not possible.

"Hey, you're cute, kid. A little bomb all set to go off. Yes, sir, a cute little bomb. What color they call your eyes? Ain't blue, ain't green. Aqua, maybe. aqua-blue. Real cute. A hot little bomb with aqua-blue eyes. The boys brought you along for laughs, baby, so let's put the joke on them and blow off the bomb."

She spent two hours with him and then in front of the half-drunk farmhands, impatient and waiting to catch the last ride back to their jobs before morning, she gave him back his money.

He stood staring at the crumpled dollar bills in confusion and bewilderment, while the woman gasped out in mock anger, "Don't bring me no more bombs, you bums. I may be outta commission for a week." She was the last prostitute with a heart of gold that he ever met.

In April of 1941, he stood penniless and hungry in front of a post office in Miami, Florida, gazing at a slightly swinging sign hanging from a metal stand at the edge of the sidewalk. The picture on the sign was of a bearded man in a tall hat pointing a finger at him: "Uncle Sam Wants You."

He asked about the sign, and two hours later was enlisted in the Army. The recruiting officer gave him meal chits for three days, telling him to report to such and such a place on Monday morning. He used up the chits in two meals on the same day and waited out the weekend sleeping under the shrubbery in a park, his field boots and farm clothes too warm even at night in the balmy, breezy warmth of the Gulf Stream trade winds.

He was past twenty before he fully understood that he had not killed his brother, that the poison in the blood had precluded saving him. Another five years passed before he began to believe that his brother knew he was dying before he got on the hay wagon, knew he would never reach the railroad trestle, but that he needed to cross the river to get off the farm—to die.

Nicholas did not know whose silent voice told him to carry his brother to the willow pool or why. As the years passed, he saw the spot as sacred, unchanged, permanent, enduring, the soft place in his memory to which he returned at odd hours—in the middle of the night or on a sunny April morning, during pain or pleasure. There seemed to be no pattern to his return to the white-sand river. It marked his life with a quality of aloneness that he neither feared nor shunned. He never returned to the spot except in his heart.

He rarely thought of The Old Man after Hugo died, telling the recruiting officer that he had no living relatives, and it was only after the war was over that he named a beneficiary for his G. I. life insurance: an orphanage on the North Coast of France. This place, too, he never visited, having taken the name from a list given him by an Army chaplain who brought it to him a week after he asked for it.

Since his brother's death he had lived without family or friend, and it was this isolation, this being cast adrift without anchor, with no claim to a harbor, that made him silent, watchful, withdrawn. It was soon obvious to the men around him that he was most at home in his own company, and curiously, this aloofness in his nature was neither mean nor obnoxious to them: he was simply one of those shadowy people about whom no one knew anything, who never spoke of a past or planned for a future, who volunteered for nothing and complained about nothing, yet always astonished everyone with his ability to adapt to any hardship with a kind of humorous, urbane indifference. No one ever called him anything but Knight, as though he had no given name, as though that, too, had vanished with his childhood as completely and irreversibly as its death.

When he was first tested in the Army, he heard two officers talk about him in his presence as though he were deaf.

"He's raw, but he has brains."

"What can we make of him?"

"Anything we want. He's a hayseed, been milking cows. Look at those thumbs."

At age seventeen, Knight glanced down at his own large callused hands lying inert on the table before him. He looked back at the two men with quiet interest, waiting to find out why he had been summoned. When they continued to talk as though they were alone in the room, he said with neither urgency nor diffidence, "I want to learn how to fly."

The two men going over a sheaf of papers at the other end of the table looked up. One of them took off his glasses and began cleaning them. "With or without an aircraft?"

Three years later on D day at zero hundred hours, he parachuted into an apple orchard in Normandy, struck out for a hedgerow at the side of a lighted building, where, through a window, he saw several German officers talking furiously into telephones. A shocked sentry waited a second too long upon seeing him, but the report from Knight's gun brought the officers running. He emptied his gun into the command post from the top of a wall of sandbags, then ran along the hedgerow and threw a grenade into the building before he fell flat, face down into the mud. The building rocked with several rapid explosions and roared into flames. A few moments later a woman threw a screaming child from a third-floor window. It landed a few feet from Knight's raised head. He rose out of the mud, a dripping monster, and in the bright glare of the inferno stared incredulously at the small body for a few seconds before he began running.

For the next few hours he ran mindlessly into the lines of enemy positions, using up his supplies, stopping only long enough to strip new ones off the dead troopers who had jumped with him, before he began running again, unaware of his own madness or the men screaming at him to get down, or even the wound that bloodied the back of his head.

By nightfall, the story of the American gone amok behind enemy lines had already become one of those astonishing battlefield legends that never needed embellishment to make it more bizarre and unbelievable.

Knight, awakening just after dawn under his blanket of dirt and debris in the bunker, heard muted voices arguing.

"The road only goes to a half-dozen farms, and we've checked all those out: no one has seen or heard anything, and there's no tracks, nothing. If he really was in that last town, which I doubt, he's halfway to Aachen by now, at least to the lakes. Hell, he's had all night."

"I don't think he came this route at all. If I was him, I wouldn't have come this way."

"Oh, yeah?"

"Yeah."

"Okay, wise guy, so what way did he go?"

"He went to Köln, and from there it's nothing to cut across."

"So how did he get to Köln?"

"By boat."

"By boat? Listen, all those guys are caught except the American, and two-thirds of them were caught on boats. You couldn't float a log down the Rhine without someone checking it. Only the fishes got to Köln this last week without being stopped. No, no, he's holed up near Aachen, just waiting for the right time to slip onto the base. Once he's past the guards there, he's made it."

A third voice, silent until now, spoke after a heavy yawn. "You're both nuts. That's one funny American Dietrich's got it in for. I saw him a couple of times at headquarters. He's one of those old-time crazy Americans like they had in the old days that lived alone a hundred miles from the nearest people. They don't want nobody around them. They don't fit with nobody. It's like they were raised by animals, wolves or something like that. They get along with animals, but not people. I read a story where a boy, a baby, was raised by a she-wolf, and when that boy was found—he was about ten at the time—they never could get him to eat with a fork or sleep in a bed."

"What happened to him?"

"I think he got away again and went back to live with the wolves, but that's not the point. The point is, this guy's the same way."

"He doesn't eat with a fork?" Two men laughed.

"No need to be a smart-ass, Schneider, you know what I mean."

"Okay, okay, so where is he?"

"I don't know, but a long way from here. He must know why Dietrich's after him, and if he has any smarts, he's in Switzerland by now. I'll tell you, if Dietrich was after me, I'd get the hell out of his way. In my whole life I never met a man could hold a grudge like Dietrich, and I'll tell you guys something else, Dietrich wants that American dead!"

"You're crazy. How would it look for someone to get intentionally shot in NATO exercises? Dietrich's not in love with that American, I grant you that, but he wouldn't put his career on the line because he doesn't like the guy."

"All I'm saying is, Dietrich wants him dead. I'm not saying he'd do it himself. I'm saying he's going to see it gets done."

Knight heard a vehicle, and a few moments later a fourth voice spoke. "The Captain says to break it up and move on. He wants everyone off the hills and down on the road to Mechernich at eight hundred hours."

"Why doesn't he give it a rest; it's Sunday."

"So? You want to go to church? You're welcome to go tell Dietrich that."

An engine started up, and the next speech was lost, although Knight heard laughter. He had dug out of his grave-bed and crept to the slots, straining to see the men and vehicles on the road below him, but he saw only a snowy ridge. The entrance to the bunker, too, was covered with a light drift of snow.

After a few minutes he heard vehicles move off. He pushed a hole through the bank and saw two jeeps jogging north across the white landscape, their taillights little red eyes bouncing about in the cloud-covered morning. The bunker was perched above a ninety-degree turn in the road; Knight could see the faint depression of the lane in the opposite direction as it rose sharply and disappeared over a hill toward the west.

He waited an hour, huddled back in the dirt of his earthen bed, his head throbbing and the wound on his hand bleeding again through the dirty bandage. *So they were all caught and Dietrich could concentrate on him alone. Well, that wasn't anything new: Dietrich had been concentrating on him all along. But why the grudge? "You know, old boy, I'd really like to know the answer to that one. I've never taken anything from you, never insulted you. I've never even met you. . . ."*

He heard bells toll a deep clear peal, followed by echoes bombilating across the hills, and envisioned people leaving their warm houses, heading for the churches, their faces rosy behind their fog breath. For the first time since he landed in the Taunus mountains, he felt a curious safety: he was alone in the calm of the Eifel plateau; the hunter-capture teams were ahead of him, moving into the garrison town of Mechernich; and the people were in church. Suddenly the whole world was his. *Now, if he could only be free of the pain and find something to eat. . . .*

He dug his way out of the bunker and followed the road going west, his vision blurred, his walk unsteady as the pain in his head increased with each step. At the summit of the hill which he had seen from the gun slots, he looked upon a bowl-shaped valley dotted by several farms, their buildings topped by caps of snow. He chose the one nearest the rim, where a band of evergreens marked the beginning of a forest which disappeared into the next valley, and began walking toward it. Several times he was forced to stop as the valley elongated, flattened out, tipped on its side until he felt he was slipping off the edge of the world. Each time, he rose to his feet and stumbled on, sloshing through the snow toward the objective which wavered in the distance, vanished, reappeared as two identical sets of buildings vying for the same spot, doing a little overlapping dance on the side of the hill, then vanished again altogether until he stared hard at the area while he held his hands against his ears to keep out the muffled roar that he had first heard when the voices on the road below the bunker awakened him. But the roar only grew deeper, until he took his hands away and it lessened again. He walked with measured steps, counting ten footfalls and resting, walking ten more and resting. He repeated this pattern as he circled the valley to get to the far house. Several times he stopped to drink from brooks cascading to the valley floor. Still he was unable to satisfy his thirst, even though he frequently scooped snow from the branches of trees and chewed it absently.

At moments, he was able to think lucidly of the terrain beyond the small valley: another few miles and he would be in the deep forest, and then the lake region, where there would be empty vacation cabins. He could get dry and find some real rest there. Take care of his hand, his eye.

He spoke aloud constantly now: "Do you remember, Hugo, on Sundays when the whole house smelled of dinner ... roast meat and sauces and ... and bread.... Do you remember the smell of freshly baked bread? Nothing in the world ever smelled as good. And Aunt Mary used to give us a slice with melting butter and linden honey smeared on it ... 'just to tide us over till dinnertime,' she always said. How old were we then ... all those centuries ago, when for a little while everything was good, when Father and Mother still laughed and spent Sunday afternoon, when dinner was over, in their room? Remember how quiet the house was? And sometimes we walked to the woods in the summertime, and there were lupines and foxgloves and ferns and golden birds with red eyes and an owl that lived in our barn. Remember the ravens that used to sit on the fence and we would run after them to catch them, but never could. . . ."

Two hours later he looked upon the farm buildings from a hedge of copper-beech, leafless now under the snow. He noted with fleeting interest that the main house was made of stone, but it was the garden near the windscreen hedge that absorbed his attention. He ran the last few steps, panting heavily, and fell into it, lying still until his vision cleared, and through the pain he saw the few remaining cabbages of the picked garden. At eye level he saw one of the heads quite near him as it hung, neck broken, by a few fibers still on the stalk.

He reached for it, realizing only then that the bandage was gone from his hand. He watched the torn hand in a disassociated way that suddenly brought him up short. *That's my hand. My hand! If I disown my hand, I'm dead. That's my hand! Now, pick up the cabbage. Ah, yes, yes. Now pull. There! Good. You've got it. Now eat.*

He chewed the frozen bitter leaves methodically and smelled baked apples. *That's not right. Raw cabbage ... not baked apples.* Still the sweet spice of apples with burnt sugar and cinnamon floated around him. Aunt Mary was walking toward him, her skirts brushing the snow in swishing noises. She was holding something out to him. He tried to rise as he held onto the cabbage with both hands, but his face fell back on the bitter icy leaves. He turned his head and opened his eye wide. "Aunt Mary, I've hurt my hand and Hugo's hurt his foot on the glass by the river where the people throw the broken bottles." He was crying.

Aunt Mary held something long and dark out to him, and he reached for it. "What is it?"

But she stepped back quickly, pulling the stick thing back with her. "Get up."

Inside his head, the roar stopped momentarily when he heard her voice. He raised his face again: a few steps from him stood a woman pointing a rifle toward his head.

17

"GET up."

Knight squinted at the woman, who wavered in and out of focus with that same miragelike trickery that had plagued him now since he left the bunker. He tried to rise but let himself fall back to the ground, the side of his face cushioned on the snow-crusted cabbage leaves. For a few seconds the gun near his head was astonishingly clear: an ancient Mauser, very handsome, with a walnut stock decorated with horn and silver inlays. He imagined someone hunting stags with it around the turn of the century. It was an altogether charming antique, and harmless—unless, of course, she had a great-grandfather who showed her how to load it, in which case it could kill him. And even if there wasn't some nimble-minded ninety-year-old around advising her, she could always turn the gun stock down and use it as a club. The idea made his head pound.

Again she told him to get up, her voice taut, harsh; but Knight lay still.

She came closer, the long gun a little awkward-looking in her grip, but he saw that her hands were steady. He would have to jerk it away from her violently: she was tall and looked strong. He did not look at her face, only the position of her arms holding the weapon pressed stiffly against her body.

Then, just as he decided the woman was within reach so he could grab the gun, a child of about seven darted from the house and ran toward them. Knight saw her dark stockings and ankle-top shoes race over the snow, her scamper as nimble as a fawn's. So it was all up with the plan: if that fancy gun was really loaded and he tried to grab it and she pulled it back and it went off ... and the child ... no ... no! He shook violently at the scene in his imagination of the child lying face down in the garden, the snow around her turning a deep rich red. With his left arm he pushed himself up into a sitting position, turned, and faced the woman. She moved back quickly, although he made no motion toward her, and in that moment she saw the child.

"Katri, go back to the house."

But the child, no longer running by then, stood near the woman and stared at Knight. "He has blood on him."

Knight turned the bloody hand over so that the uninjured palm faced upward. He smiled at the little girl. "It's nothing, just a scratch, doesn't even hurt."

The woman's taut arms relaxed slightly. "You are the American they are looking for."

Knight glanced away toward the valley below them, where the single road, hidden now behind a row of barren fruit trees, stretched off to the north. "Yes," he said. The pain in his head and hand was fierce, and the bitter cabbage he had eaten wasn't sitting too well on his stomach, either. "I mean you no harm. I only wish to sleep in your barn for a few hours ... and drink from your well."

146

The woman did not answer him; she was looking down at the child. "Go to the house."

The girl backed away from them slowly, her eyes still on Knight. "He has a funny hat on."

"Go."

The child left reluctantly, while the woman stood still, carrying the gun under one arm, the barrel down along her side. Her face, framed with a thick braid of fair hair, looked perplexed and a little angry.

"Please put the gun down; there's no need for it. I will be no trouble to you." He stood up slowly, carefully, as much afraid of alarming her as he was of passing out. He imagined what he must look like: some kind of wild man with his bloody hand, dirty head rag covering one eye, his clothes crusted with dirt from the bunker, and his seven-day stubble of black beard. He was surprised that the child had not cried out upon seeing him. He felt dizzy again and tried to control his shivering.

"Why are they hunting you?"

He was amazed at her question, but answered it quickly. "They think I am an escaped prisoner, but that is not true; they are after the wrong man."

"Why don't you give up, and they will see that they have made a mistake."

"The trouble is that only one man knows I am not the escaped prisoner, and that man is in Aachen waiting for me ... to clear me." Knight, listening to his own lie, wondered if Dietrich had indeed mistaken him for someone else. It was possible that he looked like someone out of Dietrich's past, someone who had unpardonably injured him. For a few seconds the scene at the NATO-forces meeting at Aachen seven days before returned to Knight sharply: Dietrich had stared at him with such a look of shock and disbelief that Knight almost turned around to see if there was someone behind him at whom Dietrich was staring. And then the shock turned into a ferocious rage, so incredibly controlled and

147

channeled that Knight was convinced he alone saw it as he looked back into the German Colonel's face. There was a mindless hatred in Dietrich's eyes. Even The Old Man, as insane as he was, had never managed such an evil visage. What bothered Knight most was his absolute conviction that, unlike The Old Man, Dietrich was sane.

"You may sleep in the barn if you wish, but the Army people may come back. This morning it was the first place they searched, then the root cellar, the hen roost, even the spring house. They will find you if they come again."

Knight was surprised that she should trouble to warn him, and started to thank her and tell her that the men would probably not come back this way; and for a moment he even believed he was talking, but he could not hear himself, and still more peculiar was his notion that she was leaning sideways in a dangerous slant. He stretched out his arms to keep her from falling, but he could not reach her. He saw her lay down the gun and come toward him, but instead he fell against her, and for a few seconds they seemed to struggle in such comical slow motion that he wanted to laugh and in fact believed that he did laugh. His legs twisted under him, and he talked steadily as he began to fall, telling her that he was sorry about eating her cabbage. But he did not fall, and he could still not hear his voice as he stumbled through the snowy garden while she held him up and dragged him along. He tried to talk louder, but his mouth filled with raw cabbage, and for a minute or longer she held him while he vomited.

He told her he was sorry, but all he could hear was the old familiar thundering inside his head. At one point it seemed to him that they stopped stumbling while she pushed at a wall in front of them, and moments later she finally stopped dragging him and let him drop—for which he was grateful. But then she pulled off his boots, and while his arms flapped with comic helplessness, she removed his uniform. He groped around him for hay or straw to crawl under, but only felt

148

fabric, bulky, yet light and slippery. He held on to it savagely, thinking for a moment that it was the carrousel tarp and knowing in the next that it was not.

He drank water deeply from a large pitcher through which a splintered light burst like fireworks. Then that ended and he drank something warm and indescribably delicious that left the taste of apples and cinnamon on his tongue. After a little while he drank some strange sweet whiskey, and with that he saw the woman's face, deeply concentrating and absorbed as she leaned over him holding the glass of whiskey with one hand and his head with the other.

When she walked away, he tried to follow her with his good eye, but she swayed and wavered and rose and fell and rose again and returned and began washing his face, and he wondered when his head rag had come off and would have liked to ask, but decided it was not important: his eye must be almost healed—even if he could not see with it anymore.

For a long moment her face was close to his as she seemed to be peering into the eye that could not even see her. For some reason he found this comical, too. But he could see her with his good eye; and as he watched her face, he wanted to touch it.

She was perhaps twenty-five or -six. It was at this estimating of her age that he suddenly wondered about the man. There had to be a man somewhere. If he were on the grounds—in the barn or other outbuildings—it would have been him standing in the picked-over garden pointing the nineteenth-century gun. So where was he on a Sunday noon when men were generally home with their women, waiting nearby for their midday Sunday dinner, which he had been aware of in the garden as he ate the sour cabbage leaves and smelled baked apples. Then, too, there was the child, the pretty fawn child, who clearly had the woman's features and light hair and who, therefore, must have a father somewhere, a man presently absent. So where was he—this missing stranger whom he was already beginning to despise?

149

He watched the woman dip his shredded hand slowly in a basin that she brought to the side of the couch or bed or whatever it was that she lowered him onto when they first entered the house. Again she worked on the wound with that same detachment and softness that made him long to touch her. But he did nothing, not even try to speak to her again. When she was through bandaging his hand, she brought him more of the whiskey, again holding his head up as he drank, although he knew he could easily have raised it himself.

Once, the child came from another room and stood nearby, looking at Knight with the same bright interest she had taken of him in the garden. The woman told her to set the table and stay in the kitchen.

When the child was out of the room, the woman began to take off Knight's torn socks, and it was then that he made a motion toward helping, raising his head off the couch and leaning on his elbows. "Please, I'm fine now. I can . . ."

"No," she said. "Lie still."

He settled back while she rolled off his filthy socks, went away with them and came back with the basin, again filled with what felt to him like warm oil that smelled pleasantly and nostalgically of eucalyptus. There had been a stand of the trees in the yard in front of the two-room house in which he and Hugo and The Old Man had lived. After storms, he used to touch their naked trunks and walk through the fallen leaves so that the essence remained with him through the day.

Now, as the woman washed his feet, Knight almost moaned with ecstasy, his desire for her mounting steadily with both alarm and astonishment, the willfulness of the heart and hardness in his groin embarrassingly beyond his control. He was grateful for the quilt that covered him.

She bandaged the boar-tusk wound which the pain in his head and hand had made him forget altogether. When she was finished, she wrapped a warm towel around his feet and left again. He could not remember a time in his life when physical comfort had given him such pleasure. The whiskey dulled his pain and made him drowsy, and the cleaning and dressing of his wounds obliterated the subtle fear that poisons from the injuries had already entered his blood and touched him with death.

But it was his desire for the woman that made him feel human again, that fully convinced him he hadn't actually died.

18

Before he slept, the woman brought Knight food. "When was the last time you ate?" Her voice had a low, husky tone, as though she had a sore throat or simply did not speak very much.

"The cabbage in your garden."

She smiled, and Knight got the notion that she did not do that much either. "Before that?"

He shook his head. "I can't remember. Two days ago, I think."

"Then eat slowly and not too much at one time." She put a plate of stew and a thick slice of dark, coarse-grained buttered bread on a small table near him. He believed the savory smell of the stew was going to unhinge him completely; but he warned himself sharply to show a little control and wait until she was out of the room before he dove into it.

He watched her move things about, her actions having

that economy that wasted no motion, took no unnecessary steps. She did not fuss, or shuffle objects randomly: she moved the table so that it stood next to him, took a spoon and fork from an apron pocket, and placed them beside the plate. He began to eat, with decorum and studied control, although he wanted to shovel all of it into his mouth at once. She lifted the loose pillows off the back of the couch and dropped them on the floor in a nearby corner of the room, thus turning the couch into a bed. On her way out she put another piece of wood on the hearth that he could not see from where he lay. She did not bend at the waist when she stoked the fire, but lowered her body with her legs the way people do who understand the dynamics of their own muscles, who know how to lift heavy objects without injuring themselves, who understand their own bones.

Briefly, her firelit face glowed a warm pink, her pale hair red-gold in the heightened flame. When she rose, she came straight up from her half-squatting position in a single supple motion, profoundly feminine and marked by a certain grace seen only in the very strong.

She left the room through a door opposite Knight's bed, which he presumed to be the kitchen. The moment the door closed he grasped the plate with shaking hands, held it close to his face, and spooned the food into his mouth with savage gusto, his whole being singularly concentrating on the delectable odors and rich flavors. He could not remember a time in his life when food was as profoundly delicious, nor did he see immediately the woman return some minutes later with a stoneware pitcher of milk and a glass. He quickly stopped his ravenous gorging and proceeded more slowly again, convinced, however, that she had already seen his voracious attack on the food. She did not speak at all but put the milk down and left again. Never had he wanted so much to see a woman naked as he did this one. He finished the stew and with total indifference to what the more decorous side of his nature was saying to him, licked the plate clean. He drank a glass of the milk and brooded over his situation: *Where was the man? And say for a moment that there was no man, he would still not be able to touch her. He imagined unbuttoning the manshirt. Man's shirt! Yes, you lecherous bastard, that's a man's shirt she is wearing and maybe he—the usual wearer of that shirt—is already on his way home, the sonofabitch. Probably drive up any minute, rush in, take her in his arms, kiss that marvelous full mouth, the fine strong neck, rub himself up against her. And she'll smile that infrequent smile and say huskily, "Not now. Later. Look there, we have a visitor. I caught him stealing from the garden. He's a crook of some kind, hunted by the police."*

The woman returned, bringing another blanket. "It is snowing again. You must stay warm. Best not to use a pillow. Keep the eye as level as possible. How did you injure it?"

"I ran into a tree."

She nodded. "Sometimes an injury like yours results in ulcers on the cornea. I cannot tell if that has happened. But even if it has not, that kind of wound heals slowly because there is no blood supply in the cornea; and when it does finally heal, the scars can be severe and cost you your vision."

Knight listened to her with awe. "How did you come to know that?" he asked with unconcealed astonishment.

"My father treated sick and injured farm animals all his life. I used to help him when he went out on calls."

"Is he still alive?"

"No."

She spread the blanket at the foot of the bed. "Keep your feet well covered; you have some frostbite. Flex your foot muscles and exercise your toes whenever you think of it. That will help. You will find a toilet through the door." She motioned to the far end of the room and started to leave.

"Is the child your sister?" He blurted out the very question he had decided under no circumstances to ask.

She turned briefly and without expression said, "No, my daughter."

For a time he heard her move about in the kitchen. Occa-

155

sionally the child's voice came through, but not clearly enough to understand what she was saying. He raged at himself for having asked about the girl instead of asking the woman point-blank the whereabouts of her husband and when he would be back. She probably would have told him. Now there was a certain awkwardness in asking her about the man, since she had volunteered no information on the child's father.

He examined the bandage on his hand. Very professional, he thought; then realized he only thought this after she had told him about her veterinarian father. It came to him that he might not have given that expert work any admiration without that knowledge, yet he knew that it was tough business to bandage a hand properly.

He wiggled his toes; the feeling was definitely coming back. His head still hurt, but not as bad, now that he was no longer running. He thought about Dietrich and his army beating the bushes in the forest near Aachen and chuckled. *Have at it, gentlemen.* He hoped the weather front stretched all the way to the coast. It was only Sunday, and he was a mere thirty miles from the base. *Ah, Dietrich, you dope.*

The ornate gun was hanging on the wall in a rack with another of the same kind. She must have retrieved it just after she helped him into the house. He fell to imagining her returning to the garden to pick up the gun, her face glowing in the cold, her step light, swift, sure. He saw her return to the house, brush the snow from her hair, replace the gun, enter the kitchen, bring him the whiskey. She smelled of fresh bread, new snow, and apples.

He wondered where she slept, his mind drifting dreamily to the other door farther along the wall, past the kitchen. It opened upon stairs. He climbed them slowly, careful that his boots made no sound, but abruptly his feet were bare and he was naked.

He came upon her suddenly in a gabled room, standing before a golden fire. She smiled, held her arms open to him, and floated to meet him; her clothes became transparent, then dissolved, then vanished. She took him by the hands and drew him down to the floor, which was not a floor at all but a bed; the whole large steeply gabled room with its two windows against which snow drifted dreamily was one huge feathery, floating bed.

She caressed him with her hands, her breasts, her loosened hair. She swam over his body, floated around him weightlessly, kissing his eyes, his lips, his chest. He reached for her but she drifted away, returned, hovered over him, drew him up to her, molded herself to him, and with ease turned him until he covered her. He held her fiercely then, his whole body becoming tight, rigid, until he cried out and dissolved.

He awakened too late, sat up thrashing about for a towel, a cloth, anything, fell back on the bed, and cursed quietly. Then he saw that everything had changed. The plate and pitcher beside his bed were gone. A dish with a baked apple in it stood there instead; and near it, a single small lamp with an opaque shade made a narrow circle of light on the table and a larger one on the ceiling. It was night. The fire hummed softly.

After a moment he heard splashing water: the unmistakable sound of someone bathing. He felt his bandaged face and hand, flexed his feet, wiggled his toes, and told himself that he was not moving from the bed. He thought of Dietrich snarling orders and shouting instructions at all those nincompoops out there in the dark looking for him. He smoothed out the covers on the bed and discovered another blanket which smelled of pine needles folded beside him. He held it tightly against his chest and thought about his plans to get onto the base. His body wasn't interested and the images faded away as he listened for the gentle splashing.

He rose slowly, wrapped the blanket around him, swayed briefly, and settled into absolute balance. The room was over thirty feet long. At the far side of it a light shone under the door he had opened in his dream. He moved toward it silently, his mind commanding his feet to stop.

When he touched the door, it moved open a few inches,

enough for him to see a room with a brass bed, table, and reading lamp. Beyond that another door fully ajar opened into a wood-walled bath, a little steamy in the overhead light under which he saw the kneeling woman bathing in a large round wooden tub, her hair unbraided now, but held up in a heavy mass with a contoured comb.

He held his breath and gazed with joy and anguish at the supple voluptuous body, the white neck and strong shoulders and full breasts. She washed her arms vigorously, her down-looking face shadowed under the golden light. She stood up and at the same moment lifted a folded towel from a stool beside the tub, and dried her face and arms. Knight stared a thrilling, unbearable moment longer at the curved hips and rich thighs, the triangle of golden hair. Then he crept away, back to the hearth, where he sat for a time in a large easy chair and stared with gloom and self-loathing into the fire. Not only was he a rotten, deceitful, despicable, lecherous, ungrateful bastard, but his dream had cheated him, too: she was a thousand times more sensuously exquisite than he had imagined.

19

"**E**RDA!"

A loud knocking awakened Knight. He froze. The woman quickly came from the kitchen, paused beside his bed, and motioned him to be quiet. She opened the front door only a few inches. "Yes, what is it?"

"It's our cow. Something's wrong with her; she won't get up."

"Get back into the car, and don't let the engine die; I'll get my bag."

She closed the door, bolted it, and turned to Knight. "Do you feel well enough to get up?"

Knight mumbled something incoherent and nodded.

"Breakfast is ready for you in the kitchen. It is best that you do not burn any lights; people know I turn them out when I leave, but it is almost daylight, so you'll not need any in a little while." She returned to the kitchen, where Knight heard her call Katri. A few minutes later, the woman, wear-

159

ing man's trousers and a hooded coat and carrying a small black suitcase, left the house with Katri muffled in heavy snow-wear so that she fairly bounced after her mother to the idling Volkswagen waiting just inside the frozen hedge.

From a front window Knight watched the car disappear down the hill. During the previous night, after hours of self-reproach and remorse, and after seeing the light in the woman's room go out, he had finally returned to his bed and slept fitfully, checking his watch hourly, as he waited for morning, hoping he would get a chance to talk to her. And now it was morning and she was gone, whisked away from him by some dumb farmer's kid whose cow wouldn't get up. He cursed all cows to hell and regretted it instantly; they had, after all, helped him cross the Rhine.

He found his uniform clean and dry, folded on a chair near his bed. It smelled remotely of wood smoke. Under the chair were his boots and a pair of clean socks. She must have worried about his frostbite; she had covered the foot of the bed with an old overcoat. After dressing, he entered the kitchen and walked into his distant past. On one side of the room stood a large oval table surrounded by six chairs, an enormous glassware cabinet, and a sideboard half the length of the kitchen. On the opposite side were the work counters and storage bins, hanging pots, porcelain sink, and a huge cast-iron stove similar to those he remembered from the farm near the Lahn. Two chairs and a footstool ringed an open hearth in one corner of the large room. Along the inner wall a stairway led to the upper part of the house, where Knight found Katri's room and another, larger room furnished with a four-poster bed, armoire, dressing table, and oval mirrors, all from another century. He laughed when he passed his own reflection; he was down at least fifteen pounds, and with his black beard and bandaged head he looked like a pirate.

In an ornate frame on a nightstand he saw the picture of a man and woman and two young children in the soft sepia tone that always made him think that the people were long dead. He expected the picture to be dated in the eighteen hundreds, but when he looked at the back, the date was 1939.

He returned to the kitchen, poured himself a cup of coffee, and found bread, boiled eggs, cheese, and a basket of winter pears on a counter near the stove. He drank two cups of coffee and wished he had a cigarette, although he had given them up three years before.

There were two other doors in the kitchen: one led to the outside, where firewood was stacked under a partially open port. The other entered the bedroom through which he had watched her bathe the night before. He looked for signs of a man living there—clothes, razor, boots—but found nothing. For an enthralling minute he stood in the doorway of the saunalike bath and stared at the smooth round wooden tub, his mind conjuring her up instantly as he had seen her at her bath. He returned quickly to the main room.

He left the house and stood in the snowy yard between the barn and the kitchen's back door and looked toward the valley. All was quiet under the eternally overcast sky. It was barely seven; if he left now he could be on the other side of Mechernich by noon, circumvent Kommern and Roggendorf, and be in the lakes region before nightfall. He saw the memorized map with its twisting lakes before him. If it snowed again, all the better. While those hunters were covering their asses, he could make it to Heimbach, go north around the lakes, and cut straight through the forest to Aachen. There was absolutely nothing the matter with that plan, except that he really should thank her before he left. Didn't he, in the very least, owe her that? After all, he could have frozen to death in her garden. And she had patched him up, fed him, and not even harangued him with a lot of questions, and then this morning she had protected him again—deceived someone to keep him from being detected. He couldn't very well just take off without thanking her. That would have damn little class to it.

Cut the comedy, Knight: you want to thank her, all right. You want to thank her in the way you know best, you letch. And you might notice while you're at it that she gave you no encouragement in that direction, absolutely none, no coy looks, no innuendos.

All right, all right, so why did she help me?

Because you were hurt. She would have helped a mangy yellow dog just as readily if he were starving and wounded. She's not hot for you, so don't flatter yourself.

Yeah? Well, just give me time.

Well, then cut the thank-you crap, and let's keep it straight as to just why you are waiting for her to come back. From here, Aachen's a breeze, and that plan can work tomorrow just as well, or even Wednesday.

His two arguing selves swore angrily at each other as he walked to the barn. Like the house, it was made of stone. He entered it through the seed room, whose battened half-doors with their iron hinges were protected under a gabled hood. It was clean and dry and in the cold half-dark interior Knight stood quietly and listened for the barn sounds of a winter morning: awakened animals feeding methodically, serene and content.

A large orange cat on a ledge above the filled grain bins stared down at him with topaz eyes, secretive, watchful, suspicious, then followed him when he descended three steps into a stall where two cows turned in unison to look him over. Knight talked to the animals softly, moved on through a forebay circumventing the hay-filled mow, and dropped to a stable on the other side, where a silver-gray horse looked back at him with huge limpid eyes. He patted the handsome animal's warm flank and moved on through a harness and wagon room, the cat following him, its twitching tail raised imperiously.

The barn was steep-roofed with long vertical window slits at each end letting in the morning light. To Nicholas it looked permanent and ageless, as though the man who built it marked time only in centuries. He returned to the outside, the cat stopping at the door. A chicken-and-duck yard ran adjacent to the barn; the birds were out of the henhouse eyeing him brazenly as they fluttered and squabbled at a feeder under a shed. Behind the barn, he climbed into a small terraced orchard of mixed trees staggered between a pasture that vanished in the woods at the top of the hill, and the garden. He walked along the perimeter of the garden plot, passing the springhouse, which held a storage tank and pump. Here he stopped; above him the blades of a windmill (a tool he knew was an anachronism to this area) rose over the shoulder of the hill that protected the farm. A whisper of wind stirred the wheel, feathering it faintly. Knight scanned the valley before him. All was quiet. Snow was falling on the hills to the north; in a little while it would advance southward, obscure the other farms, the webbed and withered trees along the single road, and finally reach the spot where he stood and engulf him in the pattern of the land.

Behind him, a few noisy ravens swept from the woods, flitted past him, and landed in the garden, where long ago a woman had held a gun to his head, and briefly he had been seven and Hugo had hurt his foot on the broken glass dumped in a waste ditch over which they had to jump to reach the river. *No. That's not how it went. Hugo never hurt his foot on that glass; it was on the disk wheel, years later. That glass! Where was that glass ... the broken tubes and bottles that a truck came and dumped and we had to jump to get to the river? What river? There were other people on that river. In boats. No, on the bank, calling to him. He had left something on the bank, and they were calling him to come back.* He tried to remember if Hugo was there, but only the whirring of the windmill stirred in his head.

He returned to the house just as the first delicate flakes were beginning to fall. *That settled it; there was no point in leaving while it was snowing. ... On the other hand ...*

He flatly rejected the opposing argument and heated the

coffee, carrying the cup with him as he prowled about the house waiting for the woman to return; and all the time something kept urging him to leave. It was not the hurried voice of fear that spoke to him; the urging was calm, slow, and insistent. *Since Hugo died, I have counted on no one. By choice I have lived outside the pale. It was not that I could not trust anyone, but that I did not want to, or have to need to. And it is not even "trust" but just "count on." I did not want to need to count on anyone.*

Then you should leave while there is still time.

Still time?

Before Erda returns.

Erda?

The woman. You heard her name at the end of a dream, just before the knocking sounded. Perhaps she is expecting something of you, even counting on it. After all, didn't she prepare breakfast for you? That's not exactly an invitation to leave. Quite the opposite. Ho, ho.

You vulgar bastard, leave me alone.

Not vulgar, just realistic. She could have turned you in in ten minutes after she left here, and the place would have been surrounded an hour ago. Don't forget, Mechernich is a garrison, and by helicopter only twenty minutes away. But she didn't do that. You trust her. You are convinced that she has said nothing and warned the child to say nothing. So what do you suppose she is saving you for? She certainly doesn't need any help; all the animals in that barn were already taken care of, nice fresh straw in the stalls. Everybody breakfasting. So what else are you counting on? Better go now or figure out some way to shave.

He cursed his own mockery and vacillation, stoked the fire in the kitchen, wandered back to the main room, only to find himself in the doorway where he had been the night before, staring at her bed with its two deep pillows and neatly folded eiderdown. He turned away in anger, closing the door to the bedroom, and began to pace the main room, consciously measuring the distance: thirty-two by twenty—a large comfortable room in a stone house on a neat, self-sufficient farm in a remote valley . . . and a lonely woman. . . .

He stopped pacing in front of the gun case on the wall: she had to be alone; there weren't even any signs of a man having lived there in the recent past. Casually he opened a wooden cabinet and found three shelves of medical texts and veterinarian journals with the name Heimat on the flyleaves. He closed the cabinet, paced, stopped abruptly and told himself to leave, folded the blankets and the heavy overcoat on the bed he had slept in and returned the back-rest pillows to it. He would straighten things up a bit first, then go.

But when the bed was in order, he decided that he would build up the fire so the room would be warm for her when she returned. He did that. But he did not leave.

He was staring out of the window at the silent snow when he saw the white-blanketed car crawling along the lane like a mechanical toy. It was after ten. Knight watched the mother and child hurry to the house, the girl running ahead. He felt a heart-jolting anticipation as he waited, the beating in his chest wild, irrepressible. He wanted to laugh at the fatal feeling, but could only look sheepishly back at the little girl, who stopped short when she saw him.

Erda held on to the door a fraction of a second too long before she closed it quietly. Knight saw it at once—her expression—not anger, not fear, not confusion, merely a mild surprise: she had expected that he would be gone.

165

20

H_E should have thought it through. There were his boots, his uniform, his breakfast all laid out for him, all saying, "Beat it, buster," loud and clear. She had asked him if he were well enough to get up; she meant, well enough to get up and get out. The old coat—she didn't put it there to cover his frostbitten toes; she was giving it to him. Anybody that took care of animals the way she did wouldn't let a human being go out into the snow without some protection. What a chump he was.

But she did not voice her surprise. "Did you have some breakfast?"

Knight felt his face burn, "Yes, thank you. I was going to leave before you returned, but I wanted to thank you for your kindness." He knew it sounded weak, but at least it had the virtue of being true—in part.

She nodded and told Katri to go change her clothes, but

said nothing to him as she took off the heavy coat and hung it over the back of a chair. Knight wondered if her silence meant that she had heard more about him. If she was told about the murders, she would be afraid of him now and was putting on an act. Still, she seemed not to have changed in any way.

He cast around for something appropriate to talk about. "What was wrong with the cow?"

"Hoof infection. In the winter sometimes people forget that their animals get no exercise and so may have wet hooves for weeks at a time. The hooves swell and get lesions and then fester if their quarters are not kept dry and clean."

"What do you do for it?"

She took off her boots. Knight wanted to help her with them, but he was afraid that any move to touch her might be misinterpreted. He stood awkwardly in the center of the room, certain that if he sat down, she might think he had no intention of leaving.

She took the boots and put them into the passageway with the black bag. "Lance the infection and drain it; then bathe it with plenty of disinfectant, and, of course, keep the animal warm and dry." She moved to the fire, holding her hands out to it.

Knight looked at the long fingers, held open like a fan, at the blunt-trimmed unpolished nails. She tilted forward slightly, leaning into the warmth, the fabric of her trousers molding over the backs of her legs. He watched her movements with a kind of desperate joy, the memory of her standing naked in the tub returning to him with a nervous jolt. He wanted to cry out his anguish, take her in his arms, undress her. . . . He shook his head like a man trying to dispel a mirage and moved farther away from her. "How long have you been doing this work?" He was amazed at the normal tone of his own voice.

"Since the end of the war. My father came home from the front with only one arm, and he had to have someone to help him. My brother died in the war; he was only sixteen."

"So young?"

"Toward the end, they called everyone who was not in defense work. There were children, boys of fourteen."

"But you could not have been very old yourself."

"I was ten when it was over. I could drive the wagon, sterilize the instruments, help bandage. And my father was a good teacher; he explained everything to me. I mean, he explained it as he went along so that I could learn. After a while I could do it, too. He said I was his other arm."

Katri returned from the kitchen and went to stand beside the woman. She was one of those little girls who look astonishingly like their mothers, but Knight decided against making that comment, since it might appear to the woman that he was in some way trying to query her on the child's father.

"And so now you take your daughter with you and she is learning the same way." Knight felt suddenly foolish as he heard the unintended condescension in his own voice.

"She is already a help, but she will one day go to medical school."

"Is that what you wanted to do?"

"I went for two years." She turned away from the fire, and Knight knew the discussion was over.

He would have to think up more questions or figure out some other way to stay a little longer. "I would like to repay you in some way; is there any work I can do?" He watched her face closely for signs of fear or suspicion, but there was none.

She shook her head. "There is not much to do in the winter, and particularly when it snows. The wood is in. Our daily routines are done on a schedule."

"Nothing to repair?"

"No. Up here we all help each other when there are special needs. Someone knows best how to build; someone else repairs tools. We exchange work as we exchange other necessities: I raise no sheep or pigs, but I can exchange cheese and eggs for meat."

Again the discussion ended, and Knight sought wretchedly for another subject. "This house must be a hundred years old," he said, looking admiringly at the beamed ceiling.

"It is three hundred years old," she said.

He whistled. "Three hundred years!"

"Not all of it; only this room. The rest was added at different times. My great-grandfather built the upper floor and the kitchen; my grandfather added the passageway and the water closet at the end of it, and my father added another room and a bath."

Knight nodded. "It's a fine house. How old is the barn?"

"It was completed in seventeen-ninety, according to the family Bible."

He nodded appreciatively. "It's well built."

She turned to him then. "Did you go through it?" There was a note of surprise in her voice, and she looked at him steadily.

Knight reddened again and was glad for his beard. "Well, yes, actually I did look at it. I went for a walk while you were out. It's a fine barn ... well built." *Great guns, he was repeating himself.* "In fact ... the whole farm is ... well, it's a beautiful farm."

She said nothing, but continued to look at him, rather politely, he thought, as though she were waiting for him to finish talking, say good-bye, and leave.

Go, you ass. His angry self fumed at him. "I was raised on a farm, too." *C'mon, you dope, who cares?*

She gave a slight nod. "Oh." Still the waiting emanated from her, tranquil and unhurried.

He inhaled deeply and ventured quickly, "Would you mind if I waited for the snow to let up before I left?"

"No, that will be fine. Katri, go gather the eggs. Wear your coat." The little girl, who had been watching Knight with quiet curiosity, left the room.

The woman spoke slowly. "You might want to wait until dark."

170

He listened with astonishment.

"If you cross the woods at the top of the hill, you will come to the road to Mechernich. It is a garrison town. Perhaps you will want to avoid that. The darkness will help you."

Knight released his held breath. "Thank you. You don't know how indebted to you I am." He wanted passionately to kiss her.

"Well, then, if that's settled, perhaps you'd like some coffee." Her expression was warm, kind, helpful.

"Yes, yes, very much. Ah . . . here or in the kitchen?"

She looked as though she were going to laugh, but didn't. He saw at once that she was aware of his discomfort. He tried to look nonchalant, failed, felt foolish, and gave up trying.

"Why don't you just sit down somewhere, and I'll bring it."

After she left, he fell into a chair. *Oh, Knight, what an ass you are. You haven't said one intelligent thing. It's obvious that she thinks you're a cretin that has to be led around by the hand. "Mighty nice spread you got here, ma'am." No more westerns for you, buddy. You've turned into a mumbling moron.*

But what does she think? No way did she believe that story about someone in Aachen waiting to clear you. She's no dummy.

No. She's magnificent. She's wonderful . . . beautiful. . . .

And you are a fugitive, hunted by a bunch of bastards, led by a bastard who wants you dead and who will stop at nothing to kill you, even if it ruins him.

What a stupid time you picked to fall in love.

You call that love?

Shut up. It's not just that. . . .

No?

No. It's more than that. She has everything.

I'll say. Nice knockers.

Listen, you lascivious sonofabitch; get out of the dirt. She isn't just any woman. She's ... She's ...

Still waiting on this end. You tell me how she differs and ...

I don't have to tell you anything. You're a swine, a foul-mouthed, evil-minded swine. You think that that's all there is? You disgust me.

I disgust you. That's a good one. You tell me how she differs from the hundred others you've banged....

Disgust! That's what—disgust. For your information, I don't intend to touch her.

Really? Well, well, well.

That's right!

Knight leaned back in the chair, sighed deeply, and tried to think of other things. *What town came after Mechernich?*

After what?

Oh, God!

He got up and wandered around the room, picking up objects randomly and putting them back with impatience. He found a national news magazine mailed to her: Erda Heimat—and then the address.

The question that he had pushed away crowded forward again: where was her husband? Katri's father. There was no mention of him when she talked about exchanging work with the other farm people. It was inconceivable that any man could abandon such a woman. No, he had to be dead. Perhaps an automobile accident. She had no car. Yet the layout of the yard indicated one; the large opening through the hedge in front, *that* was space for a car. The wagon in the barn had its own hedge opening farther down. There had been a car. Her husband died in a car crash.

Now she was alone. But he envisioned a young farmer reroofing the barn for her; another was repairing the water pump; a third, equally muscular and blond, was chopping wood like mad. All of them were leering at her as she brought them lunch in a pail. He hated them, all those hot young farmers breathing all over her.

She returned and placed a tray holding coffee, two cups, and some pastry on the table near him. "I made it fresh. Do you want milk in it?"

She was quite close to him, so that the long curve of her white neck between the thick braid of hair and the blue home-knit sweater she wore was directly in front of him. She turned to face him when he did not answer. "Milk?"

He nodded his head, his helpless heart beating wildly, his clothes ready to burst at the seams in the wrong place, his muscles turning to water, his bones to melting clay. For one mad moment he saw himself kiss that expanse of lovely naked neck, saw her pull away in revulsion, or rage, or contempt, and demand that he leave at once. Fortunately he was too miserable to move, and he merely watched as she prepared the cup of coffee, cut him a piece of the fruited pastry, and placed it before him.

He ate methodically, murmured some comment on how delicious it was, looked up and saw her watching him. He stopped eating.

"Did you really kill someone?"

Her expression was one of concern, compassion; her voice low, soft, unafraid. She had eyes the color of the North Sea, a dark gray-green with deepening centers into which he seemed to melt, without will or control.

"No, I *swear* it," he said with all the feeling his heart could bring into his voice.

"Can you truly clear yourself in Aachen?"

"Yes, absolutely."

She picked up her cup. "It is being said that all the roads into Aachen are watched. They must be expecting you. How will you get there?"

"I don't know yet."

They were silent, but the opening made Knight joyous.

173

"Why did you help? I really could have been dangerous."

"You were hurt."

"But when you returned today and I was still here, I saw that you were surprised. For all you knew, I could have been a madman."

"No, you tried to spare Katri the sight of blood. Anyway, it sounded so ridiculous."

"Ridiculous?"

"The odds. Yesterday morning those men in the jeep said the entire German Army was looking for you. Today I hear that the police, the rangers, even groups of private citizens are hunting you. That seems like too many people for just one man who is not even armed."

As she said it, Knight, too, saw the absurdity of the odds. He had, of course, seen it all along, but had not given it much thought. It was, after all, still a game; and in time, it would be over and everyone would go home. He could go back to the base at Wiesbaden and ride around in his touring car looking for something to break the monotony; Dietrich could continue being a sonofabitch who nurtured grudges; the General could continue his lousy golf games; and Tyler— Knight shrank inwardly—Tyler could continue being dead.

"You speak very good German for a foreigner."

"I was born less than fifty miles from here."

"In Germany?" This time she did look surprised.

"Yes, near Lahnstein. My name is Knecht. In America no one could pronounce it, so when my brother and I started school and didn't understand any English, someone simplified it into Knight. It stuck. It was close enough." He laughed. "Of course, it has quite a different meaning from Knecht." He told her what his name meant in English, and she smiled.

"And your first name?"

"Nicholas." He hesitated. "I know yours already. I was snooping and found it." He glanced toward the magazine lying on the table. "Also, whoever knocked on the door this morning called you by name."

174

He wanted to tread carefully, but blundered on helplessly. "Why did you quit medical school?" He knew that if he asked enough questions, the husband would show up in the answers somewhere, even if only obliquely.

"My mother died; I came home to help my father."

That seemed to be the end of it unless he wanted to ask her directly, which, of course, he did want to. He picked at a thread on his bandaged hand and listened to the silence between them.

"If you wish so much to know about my daughter, why don't you ask?" She spoke without anger.

He blushed furiously. "It's none of my business. Why should I ask about your daughter? I assumed your husband was dead, or you wouldn't be living here alone."

"That is a false assumption, and I am not living here alone: I have a daughter.

"Mr. Knight. Three million German men died in the war. That created a very bad imbalance. It's still with us. When I knew I had to leave school, I picked out a man I respected: he was intelligent, healthy, and willing. I did not want a husband just to have a husband, and anyway, I did not fancy anyone, not even him. But I wanted a child. We became lovers long enough for me to become pregnant. I finished out the term, then I came home to help my father."

"Didn't he want the child, too?"

"Who?"

"The father—that intelligent, healthy ... whatever."

"He didn't know about the pregnancy. I never saw him again after I left school. I'm the one who needed a child."

Knight looked at her argument and felt quietly outraged for that intelligent, healthy, willing dupe who had a seven-year-old child and didn't even know it. But, of course, she was right. She must have reasoned that when her father died, too, she would be alone, so she prepared for it. She worked around the shape of death in the same way she cleaned out a wound—with care and intelligence and understanding.

"When did your father die?"

"Three years ago."

Katri walked into the expanding silence a minute later, came to the table, and took a piece of the pastry. "There are nine eggs, and the duck with the bad foot is hopping around. Should we put him alone until he is healed?" She bit into the pastry with much lip-smacking.

"No, he'll be all right. If the others bother him, we can do it later."

"They weren't bothering him. *He* was mean, running at them, and *very* noisy."

"Then he's well."

Knight finished his coffee. "What did you mean a while ago by 'private citizens'?"

She shook her head faintly, motioning toward the girl. "Katri, get the things ready for the Christmas cakes, and I'll be out in a few minutes. We'll get them started today."

The woman waited until the child was out of the room. "I heard this morning that groups of men, hunters mostly, have gathered all through this area, from here to the Belgium frontier, to look for you."

"You don't mean the soldiers, the guys in jeeps and trucks?"

"No, ordinary men who already belong to clubs. They are very gun-minded, and hunting is not now in season, so. . . ."

"So, I'm in season."

She looked distressed and anxious, but she nodded.

21

ERDA did not know much about the organizations of civilians except that they were shooting clubs and that her father had thought them a bunch of damn fools who did not have enough work to keep them busy. They usually marched around in snappy green outfits, held a great many marksmanship contests, and lied a good deal about ancestral exploits which supposedly took place when shooting clubs had had great social standing in the nation. She remembered one other thing her father had said about them: most of the members were ex-soldiers. Knight recalled then that immediately after the war, the Allied powers had killed off the zeal for such clubs; but after a time things became more relaxed and the organizations came back to life as naturally as snakes shedding their skins, and about as modified.

He asked her about the guns on the wall. "They were my grandfather's; he used them to shoot the deer that used to invade the garden and orchard."

Knight admired them. It dawned on him as he did so that it never once occurred to him to steal a weapon with which to protect himself: he was still playing by the rules of the game! How ridiculous of him, since the other side had long since broken every code of safety which the games normally observed. Civilians were clearly not to be involved in any serious way. What Dietrich started had gotten so far out of hand that there was absolutely no logic left in the whole business, nor was there any way of stopping the madness now. Then, too, a gun would not help him: whom could he shoot? A private citizen? A park ranger? A policeman; a soldier?

The blame lay with Dietrich alone. Knight was beginning to suspect that the German Colonel had probably covered his actions more subtly than he had first believed. The more he considered his own situation, the more likely it seemed to him that the enormity of the hunt would create exactly that confusion that would conceal Dietrich's hand in the affair. If Knight were killed by a private citizen who "had heard that a killer was loose," it might take months or years of investigations before a report of responsibility was made, and even then it would probably be too vague to single anyone out, particularly since the Army would be doing the investigating. And since he had no family that cared whether he lived or died, there wasn't even anybody left behind to write an irate letter to his congressman.

Dietrich must be fairly out of his mind by now and frantically sandbagging every entrance into the base at Aachen. It was one P.M. on Monday. He totaled the amount of time he had left before Thursday noon: about seventy hours. Five of these he intended to spend with Erda and Katri.

For five hours he would pretend he had a family. At the moment the woman and her daughter were in the kitchen baking Christmas cakes. He could hear the sounds of pans and dishes being moved about. Over the whirling of an eggbeater, Katri's bright, quick banter, typical of precocious children, and Erda's sudden soft laughter touched him with sadness and regret, both familiar and alien.

He would forget Dietrich for these few hours, and everything that came before Dietrich, the years of nothing that he filled with props he did not really want and populated with people he did not really care about. He had lived carelessly, consuming each day and storing up nothing, no friend that worried about him, no woman that loved him, and worse—no woman that he loved, and no child.

Seven days ago the only thing that had mattered was to have Dietrich lose the challenge. But if it were over now, and he had won, of what value would that victory be to him? And if he had been caught and brought in with the others, what would he have lost in the defeat?

"Winning is the prize," he remembered the boy saying as he shot the carrousel animals. What was there left to win after Tyler died? How absurd of Knight to think that by going on and reaching Aachen he could in some way, however small, vindicate Tyler's dying. Not even if blood instead of wine flowed from the grapes in that vineyard after this, could that boy's death be vindicated.

A deep melancholy came over him when he thought of Tyler lying on his shroud, his eternal kid's face with its last look of disbelief and astonishment still staring up with that same baffling surprise at the changing sky. Knight stood at the window and watched the snow and listened to the woman and the child he pretended were his. He would soon have to leave them, walk away from this house that he had come so quickly to love.

"Why don't you join us?"

Knight turned to Erda, standing in the kitchen doorway drying her hands on her apron, her face rosy and smiling. As he passed her, he thought he saw pity in her eyes. He was not sure that that was what he wanted her to feel, and stood uncomfortably beside the table until she drew back a chair and bade him to sit. She placed a chopping board and a

179

basket of walnuts in front of him. Katri brought the nut-cracker and two shallow dishes.

"If you get whole ones," she said, "they go here; if you get pieces, they go here." The child pointed at the dishes, her face serious, sober, even a little grim, he thought.

"What if I don't get any?" he asked.

Katri looked at him and frowned, then looked at the dishes. "If you don't get any, you don't have to put them anywhere."

Behind him, Knight heard Erda stifle a laugh.

"Right," he said, and began cracking walnuts with the kind of hasty earnestness that meant there would be very few whole ones.

At one point while Knight picked the squashed nutmeat out of the shells, Katri picked up the nutcracker and with a deliberate show of demonstrating, cracked one of the nuts carefully in her agile hands, and placed its two halves into the still-empty bowl. Her North Sea eyes never left his face.

He nodded slowly and took the nutcracker, following her silent instruction, then holding the two perfect halves in the palm of his hand out to her before he placed them into the bowl. She nodded solemnly and returned to a bin from which she had been scooping raisins into a pan.

For a time they all worked without speaking, Katri having fallen silent at Knight's arrival in the kitchen; although as she went about her tasks, she continued to stare at him with open curiosity whenever she passed him.

After a time, things seemed to be finished, or so it appeared to Knight as he watched the girl and her mother clean the counters and put away dishes. The smell of the baking cakes tickled his tongue and made his mouth water. He inhaled the aroma with immense pleasure, lifting his face toward the oven and inhaling deeply, then sighing loudly.

Both mother and daughter stopped their work, glanced at him briefly, then gave each other significant looks, or so it seemed to Knight. He left the table and brought in wood from the outside, stacking it near the hearth. When he saw that they were still busy, he repeated the chore in the main room. He wished that there were other things he could do except stand around feeling foolish, and at the same time trying not to think of the passing hours and the moment when he would have to leave the warmth of this house with its three centuries of endurance and stability and its two incomparably lovely people whom he wanted to embrace as his own forever, pouring out to them the love and longing that came to him now in such overwhelming abundance and with such incomprehensible joy and despair.

The truth was, he did not want to leave at all. He could not remember a place in his adult life that he did not think of as temporary. He had at times mused upon the idea that *he* was temporary, that the next takeoff or landing or in-flight fueling would end in a sudden sunburst explosion in which he disintegrated and disappeared back into the vast indifference of things as easily as a shower of fireworks in a black sky.

But now he saw the seasons change from the window of this wonderful room. Even before the snow melted, lavender-blue crocuses clustered near the white walk to the hedge already burgeoning a golden green. In the summer, all was shade from the walnut trees, and the sound of the windmill hummed in tune to the breezes off the Eifel. Autumn turned the beeches copper and the musky odor of wood smoke perfumed the edge of evening. And then it was Christmas again with the snow mounting on the sill and the house smelling of cakes baking, and cinnamon apples and mulled wine.

He saw himself chopping wood while Erda brought him his lunch and talked about the coming market day—how many eggs there would be, how many baskets of pears, how many cheeses.... And always he saw her bathing while he lay in their bed and watched her, his head resting on the immaculate downy pillow while his hot eyes looked and

181

looked, and his body, having reached that plateau of anxious joy, simply not of the conscious world, waited the eternity it took her to step from the tub, dry her ivory skin, and walk naked into his arms.

Erda entered from the kitchen, bringing him a glass of wine, and Knight, gripped in the ecstasy of his voluptuous fantasy, took it from her with a shaking hand and gulped it down.

"Do you feel ill?" Her voice dropped to a near-whisper and her eyes darkened with concern.

He shook his head, still speechless while the burgeoning organ that crowded out any sensible answer from him behaved even worse as she stood near him, her hand feeling his half-bandaged forehead and left cheek for a fever.

"Is your eye very painful?"

He nodded, lying, holding the empty glass out to her. She took it and led him to a chair. "I better have a look at it. I was going to change the bandage on it, anyway, before you left. We might as well do it now."

Katri came to watch as Erda removed the dressing and examined the eye.

"How does it look?" asked Knight, calmer now and almost in control again.

Erda sent the girl to get a mirror. "Does this hurt?" She pressed the area below the eye.

"Somewhat."

"Here?" She pressed another spot.

"About the same."

"I don't think there's any infection. It looks quite clean. But the eye is always unpredictable."

Her face was close to his, and he looked intensely into the deep centers of her eyes. She drew away quickly and stepped back. "Perhaps we overworked you," she said in a droll voice, her eyebrows raised and a look both humorous and skeptical warming up her face.

"It's that perfectionist kid of yours, making me think I've

got two left hands," Knight said with pretended miffed feelings. Erda laughed.

Katri returned with the mirror and gave it to her mother.

"Now don't be alarmed. It probably looks worse than it is," said Erda gently.

Knight stared at the stranger reflected before him. "My God." The skin around his right eye was shades of green and black except for a red gash that ran from the edge of the lower eyelid jaggedly to his hairline above the ear. The cornea itself was a scarlet explosion in which the aqua-blue iris appeared diffused and watery. He touched the raw scar with his fingertips.

"Never mind that. Close your other eye and cover it completely with your palm." Erda took the mirror from him. "Now, can you see anything?"

"Light, some sort of light." He removed his hand and saw that she held a pencil-slim flashlight close to his right eye. "I'm not blind!" He laughed with surprise and relief.

"It's impossible to say at this point how much sight you have. You should get to a specialist as soon as possible."

"As soon as I get to Aachen." He made the statement almost lightly, and at once saw her turn away quickly to the instruments laid out on the table.

"Katri, please take the mirror back."

The child looked at the damaged eye with great interest until Knight covered it with his bandaged hand. "Isn't she too young . . . for . . . for this?"

"No." She faced him. "Why can you not phone this person in Aachen who can clear you? There is a phone about three miles from here."

Knight thought quickly. "Because he will not be there until Thursday."

"Why don't you remain hidden until Thursday and then phone him when he is there?"

Knight almost gasped at the look of dismay and anxiety in her face. *Was she inviting him to stay?* True, their eyes had connected in that wordless communiqué that leaves no doubt between the minds, that is clearer in meaning than a library of explanations. "It's not that simple," he began. "In fact, it's very complicated, and getting worse by the hour." He heard himself mumble, and stopped. He knew that she did not believe him anymore, could not believe him.

She seemed to shrug away the disbelief and returned her attention to his eye, cleansing the wound and rebandaging it in silence.

The mood in the room turned gray, and he did not see her smile again. He looked at the fire that burned in the same cheerful way; the world outside still looked like a Christmas card; and the aroma of the cakes filled the house, but something was gone.

"Would you like some more wine?" she asked, picking up his empty glass.

"Very much, please." He smiled and tried to bring back the indefinable sense of cheerfulness to the room, the collection of major things in minor amounts—humor, security, trust—that make gaiety such a mystery. But the color did not return.

He asked her if she had a map, and she produced an old road chart that she said her father had used when they still had a car. Upon asking more questions, he discovered that the car had been quite old, and when it broke down she would have had to sell the horse to pay for repairing the machine. She said quite matter-of-factly that she let the car go and kept the horse. When he laughed, she could see nothing amusing about the situation and looked at him as though he were a little mad.

He studied the map with some care, although it was only a crude approximation of reality, and asked her questions about the terrain between the farm and Aachen. She mentioned the nature parks heavily patrolled by rangers, where every animal and plant is government-protected, "Even the toads and lizards.

"Generally, though, the Eifel is treated like a poor cousin

in Germany. Most tourists do not come here as they do to other places—the Rhine, the Black Forest, the big cities. But it is truly beautiful, sometimes bleak and sad, but even that has its own passion."

The word startled him, but she went on without stopping. "There are several lakes with dams and power plants. But the area is not greatly populated until you near Aachen. . . ."

It was clear that she did not think she had to say anything further about the city.

Toward the late afternoon, Erda prepared food for the three of them, and they ate silently, Knight miserable with regret at the loss of the earlier mood. Again and again he considered telling her the truth—step by step—from the very beginning. And each time he thought better of it.

When he was getting ready to leave, she brought him the overcoat he had found on the bed that morning. "It's from the war. I have no use for it." It was an overlong olive-green German infantryman's coat from World War II, without any insignia on it. She took a varicolored knit cap from one of the pockets. "Bring it as far over your eye as you can."

He did this while Katri, seated at the table, her face propped on the heels of her hands, watched him with her large interested eyes. Erda gave him a pair of man's work gloves, which he promised to return. In fact, he promised to return everything, or at least pay her for everything—personally. But she only nodded and wished him well. He saw that she did not believe he would be alive long.

When it was finally time to go, he stood at the back door to the kitchen while Erda and Katri waited. It was dark outside, and it was no longer snowing. The conditions were right, ideal in fact, but still he could not leave. Twice he opened the door and looked out at the night. Each time, he drew back from it as the woman and child watched him in silence. Both were close enough to touch, to kiss. He did neither. Both looked at him with their mysterious, sober faces that he could not read.

He knew that in an hour from now he would be railing at

himself for not having kissed them good-bye, for having left them at all. For the third time he thanked them for everything they had done for him, opened the door resolutely, and walked into the night without looking back.

Seven days before, he had wept for Tyler, and now, with regret and pain and love, he trudged through the snow weeping for himself.

22

A<small>T</small> the top of the hill, Knight turned and looked back at the single square of golden window set in the night-hidden house that in all his empty, houseless world had been so briefly home. The snow shone mirror silver under the black-bedded stars and for a perilous moment he felt the lure of that light draw his soul back to the woman and child. *Damn you, Dietrich, take your tawdry little victory. What I want is back in that farmhouse.*

He gazed at the light with astonished longing. *How did I get to be thirty-eight years old and not feel this before?* Elation welled up in him, convinced as he was that he had seen in Erda's face some reflection, however faint, of his own feelings. And then there was that anxious concern for him in her eyes when she told him about the civilian hunters who were gathering to search for him. *Yes, she felt what I did. Not as much, but there was something left unsaid between us. The silence at dinner confirmed that.*

C'mon, Knight, there was nothing left unsaid between you because there was nothing to say. She thinks you're some kind of gangster.

No. She does not believe that. I saw in her eyes that she did not believe that.

All right. You figure it out. You tell her some cockamamie story about someone in Aachen who can clear you, but only on Thursday, at high noon. Where do you think you are, the OK Corral?

I shall give up.

Really? That's clever.

Hell, yes. There's a garrison at Mechernich. I can turn myself in there.

You think it's that simple? Well, try this on for size: only the hunter-capture teams know who you really are; and probably none of them would shoot you, unless, of course, Dietrich has hired a few professionals to commit an accident. In that case, it's fairly chancy to surrender to any of them. Now, let's consider the rest of the German Army. What do they know about you? Maybe they know who you are, and maybe they don't. The rumor is that an American has escaped from a military prison, and that so far he has shot four people, not accidentally, mind you, or even to save himself: this killer is some kind of psychopath who shoots without provocation, who gets a thrill out of it. Now, do you really want to surrender to one of them? How about the local police; those weren't noisemakers they aimed into the water back in that walled town. If you think so, you better unwrap that nice fresh bandage on your hand and take another look at what's under it.

Would you like to consider the shooting clubs and their itchy trigger fingers? You think you can get close enough to a bunch of them to surrender? Good God, look at yourself: you look like a Mauldin cartoon of a Russian prisoner of war. No. No. You were right a couple of days back when you were

188

thinking a little straighter: you can't surrender. No one will let you. You have to see this thing through to the bloody end—which it may be.

As for that pretty woman back there, well, you're not exactly a knight in shining armor to her; you're a fugitive being hunted by the law for some crimes heinous enough to make the whole county search for you. You're just lucky she didn't turn you in. Maybe she still might tell somebody your general location, and even accuse you of having forced your way into her house, stolen a coat and . . .

No. She will not do that.

You know, Nicholas, old boy, love usually turns people into lunatics: they get careless, feel invincible, indestructible. It's called the loveconquersall syndrome, and there's nothing more ludicrous in this whole world than a love-struck dope who thinks all the world loves a lover. You better watch it, or you'll make a false move, and POW, you've had it. I have to admit, though, that's one classy broad. "I gave up the machine and kept the horse." That's rich. Yeah. I like that. And getting herself knocked up on purpose—isn't that a kick in the head. You should have asked her if she'd like to try for a son.

Shut up!

Anything you say, but I suggest you stop this mooning and get your ass the hell out of here before somebody fills it full of lead. Those vigilante types aren't afraid of the weather; they're the kind that think getting up at four in the morning just to tromp around in the snow to shoot an equally early-rising deer is one of the great joys of the world. Unfortunately, when the season's over, it's back to target practice. How much more fun a running human target would be, after all those stationary inanimate concentric circles that keep right on staring back even after you shoot the hell out of them. I'd keep an eye peeled for those guys: they're real trouble.

Knight turned and dropped over the crest of the hill,

189

following the star-pale paths among the trees, occasionally sinking into snowdrifted darkness from which he plunged again toward the fragile light.

He came upon the road abruptly and rushed back into the trees when he realized where he was. Erda had told him about the road, but he assumed he would see car lights long before he got to it. He followed it, remaining concealed in the forest's darkness until the trees became scarce and he came upon the first outlying houses of the village.

From a hill above the town he saw immediately that something was wrong: the military base looked like an anthill that someone had kicked apart with a boot. Jeeps scurried about in all directions under the burning floodlights, while the sirens overlapped each other's screams, wound down to guttural drones, and rose again. The whole town was awake, as though there had been a general call to arms. He could hear occasional yelling, and someone with a bullhorn was barking sharp commands, too fast and too faint for Knight to understand.

There seemed to be some kind of convoy forming. He crept under a snow-laden tree and watched the curious activity below him. Men, carrying guns, climbed into the backs of a row of covered trucks whose motors Knight could hear revving up in the cold clear night. He glanced at his watch: Monday, twenty-two hundred hours. A few minutes later, with two jeeps in the lead and one bringing up the rear, the line of vehicles moved out of the base toward the main road and headed south, passing several hundred yards below Knight's position.

He considered the possible reasons for this obviously sudden and unplanned troop movement. He knew that the military frequently aided civilians in times of disaster: forest fires, floods, storms. But for these they would not need to go armed, except in the aftermath of such tragedy to discourage looting. They could have been called out for a riot or some other sort of political trouble. But that was a drastic measure taken only when local police were not able to control the problem, and he knew of no current crises that had been forming in that speck of the world that could possibly call for martial law for order.

The trucks roared in the night, their engines laboring briefly as they climbed the hill and vanished around a turn on the descent. In the camp below, things were quieting down. Knight scanned the village for activity, but it, too, had become quiet, although a few neon signs designating restaurants and beer halls made the area look more inhabited and lively.

He crept slowly toward the town, entering it through an alley and moving only in the shadows, avoiding the luminous garden plots and pausing periodically under the snow-draped, icicled buildings to listen for human voices from the streets or even from inside the buildings themselves, although he knew the closed windows prevented this. He felt an unreasonable need to discover where the convoy went and why, dismissing the voice in his head that kept telling him to get the hell away from there and strike out at once for the lakes. Something was certainly wrong when a dozen trucks filled with armed men, roused from their barracks by sirens, raced down the highway in the dead of night. He crossed a side street and spread himself against a dark wall as a door opened at the corner of the building. Two men, bundled in overcoats and fur hats, made jokes and said good-bye to people inside.

"You just remember, Carlie, that I got a fiver on him," said one of them over his shoulder.

"That's unpatriotic," someone shouted with mock outrage from inside.

"Only if I win," the man on the sidewalk yelled back. Both men roared with laughter and started off down the street, their footfalls crunching the snow like muffled blows.

Knight slipped to the back of the building and saw at once that the place was a restaurant. He followed a narrow alley

191

where garbage cans and an occasional brick furnace stood under caps of snow. At the next side street he heard the men again, but they talked in lowered voices and their coat collars were turned up around their ears so that their words were muted and unclear.

Warily and with uneasiness Knight returned to the back entrance to the restaurant and waited under a flight of external stairs built beneath a wide overhanging eave. He could not say what commanding obsession made him stay in this town, except that he had to know what the Army was up to. He'd been out of circulation for almost eight days, had heard no radio, seen no newspapers, and this sudden rushing away of troops made him anxious. Still, the two men leaving the restaurant did not seem to be in any kind of panic; although it was obvious from his earlier vantage point on the hill that the town knew what emergency had sent the soldiers off into the night.

Someone came out of the back door to the restaurant and placed a wooden crate of bottles on top of a stack already there, not ten feet from where Knight, crouching under the lower stairs, had pulled his coat over his head and plunged his gloved hands into his pockets so that he appeared to be only a shadow among other shadows. He held his breath and waited while the bottle carrier, whistling some kind of unfamiliar tune, looked skyward as if to check the weather, then stamped the snow from his shoes and reentered the building.

Knight breathed easily again and considered his course of action. It would not be wise to follow a road, not with the Army loose. He would wait until midnight: possibly he might hear some conversation from the back door when cleaning up and closing time came around. If he heard nothing by then, he would leave the town and cut across the fields to the woods, where he always felt safest, anyway. He took out the food Erda had packed for him and discovered a piece of the

Christmas cake. He ate it all ravenously with great delight, although he was not particularly hungry.

Then without warning a small car with headlights darkened drove into the alley and stopped behind the building next to the restaurant. A man wearing a soldier's uniform got out, closing the car door silently with a kind of studied stealth suggestive of planned mischief. Knight watched, first with alarm, then amusement, the man's comical tiptoeing in the snow to the stairs. He realized that if he jumped out of his hiding place, the poor fellow would probably drop dead of a heart attack.

The soldier climbed the stairs, and Knight heard an obviously coded knock: tap-tap, tap-tap. A moment later a door opened and a woman's loud whisper broke into Knight's intense listening. "You're too early. He's still up. We agreed—"

"I know, I know, but I thought that with all the excitement I might not have the chance to get away later because there's a different guard tonight. Joseph went off with the others. It's a damn nuisance, I know, but can't you think of something to tell him?"

"Like what?"

"Say you're visiting a sick friend."

"You're mad! In the middle of the night? He may be old, but he's not stupid. Anyway, he knows all my friends and would want to know who and all that. No. Come back in an hour."

"But maybe I can't get away in an hour. I'm here *now*."

"Too bad. I can't now. So we'll just meet tomorrow."

"I can't wait until tomorrow," grumbled the soldier.

"Poor baby, can't wait." The woman giggled and whispered something too softly for Knight to hear.

The man laughed excitedly. "In that case, I'll wait."

She shushed him. "You want him to hear you? If he finds out about you and me, he'll kill us both."

"All right, all right. In exactly one hour, then. Keep it boiling."

They both giggled, and the house door closed with that same stealthiness generally attributed to the manner of burglars.

The soldier descended the stairs, cursing quietly, not in any violent way, but merely with that steady, almost monotonous tone of repetitious swearing that had no rage behind it except that calm one indicative of an accepted frustration. He stood at the bottom of the stairs for a few moments, starting first toward the car, then turning abruptly to the street.

Ten minutes after the soldier disappeared around the side of the building and Knight was just considering leaving the town, he heard the trucks returning to the base, their loud engines lumbering without haste through the midnight calm. He felt a curious dread as he listened to their heavy, unhurried return. A few moments later the soldier came running back, jumped into his car, and backed out of the alley, his lights burning this time, apparently forgetting all the caution and vigilance he had been so careful to exercise before.

On the stair landing above Knight, footsteps suddenly pounded on the wet wood. "Rudi, wait!" A woman ran to the halted car. "What is it?"

"It's off for tonight. I have to get back."

"What's happened?"

"They got him."

"How do you know?"

"I just heard it from one of the drivers. It was a regular war. Plenty of shooting."

"I thought there was only one."

"No. They said he had help. We don't know how many; some of them got away."

"When will I see you?"

"I don't know. I think we're going to get some brass in

from Aachen, and maybe I'll be tied up for a couple of days. There's some kind of trouble."

"What kind of trouble?"

"Well, one of our guys got shot."

"Dead?"

"Dead."

"How terrible, and in peacetime."

"And three of them."

"Three? Dead?"

"Including the American."

After the soldier drove away and the woman returned to the flat above the restaurant, Knight, still curled up in the World War II German infantryman's coat, rose slowly from his cramped, crouching position without any feeling in his feet and legs at all. *How appropriate, since I'm dead, anyway.* The temperature, too, had dropped drastically, and a crust of glistening ice covered the snow. Under the aloof unsleeping stars, Knight slipped out of the alley and followed a side street to its end at the edge of a field. He trotted along a hedgerow that bordered the open area and moved steadily northward, a dark, implacable depression possessing him.

Good God, Dietrich, look what we've done. Four more men are dead! And for what? What the hell happened? Some dumb report or rumor ... some stupid, deranged blunderer shooting in the middle of the night ... probably at anything that moved—and instant carnage.

And who, in this bloody night, has died in my place?

23

KNIGHT circled the next town and turned toward the west. He was in no mood to run into any additional war news. He knew too well how these ghastly mistakes came about: someone reported seeing somebody who looked or acted suspiciously, and everybody for thirty miles around with a gun went out to have a look for himself, with the secret sly hope of becoming a hero, including the Army. He imagined a drunk or a hitchhiker being mistaken for the American killer and getting caught in the crossfire between some local sharpshooters and the troops from the garrison. It was worse than madness, because most of the people involved were relatively sane. Now there really were four murdered men. He would have liked to see Dietrich's face when he got to the garrison and looked at the dead American.

West of the town, he made his way through a pine forest and headed for the lake country, his mind still pondering

Dietrich's reaction to the killing of the wrong man, when he came upon another town—clearly not on the map. He had vaulted a fence of some kind at the bottom of the hill, not paying much attention to it at the time, only noting in passing that he had probably entered a national forest reserve or perhaps one of the numerous nature parks for which the region was known. What did Erda tell him? "Even the lizards and toads are protected." That was fine as long as the protectors were sleeping snugly in their fairy-tale cottages. From what he knew of park rangers, they were an easygoing bunch that liked to please the public and keep things peaceful and pleasant at the same time. But they were also very protective and possessive of their domain. They had more of the sentimental romanticist about them than the aura of the policeman, and they tended to settle disputes by talking and compromise rather than gunfire.

Still, Knight had no desire to verify his knowledge of the matter by waking one and putting his ideas to the test, so he crept quietly along the periphery of the unmapped village, searching for some sign that would fix his location. When he saw a seventh-century watermill he stopped creeping from house to house and examined one of them more closely. There was something strange about it. He looked at another. They were old-fashioned but not old, at least not old the way Erda's house was old, yet they had windmills and watermills that went back several centuries.

He stood in the middle of a narrow deserted street and looked both ways; there was not a single snow-hooded car parked in front of any of the houses. It was as though some malicious piper had spirited the inhabitants away centuries before. Then he said the word to himself before he even had time to think it through: *uninhabited*, not abandoned and not even temporarily deserted, but never lived in at all, never inhabited. It was a display of some kind. Everything was in good shape: no roofs were caved in, no windows broken, no snowdrifts piled in the parlors, where doors should have been missing. In fact, all the houses were in excellent condition. Knight walked among them, realizing that he had entered another century. He used his flashlight to examine interiors through gabled windows. In one of the houses he saw a spinning wheel and butter churn. A barn had hay in it, but no animals. He flashed the light into another house and at the same moment felt a gun jabbed into his back.

"Don't move. This time I've got you! Turn around slowly and don't try any funny stuff."

Knight continued to hold the light against the window, although his heart was beating itself to death.

"No running now," said the voice.

Knight remained silent, turning slowly. If he could blind the man with his light, he might knock him down and get his weapon. But if there were others, that would be it: they would kill him on the spot. Maybe this was intended. A trap. He'd obviously been followed. What an idiot he had been to hang around that garrison, and he had been none too careful when he left it, either. He wondered how many eyes were looking at him through gun sights at that very moment.

When he had fully turned, he saw that the weapon now pressed against his middle was not a gun at all but a knotty, crooked walking stick. Knight laughed with relief, although he felt physical pain in his chest.

"Here, here, young fellow, what do you think you're laughing at?" A stern face with a great white droopy mustache frowned back at him.

"Well, sir, it's just that you look like . . ."

"Like what?" snapped the old man.

"Like . . . von Bismarck . . . sir," said Knight solemnly.

The cane relaxed from Knight's midriff. "Well, that's a very decent thing for you to say."

"I meant no disrespect. I'm sure you must have been told that before, sir."

"There has been a time or two when that observation was made." He leaned on the cane and adjusted a scarf inside his greatcoat and straightened his military-looking visored hat. Then he squinted into Knight's face. "You're not one of the rapscallions that's been here in the past?"

"No, sir, I've never been here before. It's a fascinating place."

"Well, I see now that you're a responsible man. I've had some trouble with a couple of hooligans. They think nothing of breaking things and even stealing."

"That's unthinkable to me, sir."

"I should hope so. A walk around costs a mark when it's open, and well worth it. But what are you doing here now? Can't you come by day? Winters it's open from ten to four. You'll not see much with a flashlight, I'll tell you that, and you don't look like one who would cheat the nation out of an entrance fee."

"No. No. It wasn't that. I just knew that I might never get to see it. When I got here today a few minutes after four, I tried to urge my money on the ticket taker, so I'd get in, but no—'Closed!' I was told. 'You are too late.' And I'd set my heart on it. . . ."

"Well, couldn't you come tomorrow?"

Knight shook his head dejectedly. "No, today was the only day I had. Tomorrow it's back to work, back to the mines."

"That's a damn shame. Can't you come during your holiday? It's open all year, and in the summer it's much more pleasant, anyway, what with the flowers in bloom and the grass all green. It's worth it to make a special trip."

"I wanted to, but everyone was shouting, 'Let's go to Munich' or 'Let's go to Hamburg . . . or Berlin.' I was the only one that wanted to come to the Eifel, so the majority won, and do you know what we got for a holiday?"

"What?"

"Cities full of crazy speeding drivers, the air so polluted with smoke I'm surprised I survived . . . and *noise*—the noise was so bad I wished I was back in the mine. So I said to myself, 'Take your vacation in the mine in the future. It's

200

safer, cleaner, even quieter. Then this afternoon, when this opportunity to see what I've heard about for so long finally came, well, I just had to take it. A friend who was passing through asked if I'd like to go. You can imagine how I jumped at the chance." He sighed. "But I'll leave now, sir. I swear I did no damage, took nothing. But at least I've had a glimpse, and I'll not forget it."

The old man hesitated for some moments, stroking his chin before he answered Knight, who made no move to leave. "Well, there's no sense in your leaving now when you've come this far. Come on over to my place. I've got a little something to take the chill out of the marrow."

Knight protested feebly. "Oh, I'd not wish to disturb your family, sir."

"My family? Ho, ho. That's rare. Why, I've no family, none to speak of. Nobody visits. I'm too far out, you see; but mind you, I'm not complaining: I like it that way. I don't mind it at all. When a man's his own good company, he doesn't get lonely, I always say. No. I'm not lonely: I keep an eye on things here at night, and that keeps me busy. Never needed much sleep, anyway. I snooze a bit in the afternoon."

"I see, sir. So you're the security officer, then?"

"Well, the big muckamucks call me a night watchman, but I can see you've got the truer picture of things."

"Desk-sitters don't understand this kind of responsibility. To them, it's all simple. You take their official stamps away from them, and their fill-out forms, and they'd go all to pieces."

"By God, you've got a head on your shoulders. That's just what I've been saying for years."

Knight followed the man to a small cottage at the far side of the museum, keeping track of his lies. It would have been easy to run, but that would only make the man suspicious and he would call someone, and all hell would break loose at the garrison again and who could tell how many more men would get killed.

Once inside, the watchman motioned him to a chair. "Just have a seat and I'll get a couple of glasses." He busied himself in a small kitchen, while Knight, warming his feet at the potbellied wood burner, cased the main room. There was a telephone as well as a radio. Was the old man wise to him, playing him for a dope?

"Here you are." He handed Knight a half-glass of pale liquor. "Say, what's wrong with your eye?"

"Old war wound. The infection returns when I get an excess of coal dust in it. That's how I got off today, had to get it treated."

"And you came to the Eifel! That's a compliment. I drink to that." He took a long swallow and expelled a deep breath. "Good stuff."

Knight raised his glass, drank deeply, and realized his mistake at once; but he managed to nod and even smile as his throat burned and a fine thin quiver of electric heat ran all the way down to his toes. "Terrific," he said when he found his breath. Enough of this stuff and he could just flap his arms and fly to the Aachen base. "Where do you buy this? I've never tasted anything like it."

"Buy? Who buys? I make it myself, from potatoes, but I have a secret way to give it that little extra something."

"It's a great extra," said Knight, licking his lips. "Fantastic."

The watchman beamed. "You know, I'm glad you came. I generally don't like a lot of people around, but you're very good company." He gazed at Knight fondly.

Knight smiled back, sipping the concoction more prudently.

Suddenly the man pointed his forefinger at him. "Now, I've got it. I couldn't figure out before what made you so familiar, but I just got it."

Knight stiffened, continued smiling, and gauged the distance to the door without looking away from his excited host. He was an old man: he could keep him from doing anything just by hanging on to him. Then he could rip out the phone wire, check the bedroom for a gun, get to the front door, let the old guy go, and beat it the hell out of there. It would take the old fellow some time to get to the village to rouse anyone.

"It's the coat!"

"What?" Knight looked at the spot on his coat where the man was pointing.

"Let me guess. Let me guess. Now, don't tell me!" He waved his hand excitedly. "You were a mountain trooper." He named a division and regiment.

Knight gasped in amazement. "The very one. How did you know?" He wanted to laugh aloud with relief and delight, but controlled himself. "Come on, now, tell me how you knew."

"Oh, I had a lot to do with you fellows in those days, and I remember the Alpine patch, the little flowerlet on that spot there where it's been removed." He took another big swallow of the liquor and looked at the glass wistfully. "Ah, such days . . . and nights." He winked.

"I had a job on the frontier then with the Forestry Service. Used to run into you fellows all the time, out on some kind of mission, or patrolling. You know I always thought it could have been a very good war if it was run right."

Knight took another swallow and discovered that the taste wasn't half bad, and the stuff went down more easily after the first jolt. He smiled. "Yes. I agree. It could have been run better. How do *you* think it should have been run?"

"Well, to begin with, we picked all the wrong people for our side. We should have let the Italians go and taken the Americans on our side. What do we have in common with the Italians? Nothing. Now, I look at it this way: the Germans and the Americans and the English are alike . . . we think alike. The Italians and the French and all those others . . . that Spanish bunch . . . *they* think alike."

Knight nodded and held out his glass when the watchman

raised the bottle to him. "How about the Russians?" Knight drank again.

"Now, that was another mistake. Left alone, the Russians would have stayed out of it. They were too poor to run a war properly, anyway; and if they had stuck their noses in, don't you think we would have beat them?"

"You mean the Germans and Americans and British?"

"Exactly."

"Absolutely."

"So you see, there it is. If you're going to have a war, make sure you got the right people on your side."

"That's sort of where we are now."

"No, no, it's all over for wars now. They're too dangerous. Was a time when a good war shook things up, made a few changes, reorganized people's thinking about things. Trouble with too much peace too long is that it gets boring. Now, you take eighteen-seventy. That was a good time to be alive. Plenty opportunities." He wagged his finger in Knight's face, drained his glass, and refilled it. Again he tipped the bottle toward his guest.

"Why not?"

"Sure. I got plenty more in back."

Knight smiled. "Great." He knew that he could drink one more glass and still walk. He was waiting for the watchman to pass out, then he could lift off quietly. The cold would sober him up quick enough. It was two A.M. If he left within a half-hour, he could make it to the lakes before full light, borrow a boat, and be in the dense forest on the other side—safe—and near enough to Aachen to reach the base by early Wednesday morning. In the meantime, why not enjoy this sweet old lush and his dopey ideas. All he had to watch out for was getting too drunk.

He settled down to listen to his host, whose head was back, his cloud of white hair flattened against the cushion of the chair, his eyes looking at the ceiling or perhaps only at something midway between himself and the ceiling. "When I

204

was a boy, wars made sense. You got prizes for winning them. If you won the scrap, you got the other fellow's land or at least a good portion of it. Today, if you win a war you end up with nothing but trouble: you end up taking care of the fellow you beat. Wars are finished. No one can afford a war now. Costs too much if you win. Too much danger of bankrupting yourself. There's no more profit in it."

The watchman droned on while Knight made agreeing grunts and nodded pleasantly to every theory the man wanted confirmed. But after a time his head swam just listening to him. Why didn't the old guy pass out; he'd drunk two drinks to each one of his. By all counts he should be unconscious.

The watchman started to fill Knight's glass again. "No, no. No more. I have to go. My friend will be coming for me down on the road." He drew his wrist up quickly to look at his watch, and smacked himself on the nose. Four watch faces jumped around in front of him, saying either two-twenty or four-ten. Knight rose, swayed and sat down again.

"You can't leave now. We're just getting down to things."

"No. Really, I have to go. It's back to work tomorrow. It's been splendid talking to you. The best chat I've had in years." He got up again, carefully, resolutely.

The watchman, too, rose. "Please, please, don't go. You have such a head on your shoulders. I've never heard such sensible intelligence."

"I'm sorry, but it's the mine, you see."

"Give up that job. A man like you shouldn't work underground. It's undignified. Let blacks do that. They're fit for it. The right color, too." His giggle sputtered into a wet laugh as he grabbed Knight's arm to steady himself. "You can stay here. Sleep on the couch there, and tomorrow you can see the museum. I'll give you a private tour before it opens to the public. Prob'ly won't be more than a few kids and an old folk or two, anyway. It's not pop'lar in the winter. Sometimes no one shows up. It's lonely then. Say you'll stay."

"I can't. I'm sorry."

"Don't be that way. Please don't go. You have fine ideas. The best I've ever heard."

"I'm sorry. I can't."

"You see, it's almost Christmas again, and I like to have someone about then. It's a sad time to be alone. I have no family ... no wife ... no kids ... It's lonely then...." Tears rolled out of his rheumy eyes, which seemed bereft of all color except a transparent tint of tarnished silver which glistened under his white brows.

"I can stand it most of the time, but not at holidays. Oh, say you'll stay."

Knight unwrapped the knotty hand from his arm. "I'm truly sorry, but I can't."

"Will you come back again, then? Give me a promise to come back, and I'll have something to look forward to. I'll spread out a feast for you and we'll drink to old times, to the mountain troopers ... to ... to old times." He suddenly grabbed Knight's arm again. "Wait, I have something to show you. It will only take a minute." He stumbled to a chest set against the wall and pulled up the lid. "Look. Look here." Knight staggered to the chest. The watchman pulled out a World War I uniform, unfolded the coat, and held it in front of him, the smell of damp cellars and rot emanating from the garment like a thick, defiant vapor.

"Mine! You see, I had my day, too. I did my best for the Fatherland. I was gassed. God, how we suffered. So many dead. But it was for something is those days.... There were reasons, then, sound ones."

Knight was not sure at exactly which moment during the watchman's pleading that he began to feel sober. The odor of the decaying contents of the chest filled the room in seconds. Knight looked down into the container with its absurd mementos, the folded flag of the old empire decomposing in a glass-covered box; a gas mask looking like some monstrous prehistoric insect—sleeping; and beneath it a curved sword in a black sheath.

"That's a Russian sword. Got it off one of their officers. He was one of those prancing dandies. He didn't prance long, I'll tell you that. Hee, hee."

The watchman swayed toward Knight, dropping the coat as he fell. Knight caught him and carried him to his chair. He surveyed the room briefly, picked up the uniform coat and returned it to the chest, which he closed quickly, the close smell of it making him gag.

The old man's mouth was open and he snored and wheezed colorfully. Knight covered him with a soiled blanket he got from the bedroom, a dismal place which smelled of sweat and urine and the odor of an old man living alone with death.

He left the cottage quickly and breathed deeply of the night air. A moment later he vomited the harsh whiskey and, unfortunately, Erda's lovely Christmas cake. With a curious anger and disgust at himself he headed west for the lakes.

24

In the silence of deep night, he moved easily across a snow-covered open landscape that stretched for some miles as flat as Kansas. But he felt fearful out in the open and sometimes found himself half-running, unaware of the exact moment when his anxiety had spurted him forward, conscious only of the whispering in his mind that told him that a good marksman could pick him off with ease from the occasional clumps of pine and spruce that loomed up suddenly on either side of him.

He had no reason to believe that anyone was out in these open fields waiting for him; yet all his life it seemed to him that he had a kind of irrational, animal ability to sense impending danger. He knew that somewhere in his past he had walked into a trap. Sometimes in dreams he heard his own cries, saw himself a child again, running toward the failing sun, while from the long shadows of angular houses, violent screaming figures raced toward him. For years, long

209

after he reached manhood, the recurring dream haunted him, and always after he awakened, he lay shivering with the horror of the single certainty which the nightmare forced upon him: those howling demons streaking out of every alleyway were going to kill him.

He reached the forest long before first light and felt safe again, stopping briefly under an animal shelter where rangers had dumped fodder for deer. Here he ate some of the dried pears and cheese Erda had packed for him, angry at himself for having greedily devoured all of the Christmas cake at one time. *How bloody typical of him not to have thought ahead even one day.*

Knight followed the crude road meant for the ranger's truck. It cut through the thickest part of the forest, meandered around hills, and sank into narrow valleys where log bridges crossed small streams, now gurgling under crusted snow and ice. Although the Army coat kept him warm, his feet were numb and frequently he ran briefly only to bring feeling back to them. He knew the temperature had dropped again, and although this was dangerous for his freezing feet, it also meant that the rangers would not be eager to go out early and no one would be about the lakes on such a bitter morning. He crossed a major road with its usual signs of leaping deer and directions to Instructional Paths, detailing the types of flora and fauna native to the area, and admonitions about disturbing any of these. Erda had told him that even lizards and toads were protected. And so was everything else apparently: a marker ordered him sharply not to touch a single leaf. He was amused at this stark warning. As he read a sign laboring the sacredness of the nation's woodland's creatures, he hoped he was included in this fine sentiment.

In the thin light of dawn, he stood on a bend of the rangers' road and looked down upon an irregular-shaped lake. Trees hid the shoreline and snow covered the roofs of the tiny resort villages, deserted now in the winter. The lake was clearly man-made, its fjordlike stretches inundating the forest where Charlemagne once hunted stag and boar to the lilting call of Roland's horn.

Knight made his way with special care to the lakefront: he needed no more watchmen or caretakers, or even security officers for that matter, however sad and lonely they were or generous with their homemade moonshine. He had hoped for an overcast day; but minutes after he reached the shore, the sky turned a brilliant sapphire under which the lake changed from black to purple before his eyes, its surface velvet smooth in the stillness. He had no trouble removing the lock from a boathouse overhanging the lake and lowering one of the boats straight down into the water.

He rowed steadily but without haste, pacing the pull of the oars to the metronome set in his head. Behind him, the rippling wake widened into an opening fan ribboned with silver sides. The beauty of the lake touched him with melancholy, and his mind drifted. Later, he was to wonder at what moment he had actually stopped thinking about the rowing and begun pondering Dietrich's position.

What was the man going to do now? If that tomcatting soldier from the garrison was correct about the four deaths, Dietrich was going to be a wild man when he discovered three civilians had been killed by the Army. That was going to be a little harder to explain than the accidental death of an American survival-team-member airman playing at war games, who had been killed because of an unfortunate rumor about his being an escapee from a stockade. Dietrich could probably build a fairly good story about Knight's death if the killing was done by private hunters or even the Army or the rangers or the local police. There were always accidents in the games, and not just of Tyler's kind. But three dead civilians? Shot? That should be an interesting explanation to contemplate.

He thought of Erda. She was up now, probably in the kitchen with Katri, the two of them eating breakfast while the child talked about Christmas, Erda smiling as she listened. They made plans. There would be visitors. He saw them around a Christmas tree. They were singing, and then there was cake and cocoa and oranges for the children and wine for the adults.

Abruptly his thoughts were disturbed by the sound of an engine. He stopped rowing. The graveled beach was about a hundred yards ahead of him. He looked back across the vanishing wake to the shoreline from which he had come. He saw nothing on the lake, yet the sound of a motor continued to reverberate over the water. Knight pulled at his oars and spurted ahead. He was still two hundred feet from shore when the powerboat roared out of a fjord arm less than a mile away, skidded as it turned, straightened, and bore down on him.

He rowed furiously, his head down, his feet braced against the rib-boards, his concentration spread into his swiftly moving arms and heaving chest so that he did not look at the speeding boat at all, but kept his pace until he heard the scrape of the boat bottom on the gravel. At the same time the first bullet thunked into one of the oars.

Knight rolled out of the boat into several inches of water, then scrambled crablike onto the bank and under the nearest snow-covered shrubbery. He could hear the bullets pound into the ground behind him, the rifle shots echoing throughout the steep, wooded hills. He began to run while he was still crouching, his mind outlining the situation almost calmly: their craft was too big to run upon the shore; they had to stop the engine first and lower a rowboat. By that time he would be half a mile away. The forest was thick, thus it was no easier for them than it was for him. So much for the advantages.

He wondered how many of them there were. They could spell each other. They could fan out and encircle him. They could phone ahead for reinforcements. They had the guns. It was all stacked against him. His only hope was to find a place to hide. But his own tracks in the snow would give him away. He glanced up at the clear sky and asked for rain, snow, fog, anything to conceal his tracks. But the sun shone brightly, turning the trees into blazing torches of sparkling light, at times blinding him so that he stumbled over low-growing bracken and raised roots.

He climbed the first hill which rose from the lake, dropped over the top, and alternately slid and ran into the ravine below where a small, fast stream cascaded around snow-capped rocks. For a few seconds he stopped and listened for his pursuers, but heard nothing. Quite near him a branch cracked under its burden of snow, the noise sounding singularly like a gunshot.

He stepped into the water and began running with light careful steps. A few hundred yards later he got out, ran over the top of matted shrubbery, and bumped headlong into an outcropping of pink limestone, the color as incongruous among the shades of green and blue and white as a full-blooming rosebush might have been in that winter world.

The wall of stone was too steep and too high to climb. He followed it to the top of another hill and found the ruins of a castle at its summit. Only the floor and a few feet of a crumbling wall remained of the ancient stronghold, but from this vantage point he could look down upon parts of the lake and the first hill he had climbed.

A light wind played on the promontory and Knight shivered as he searched the landscape below for movement. Then, on the summit of the first hill he saw a momentary flash such as a mirror or shiny piece of metal turned for an instant toward the sun might make. He telescoped his hands in front of his eye and scanned the area. Looking back across the same ravine were two men dressed in bright green. In following the pink outcropping, Knight had returned to the spot where he had entered the stream. Instinctively, he ducked behind the wall, scraped a channel through the pile of snow on top of the stones, and examined the men. "They wear snappy green outfits," Erda had said. " . . . and most of the members are ex-soldiers."

Two more men reached the top of the hill and stopped beside the others. One motioned in various directions with his arms, as though he were conducting. Knight watched them fan out and descend toward the swift stream below.

He turned and looked at the landscape behind him: more wooded hills, though none as high as the one on which he stood. Smoke rose from the chimneys of a village several miles away. Knight headed for it, running when he could, but frequently obliged to climb laboriously as the terrain became steeper. As he stopped on top of the last hill before the town, he caught sight of a road winding midway down the incline. He ran to it, walked along its shoulder for some distance, listening now for both the civilian hunters behind him and the sound of cars.

After a few hundred yards he stopped, walked back and forth in the space of a few feet, then vaulted into the middle of the road. From there he leaped to the other side, found a long stick, and erased the footsteps in the middle of the road. Walking backward to the edge of the road, he erased the remaining steps except for the spot on which he stood. Below him was a steep drop of about ten feet. He lowered himself over the side, and stood on an exposed root protruding from the side of the built-up road foundation. Carefully he removed the last footprints, and then dropped to the ground, which turned out not to be ground at all, but garbage.

He picked up a large carton, careful not to remove its snow cover, pushed himself into the loose mass of decaying waste beneath it, flattened out the snow where he had landed, and brought the carton slowly back over him. He could see light through several holes in the garbage, and when he moved his face away from these openings, the smell of corruption closed in on him like a physical touch. He waited and prayed silently for traffic. A truck passed only a few minutes before he heard the green hunters.

"Look here, the tracks stop. He got a lift. Goddamm it, now someone else will get him!"

Knight heard stomping from the road above.

"What's over there?"

"Only a dump."

"Hell. I was sure we had him. When I got up this morning, I said to myself, 'Ernest, this is going to be your lucky day.'"

Knight heard a gun being readied for firing. "Freddy, go down and line up some bottles; better yet, kick up the place a little and scare up a few rats."

"Do it yourself; I'm not your servant. Anyway, why should I muck up my uniform in that crap just so you can shoot at a few rats. You couldn't hit one, anyway. Look how you missed him back at the lake."

"Cut the bickering, you guys; we all missed him back at the lake."

"Gus is right. We've got to get to town and call the police and let them know he's in a car on this road."

"You're crazy. I don't intend to let anyone know we almost had him and then let him get away. How would that look? National trophy winners! We'd look like fools!"

"Listen, Ernest, you're just thinking of the club. The man is dangerous. God knows how many more people he'll kill before they get him. We've got to let the police know when we saw him and where he got away. It's in the national interest."

"The national interest! You think the government's going to fall because one lousy American gangster is loose in the country? Let the Army worry about him; he's one of theirs."

"Look, Ernie, we agreed we'd hunt him until he was caught. Now you want to quit just because of a little setback. We'd still look pretty good if we were the ones that led the police to him."

"Crap. I don't want to lead the police to him. I want us to get him. We were the ones that figured he'd come to the lake. We paid for the lookout. . . . And that's another thing: how come that nut didn't call us sooner? If he had called us as soon as he saw the boat, we could have blown that killer right out of the water. He would never have made it to the other side."

"He did call us as soon as he saw him. He just didn't get up early enough. He has to sleep sometime. You expect one man to pull a twenty-four-hour watch?"

"This is wasting time. Come on, Gus, I'm for walking into town to call the police and tell them what we know. If you and Freddy want to stay, Ernest, it's okay by us. We'll pick you up as soon as we can get a car and get back."

"Okay, okay. I'll go. You think I want to stay here and freeze my balls off? Just give me one minute. I want to fire a round into the dump."

"If that will make you feel better, go ahead, but hurry it up. It's going to be a cold walk unless we catch a ride."

Knight lay paralyzed under the covering of garbage, waiting for the shooting to begin. If he jumped up now, they would kill him at once. His only hope was that the disappointed, crabby Ernest would try for distance.

The firing began, the bullets smashing into the debris with muted thumps, the shots not even very loud.

"A rat! A rat!"

"Where?"

"Over there."

"Yeah, yeah, I see him."

The firing came again.

"I got him. Did you see the little bugger jump? Ha ha. Very comical. A gymnast, that rat. An aerial rat. Do you see any more?"

"No."

"Throw some stones."

"Come on, Ernie, you said one round."

"Okay, okay!"

Knight listened to more grumbling, then footsteps crunch-

216

ing on the snow. He shivered. Within a minute the sounds from the road vanished, and he became more acutely aware of the stench. The smell was not of garbage, but of a deeper decay. He moved his head, and the smell increased hideously. Quickly he pushed the carton to one side. Quite near his face was a small dead animal. Knight pulled himself up on his elbows and looked at the half-decayed thing with maggots crawling in its ruptured belly. It was a cat.

Carefully Knight extricated himself from the hole he had burrowed into the garbage and surveyed the dump. He examined every snow-covered mound from where he stood. Some twenty feet away, he saw the configuration that he was looking for. He tore off the lid to the carton that had concealed him and walked gingerly toward a large hump of snow, erasing his steps with the carton lid as he went.

Three minutes later he was kneeling on the back seat of a wrecked car. The upholstery was damp and badly shredded and the windows were all shattered, but the roof was sound under its hood of snow. The forward part of the car, the engine, steering wheel and dash, were missing. The only opening was through a partially crushed windshield, and it faced the valley, away from the road.

It was eleven in the morning when Knight curled up tightly and thought of sleep. It was Tuesday. He had forty-nine hours to go before he was free. He knew now that only in the presence of the NATO Games Commander's meeting at noon on Thursday was he safe from getting shot. With the hunters out looking for him and the police soon to be notified of his last known position, and the sun shining upon a beautiful winter's day, revealing even the movement of a rat, he elected to lie low. But he could not sleep. There was one more event he could count on for that morning, and waiting for it kept him awake.

An hour later he heard the first singsong siren and the squeal of brakes of several cars on the road, then loud voices.

"Are you sure this is the place?"

"Positively. Right opposite the dump."

"Where are the footprints?"

Silence. Then: "Well, we walked all over the area. We were following him, don't you see?"

"And you managed to tromp all over the evidence! Idiots!"

"But we clearly saw where he stopped walking, and there were no more tracks after that. And a car passed just before we got out of the forest.'"

"Amateurs!"

For a minute there were only footsteps pounding the snow. Then Knight's heart skipped a beat.

"Did anyone think to check the dump?"

"Yes. We did. In fact, we shot some rats." Knight recognized Ernie's placating voice.

"You were shooting rats and letting the criminal get further away? What idiocy!"

Car doors slammed, and a few minutes later the vehicles rumbled over the snow. Silence settled on the bloated heap of garbage, and Knight, almost warm in his greatcoat from another war, slept.

25

THE rats awakened him. He had actually been hearing them in his sleep for some time, their squeals entering his dream and becoming a part of the events that his silent self dredged up from a past he no longer remembered.

He and Hugo had to walk through a town to get to and from their school. It was the walk home that they thoroughly enjoyed, stopping from time to time to gaze into one or another of the store windows; the tobacco shop with its meerschaum pipes and pyramid of boxes with glass-sealed cigars from Cuba, and a larger-than-life wooden head of a man from whose open mouth smoke, or something that looked like it, puffed every two minutes, while his wooden painted hand, holding the cigar, moved to and from his face with slow mechanical jerks. The bakery sometimes featured a tiered wedding cake or one shaped like a locomotive or a ship for a party that the boys could only guess at. There were other shops, but their favorite (except for the smell of the confectionery, where the aroma of chocolate made them a little mad) was the watchmaker's establishment with its windows of mechanical miracles. The scene was of a court ball in which three-dimensional Lilliputian figures acted out their appointed parts, the king and queen sitting on their thrones, nodding approvingly to the entertainment spread before them: acrobats and dancers, jesters and jugglers, drummers and fifers, all performing with the most glorious precision, their brilliantly colored costumes as glazed as colored lights. On the hour, all movement stopped and every head turned toward a winged trumpet-bearing angel that lowered slowly and majestically, like the heavenly spirit it was supposed to be, from somewhere above the king's chair and blasted forth the hours as though God had invented time.

The boys loved all the shops and were always sorry when the last one was behind them and they came to the edge of the town, where a huge three-story, windowless, dirty stone building faced its blind wall toward the street. There was no mystery about the building; it was a chemical factory whose doors and such meager windows as there were looked across a strip of puffy marsh to a river.

One day after school, Hugo and Nicholas discovered a loose board in the tall solid fence that encircled the three-acre yard adjacent to the factory. On occasion they slipped through this opening and looked into the glass pit—a deep narrow trench where broken bottles and shattered tubes were dumped by the cartful.

The establishment was closed on Sundays, and it was on one of these pleasant afternoons that the boys, coming from the farm that day instead of school, stopped and pulled aside the board to see if more glass had been thrown into the pit. It was summer and the grass was thick, allowing them to move noiselessly as they came upon the half-filled trench, seeing at once the large brown rats that ran nimbly over the broken glass with their delicate handlike feet. Both boys stopped and watched with fascinated amazement at the little beasts' arrogant defiance of the razor edges and jagged, glistening saber points. "They're eating the stoppers," said Hugo, "and the stuff that spilled from the bottles."

The rats scattered down into the pit of glass at the sound of human voices but returned brazenly moments later and resumed their scavenging, squeaking stridently as they darted about, their narrow bewhiskered heads twitching and sniffing continually. The boys sat on the ground and watched these amusing antics for a time and then went on to the river to swim. But that was over thirty years ago.

In his dream in the wrecked car, Knight was inside the glass pit, paralyzed with fear that he would be hideously cut if he moved to get out and at the same time half-mad with horror at the knowledge that the rats were eating their way toward him. Something flickered against his face, something whiskery that sniffed his skin and nipped hesitantly at the bandage over his eye. He awakened screaming, hitting at his own face with flailing arms; the rat leaped off Knight's head and onto the seatback, where it halted briefly on its hind legs, squealing horribly, its little hands raised in agitated motions as if to fight back. Knight kicked it backward into a pile of debris, where he heard it scurry away, still squeaking shrilly. He heard more of the rodents around him, and as he awakened fully, he saw rat eyes staring at him, flashing like black diamonds from a dozen different holes in the garbage around the mutilated car. He shuddered and sat up.

It was twilight, a time of day that all his life had infused him with insuppressible fears and vague desperation which gnawed at his mind and subtly reached into his body as though invisible boneless hands were touching his raw spine. Everything failed between sundown and darkness: warmth, light, strength. When he was a child, he thought of it as The Bad Time and made certain he was not alone then. If Hugo was with him, the fears kept their distance. Even among strangers he felt lost and anxious, in the haunting layers of gray between light and dark.

He looked out over the sloping fan of the refuse heap

toward a tree-cluttered ravine. Some of the snow had melted or slid from the trash during the full day of sunshine, uncovering patches of foul-smelling rubbish in which large black birds pecked and gulped, lunging at each other from time to time with necks outstretched and wings spread wide.

Knight felt stiff and exhausted; the sleep had been restless, uneasy, uncomfortable; yet he hated going out into the twilight, crawling down through the garbage and into the dusky ravine where he knew the snow was deeper, the thickets more thorn-covered, the footing less certain over the frozen patches of black ice. He decided to wait until dark.

He stared vacantly out upon the dying day. It was December, and the year ... the year was 1962. Christmas was a few days away, and for the first time since Hugo died he wished he had someone to be with during the holiday. He realized then that he was lonely, had perhaps been lonely for years but had mistaken the feeling for boredom. He had spent almost his whole adult life in the tedious, dreary business of being ready for war. Why shouldn't he think he was only bored? He had chosen the safety of military life in favor of the dangers of living outside the fortification. How neatly he had escaped having to live his life, having to face making terrifying choices that might be wrong, or thwarted, or ruinous. It was not that he was rootless; the U.S. Air Force was home no matter whose country it was in.

He felt disgust at himself, at his indifference, his cowardice. He had botched his whole life. After the war, he had gone to school for a few years with no particular design for the future. His old desire to be an actor seemed frivolous at the time, and the dream embarrassed him, although he read plays passionately, voraciously, secretly memorizing long Shakespearean passages. At college, he soon discovered that his reticence and detachment made him interesting to women, more exciting. In time, he played the role of the unknowable, mysterious man to the hilt: he was Hamlet, the Count of Monte Cristo, Cyrano (with a more fortunate nose).

When he was alone, he roared at the absurdity of it all.

He returned to the military out of inertia. There was no other business that he understood as well; then, too, it was a good stage: there was always an appreciative audience of hopelessly bored and leisure-wearied spectators. But most of all, it was safe.

He had exchanged freedom for safety. In a year and a half he would be forty and entering a new kind of twilight. Why had he never promised his life anything? Again, it struck him that he had nothing of value to lose since he had placed no value on anything. In all those years, he had even missed the only divinity of which man is capable—love. He thought of Erda choosing her life, then being denied her choice, and so revising her plans and choosing again. And he had escaped it all—the decisions and revisions, the uncertainties and doubts, the failures, and most of all, the contributions. That was the worst part: he had contributed nothing. He felt old and friendless and useless. In another thirty years he might be a night watchman in some warehouse, snoozing in the afternoons, collaring strangers when he could, to show off his disintegrating military paraphernalia, and talking desperately about old times to anyone who would listen.

For all his eccentricities, he had not chosen his life: he had simply and carelessly allowed it to happen, dressing it up with fripperies and grandstand plays so that it appeared that he was in control of it. For a long time now he had known that he lived only on the thin surface of his life, avoiding some dark center of his self where forces waited to urge him to face the facts of betrayal and loss. He had always averted his mind from any such unpleasant suspicions, marked by half-conscious whisperings, and played the clown instead.

Now he sat hunch-shouldered against the cold and felt time passsing. Rats and huge-eyed angry birds were tearing away at the decaying earth around him. Beyond the garbage heap an implacable, murderous enemy stalked the forests and roads in search of him. A sick despair ate into his soul. He tried to remember the tune the young nun had hummed to him at the convent of the blind fish, but failed. He sought, in the fading hour, the deep blue of the eyes of the Abbess, but all was gray. He searched for anything that would protect him from his own despair and the horrifying conviction that he would have to run forever from a Dietrich who hunted him through eternity.

He thought of Erda's absorbed face and her sure, gentle hands as she worked on his wounds. With this, he began to shake off the black anxiety and resolved to move on.

Darkness came quickly, but there was a curious cast to it, a luminous quality that was unnatural for nighttime. In the distance, the lights of the town should have been bright, clear, but instead they looked diffused, as though shimmering through opalescent glass. Perhaps it was raining in the distance. He climbed painfully into the front seat and looked through the opening in the windshield up at the sky for the stars. Only a few of the very brightest shone down, and these, too, had the same aura of diffusion and frostiness about them as the street lamps of the town. A car passed on the road, its yellow headlights cutting conical beams into the strange darkness, and Knight saw then the rapidly incoming fog from the lowlands in the north. In another hour the whole area would be socked in and the little villages surrounding Aachen would be hidden under its pervading presence. He could slip in and out of them at will for the latest news on troop locations; then, with care, reach Aachen by midnight, climb over the fence into the base, and. . . . *And what?*

First things first.

Twice he slipped on the refuse heap as he made his way toward the bottom of the hill, still hesitant to use the flashlight; but by the time he reached the ravine and sank up to his ankles in ice-covered stagnant water in the total darkness, he was forced to use it. The light was the color of buttermilk and showed only a few feet of the terrain ahead of him. He made his way through the trees and rigid underbrush, heading northwest, the pain in his feet more severe than it was when he left the dump.

It was on just such a December night in the Ardennes eighteen years before that he received the final wound that took him from the Western Front and the war. He reflected upon that series of events, wondering if Dietrich might not be in some way part of the cast of that bizarre drama. Three German armies had stopped the advancing Americans south of Aachen and swept them back almost as far as the Meuse River. The enemy had dropped a number of English-speaking SS soldiers in American uniforms behind Allied lines to murder officers and create confusion. In the dense fog, Knight, heading for Bastogne, heard two of them talking about the plan. He grasped the situation at once and brashly joined them, took command, claiming he had special orders for a secret mission from their commander, rounded up as many of the impostors as he could find; then with that same impudence and contempt for failure he led them to Bastogne and turned them over to the U.S. Army. Again he was promoted in the field.

Two days later, in the same obstinate fog, when he was headed for Aachen, already in Allied hands, a piece of shrapnel tore into his chest and took him and the three men in the jeep with him out of the war. He, alone, survived.

He mused over those days, trying to remember if he might have met Dietrich then, or even seen him. But he was convinced he had not. He had been in on the interrogation of the Germans in American uniforms: Dietrich was not among them.

An hour after he left the ravine below the garbage dump, Knight stood near the road leading into the town, its first bleary street lamps looking like fuzzy flowers of light in the dripping darkness. He tried to gauge the activity within the village by the number of cars on the road, but no cars entered or left. Still, there seemed to be a celebration going on; he could hear some kind of music, not the traditional German beer-hall songs, which he disliked, nor the popular new American dance tunes, which did not thrill him either, but some sort of eerie collection of percussion sounds—drums, gongs, bells—interrupted every half-minute by a harsh rattle which he could not identify at all.

He crept along a hedgerow that fronted some buildings, private houses from the looks of them, with the usual half-timbered architecture and steep roofs. He came within a few steps of walking into the midst of a cluster of people at a wide opening in the hedge, who appeared to be waiting for something due on the street any minute.

"I hear them! I hear them!" yelled a boy.

"Don't shout, Seppi; we all hear them. They should be coming around the corner any minute."

Knight drew back and plastered himself against the hedge as the noise grew louder, more discordant and jarring, and the unmusical rattling more frequent, more insistent. He peered through the topiary hedge: out of the fog, marching up the center of the street, came a procession of cloaked and hooded men carrying flaming torches in one raised hand and in the other, bunches of loose bones tied together in the form of wind chimes, which they shook at regular intervals. On both sides of them strode a single row of masked figures, each beating a percussion instrument, but none of them making any attempt to harmonize with the others. They wore animal skins and the masks of lewdly grinning satyrs with black horns. The bone rattlers were draped in red robes, their faces concealed by white slit-eyed visors that flashed and blinked from under their hoods as they moved in a swaying motion down the street.

When the procession passed, the group of people near Knight fell in behind them, where a noisy crowd already followed, some dressed in the lurid costumes of demons and specters. Some wore plaster animal heads. Many were children.

Knight took off his knit cap, and after cutting a hole in it for his good eye, pulled it all the way down over his head. He fell in easily with the revelers, who staggered and swayed and talked loudly, as though they were a little drunk. He discovered quickly from the ripe smells that many of them were. He suddenly felt wonderful—thrilled and exhilarated. Nothing could have stopped him from joining the crowd. Dietrich and the rats and The Bad Time all vanished in the presence of a deeper past, of a fantastic night when he was four, or perhaps five, and the grown men, his father and uncle and grandfather—yes, there had been a grandfather then—were all marching joyously up a strange and beautiful street where all the lamppoles were festooned with silver streamers and balloons. He was being carried on his uncle's shoulder, and Hugo was on Father's. The men talked loudly, and laughed much, their eyes bright and a little wild, their breath smelling of something oversweet.

Other men, also in high spirits and shouting greetings to them, came running out of the slate-front houses and joined them, until the street was a swaying river of men. The procession halted at the town's square, where all the men stood very straight and sang magnificently to Someone Wonderful as the bells rang on both sides of the Rhine and echoed down through the gorges in deep reverberations that promised to go on forever. It was all glorious and a little terrifying.

Afterward there was a feast and the men told stories of how the ghosts of drowned rivermen had rung the bells to help send the Devil back to hell. In later years, Nicholas could still conjure up the vision of the dead men climbing out of the Rhine and tramping in their soggy boots to the towers to ring the bells.

In the fog, with his knit mask hiding his bandaged face, Knight felt an exuberant sense of safety and camaraderie. He was only a few miles from the base; and he was with people, a whole crowd of people who accepted him without question, who allowed him to march with them and be part of them. He was more than delighted to help them send their devil back to hell; he was grateful. With immense joy he looked forward to the singing.

In the center of the town in front of a floodlighted church where a few ancient gravestones leaned haphazardly toward the snowy earth, the hooded procession stopped, still shaking the bones and waving the torches. Behind them the crowd halted and hushed. From the front row of the marchers, one of the visored men walked to the steps of the church, faced the townspeople, raised his torch, and demanded that all evil spirits leave the town at once.

A surge of murmuring echoed him. "At once ... at once: all evil go hence." The voices became louder, more urgent, as the torchbearers silently encircled the crowd, the satyrs sentineling into a second ring outside the first, beating their instruments into cacophonic madness.

Around Knight, the people shrieked for the evil spirits to leave their town as the bones rattled and the torches circled like fireworks pinwheels.

Suddenly a trumpet sounded stridently from the church tower, the bones stopped rattling, the musicians halted in mid-beat, and all the people inside the circles dropped to the ground. All except Knight.

There was a moment of dreadful silence as Knight, trying to reason out what had happened, stared dumbly at the prostrate bodies lying around him. He looked up at the masked men whose hidden faces were turned toward him, and realized, too late, the rules of the game.

As he began to run, leaping over bodies into open spaces of trampled snow, he saw the circles close in, the paralyzed forms on the ground rise like the dead returning to life. He hit in all directions as he felt fists pummel him. A grasping hand tore off his cap, and those nearest him washed back with gasps of surprise or shock.

He leaped then, shoving all aside, breaking through both

rings with a wild swinging of his arms, jumping high over a tombstone that loomed in his way, dashing behind the church and down the nearest fog-drenched alley. For a time he heard the roar of human voices and running feet behind him, and he ran harder, faster, his heart wild in his chest, his lungs ballooning dangerously.

The alleys and streets and yellow-thistle lights finally all vanished along with the shrieking crowd, and he was running across an open field. He could hear the frozen, cut, grain-stubble crunch like ice needles under the thin covering of snow beneath his boots. He used his flashlight: the fog was even thicker than before.

You idiot! Speak of stupid!

Yeah. Yeah. Yeah.

Next time, learn the rules before you decide to play; everybody's got their own way of dealing with devils.

Okay! Okay!

You know what's wrong with you, Nicholas? You're still living your life as though Death has lost your address.

26

WHEN Knight first heard the hounds, he thought that he had disturbed a couple of watchdogs at some farm he had passed close to in the fog. Then a few minutes later, climbing over a rock wall at the top of a low hill, he heard them again, nearer this time, their baying prolonged and harsh, as though they had treed or cornered some animal. It was two in the morning; he had been stumbling west for nearly five hours.

He stopped, cupped his hands around his ears, and looked back into the darkness from which he had come, straining to isolate the overlapping barking. There were three. No, four! Four dogs. Of course, Dietrich would get dogs. In this soup the hunter-capture units must be bumping into themselves. He ran a few steps and stopped abruptly: if he panicked now, he could consider himself dead. He had to think. There were a thousand false moves and probably only a half-dozen right ones, and he could only choose one. He felt his belly knot up at the renewed, more vigorous baying of the dogs. Cold terror, that's what that was, and if he allowed himself that, he was dead, too.

Think. Think. Dietrich could not be sure that the dogs had the scent of the right man. The stories those people at that demon-hunting town told the police were bound to be contradictory tales, if for no other reason than that no two people ever saw the same things in the same way. And considering the wild circumstances back there, with everyone revved up and willing to see fiends, some of those police reports had to be funnier than hell.

There he was, standing amid that sea of prostrate bodies, his head looking like a snake's with its tight cap pulled down to his neck and only one eye staring out into the fogged-up floodlights. His long military coat was black with filth and reeked of garbage and dead cats. To most of those people he must have looked like a fugitive from hell. Then when they unmasked him and still found only one eye and a face that was half-covered with black hair, he must have convinced the rest of them that a demon had indeed come amongst them. He would have liked to hear a few of those descriptions given by the citizenry of that town, especially those who were drunk.

Well, Dietrich, you're going to have to follow more than that lead; and you better move carefully everywhere or you'll have more dead civilians on your hands. You poor bastard. What are you going to find to say about those dead men?

He started down the hill, keeping the beam of his light directed on the ground immediately in front of him. There was another sound that he was beginning to pick up, and he knew what made it even before he reached the top of the next low hill and could look down upon its origin, his mind already seeing the butter-yellow lights that dug into the thick white blindness of the freeway, which was harder to cross than a river, day or night, and a whole hell of a lot more risky ... *except in the fog ... when I'm not likely to be recognized and ... and not even likely to be seen either before some maniac, roaring down the fast lane in a Maserati, knocks me halfway back to the Rhine or just kills me outright ... nothing fancy.* Well, it was a relatively small risk at two in the morning. He put away the flashlight.

But when he came within a hundred feet of the freeway, he realized that getting killed in the fog by a speeding car was not going to be one of his problems. Against the muted lights of the passing vehicles, he saw a line of jeeps parked on a secondary road, adjacent to the freeway. He knew at once that to the south, they were probably bumper-to-bumper as far as the Belgian border. And to cross that frontier in the hope of coming onto the base from the south was sheer madness: the Belgian border patrol used dogs as a routine matter, and he already had four of those at his heels now.

He loped northward, away from the base that was on the other side of the freeway not ten minutes from where he first saw the military traffic with its gnome-hunched figures inside—waiting.

He ran steadily, sometimes in near-panic as the row of military trucks and jeeps continued to line the road, it seemed to him, to the end of the world. He cursed Dietrich in short, furious, repetitive snarls, but stopped when pain began to shoot up into his eyes from his clenched jaws. His legs were wet to his knees and his hand throbbed in time to the pain in his face and head. Still he ran, no longer stopping for a few seconds from time to time to listen for the dogs, and paying about as little attention to the ground under his feet as the situation allowed. He knew he was running along a hill sloping toward the road below him and that it was relatively free of trees and bushes. Twice he crashed into some kind of low growth, but without harming himself. But he could not run until morning. So far, it was the combination of night and fog that had protected him. In fact, he could not run much farther at all: he was sure that if—or when—the dogs reached the spot where he turned north, someone would phone ahead and have him intercepted.

He glared at the silent military vehicles with a wild anger, and even after the line ended it seemed to him that he still saw them for a time, tenebrous hulks crouching along the road waiting to spring out with a great roar. It was the secondary road that had ended, abruptly, up against a freeway entrance. There were several roads converging upon the main one, looping over and under each other like a well-made pretzel. He climbed to the top of the hill and looked over the pattern, the lights from the cars giving him at least some idea of the terrain on both sides of the intersected freeway. There was one area between the main highway and one of the entrance roads that looked black, not murky semidark the way buildings and trees look in the fog, but deeply black like a pit or at least an abrupt falling away of the land.

He crouched down and ran to the side of the entry road, then on it, racing straight down the middle of it toward the east for half a kilometer. Only one car came, and the driver, apparently seeing him in the last few seconds, careened crazily on the slippery pavement, barely missing him. He heard the harsh scream of the horn as the car straightened and sped on.

Knight ran off the side of the road into the black area that he had seen from the hilltop. Immediately he began to slide down a steep slope, the thick smell of smoke or oil or both rushing into his face as he slid farther and farther away from the road.

He tried to control his speed, rolling over on his side in order to grasp the racing ground beneath him, but there was nothing to hold onto. Under the snow cover, he felt a rough fist-sized aggregate that slid with him for a few feet, stopped from some sort of bunching while he rolled on until another loosened area of the stuff slid with him and stopped again as he lurched on. He dug his knees, then his elbows, into the slippery rocks, but the momentum and the angle of the decline kept him going. Something struck his ribs a sharp blow, and stars danced around his head in the dark; but the wild rolling ended. He lay still and listened but heard only the throb in his head and chest and after a few moments in his whole body. He groaned and tried to rise, but his right ankle would not support him. If it was broken, he was finished. He lowered himself slowly to the ground and grasped his ankle in both hands. Hot spasms radiated from his ankle into his foot, up his leg, his left side; again stars gamboled before his eyes. He gulped air, gasped, and stretched out fully on the ground, his left hand coming to rest on metal. He moved his fingers over a smooth cold surface. No snow.

There was nothing else to do except risk a light. In the faded glow of the flashlight he saw that the metal was part of a railroad track on which a small coal cart squatted like a toad. Behind him was the incline down which he had crashed with such force. For an astonished moment he could not believe that he had fallen down such a steep slope without breaking his neck, let alone just his ankle. One thing was certain: the men with the dogs were not going to come that way—assuming they managed to track him to the point at which he went over the ledge. Even dogs weren't that dumb.

He pulled himself to the coal cart, and grasping its side, rose to his feet, keeping his injured foot off the ground. Slowly he pulled himself along the empty cart, but his weight pushed it with a thin squeaking sound. He held onto it to keep from falling, dragging his feet as the cart slid on the track. He swore at the pain. The cart stopped as it nudged into another of its kind. Again Knight pulled himself forward, careful this time not to lean on the vehicle without a strong hold on it. He discovered a whole string of the small carts, all empty: some of them with built-up sides, some of them only boards with wheels like a miniature railroad flatcar.

He dragged himself upon the last of these and considered his location. He was in a coal yard: either there was a mine nearby or this was a loading point. In either case there had to be some kind of building or shed where the men checked in for work and the foreman handed out the weekly pay. From some distance, he could hear the muted sounds of trucks moving slowly on the highway, but the fog was too thick for any light to pass through.

He stretched his left foot down on the track and pushed at one of the ties. The flatcar moved a few yards. He repeated the action and moved again. Lying on his belly, with his arms holding onto the sides, he could push himself farther while he kept his right knee bent to protect his injured ankle. He was moving toward the freeway.

After a few hundred yards, the texture of the darkness seemed to change suddenly; he stopped and listened for the sounds of the trucks. He could not hear them. He could hear nothing except a steady dripping of water that he had not heard before, and the darkness was total.

He snapped on the light, but kept the beam covered with his hand, letting only a small amount of it leak out. At first he thought he was inside the mine, but when he directed the full light to the walls and ceiling of the cavern he had rolled into, he saw that he was in a short tunnel. He was underneath the freeway.

Built against one wall of the tunnel were the offices for the yard. How very resourceful to build this stuff inside the tunnel. How very German. Knight knew at once that at the other end of the tunnel he would find the rest of the coal yard with a spur of regular track that connected up to the main railroad nearby.

He hopped to the office and unscrewed the hasp that held the padlock. Once inside, he dropped into the nearest chair, stretched out his damaged leg, and groaned freely as he leaned back to rest, finding, however, then that all his other pains cried for his attention, too.

He ignored them and pulled himself together, flashing the light around the room. On the wall behind a desk hung a large map of the Aachen area that had the base clearly delineated with a heavy black line, although it was not otherwise identified as such. The Germans referred to it generally as an "Adolf" camp, a name they gave any structure or installation whose origin dated back to the Third Reich. But at one time this very installation had been the most important panzer base in all Germany and some of the soldiers from that time still looked back upon those days with fierce and bitter longing. Knight had met some of them with their ill-concealed contempt for the new Army, their innuendos about the inherent weaknesses of the NATO forces due to the inferiority of some of the member nations. He had heard their catcalls hurled at German girls who married American black soldiers.

As he studied the map he saw for the first time the way Aachen was pushed into a niche between Belgium and the Netherlands. The city looked cornered, with the freeway running across the front of it as if to hold it at bay. And it was not one of those highways that appears around a clump of trees and vanishes over a hill. It was cut straight through the trees, gouged out of the middle of the hills as though the man who dreamed it up had never thought in any way except straight lines, let alone a curve through a stand of lovely beech trees or a breast-shaped rise that was pleasing to the eye and whatever other parts that might find pleasure at such things.

Knight found a washroom and looked at his face in the mirror. The bandage over his eye was black with coal dust. He filled the basin with warm water, washed his hands, and carefully removed the dressing, again feeling shock as he saw the gash along the side of his head. He tested his vision, but could see nothing out of the injured eye. For a long moment he contemplated his filthy face; then he hopped back to the outer room and again looked at the map of the cornered city.

He was five kilometers from the camp's main gate, and although the original war-games rules clearly stated that any survival teams reaching within one kilometer of that gate were safe from capture, Knight knew that he could not count on surviving in that safety zone. Dietrich intended to kill him, and in this fog an arranged accident within that kilometer was not only possible, it was sure to be the plan of the day.

It was after three in the morning as Knight stood on one foot and reconsidered the miners' map: he had under thirty-three hours left until Thursday noon, and somehow he had to walk through that front gate. Dietrich must have his forces organized in a fairly solid ring outside that chain-link fence enclosing the base.

He found a can of sardines and some stale biscuits on a shelf, a half bottle of cheap whiskey in a file drawer, and in a metal closet, various articles of heavy clothing and headgear.

He decided to see to his ankle first. After taking several deep gulps of the whiskey, he unlaced his boot and glared at his swollen leg.

He was seventeen and an Army surgeon was looking back at him a little angrily. "What do you mean you don't know anything about it? They're your bones, kid, and by God, they've been broken. Three ribs, the mandible, the right clavicle, left radius, right patella, left fibula. . . ."

"What's all that?"

"Bones. Your bones! All broken at one time or another. Now, don't try to tell me you don't know anything about any of them except your jaw."

"I don't remember."

The man sighed and lowered his voice to normal. "Did you ever have a serious accident?"

"No."

"Weren't you ever sick . . . have to spend time in bed?"

"No."

"You're sure you were never in a hospital?"

"I'm sure."

"Your people ever tell you about an accident you had when you were a small kid?"

"No."

The doctor stopped walking back and forth in front of his desk and sat down. He straightened out a disheveled stack of manila folders and picked up an X-ray photograph from a pile and examined it. "Anyone ever beat you up at home?"

"All the time."

The doctor looked at Nicholas over the top of the X-ray photograph, the picture covering the man's nose and mouth so that he had no expression at all except that which came from his eyes, musing and remote. "Who's your next of kin?"

"My what?"

"Your relatives. Whom do we notify?"

"For what?"

"Boy, you are going into the Army."

"Oh. Nobody. There's nobody." Nicholas shook his head.

The doctor looked at him a moment longer; then he returned his attention to the stack of folders, dropping the X-ray sheet casually back onto the pile. He did not look up again. "You can go. That's all."

Knight removed the linen towel from a roller and cut it into strips, binding the lengths tightly around his ankle; then he replaced his boot and laced it snugly. He rose slowly and walked on the injured foot, from chair to desk to cabinet, gasping at each step. *A crutch . . . if he could make a crutch . . . No. No crutches, not if he was going through that front gate. . . .*

He hobbled out into the tunnel and filled the sardine can with coal dust. Back in the washroom, he allowed himself a light as he carefully covered his face, neck, and hands with the black dust. His facial wound burned when he rubbed the coal into it, but his ankle took most of his attention away from that pain. When he was finished he pulled his gloves back on and examined his face closely. The injured eyeball still looked like a red-veined plum with a blue-green bruise on it, but he'd have to do his best with it.

"Yassah, sah. I got into a fight wif one dem niggahs ova at the fo'ty-secon', but I done come out bes'."

Probably too thick, but the Germans wouldn't know the difference. To them, all blacks looked alike—and sounded alike, too—so he could ham it up as much as he wanted. Knight knew all the stereotypes the Germans believed about American blacks and decided he could employ any or all of them as the need for them arose.

He took a hooded rain cape from the closet and put it on, snapping it up to his neck. It ballooned out over his coat, making him look like a walking tent with a head sticking through the top. When he was through cleaning up after himself, he left the building, careful to replace the hasp and its padlock.

It was after four when he emerged from the tunnel and again heard the sounds of the trucks and cars on the freeway above him. *All your noise can't convince me that this is a nation of cars. You don't even know what it means to be car-oriented: you should see California. I'll bet there's not a person in that whole state that would get rid of a car and keep the horse.*

He found the bicycle in an unlocked hut near the railroad spur. There were two of them, solid, well-built, with excellent handbrakes and fine racks behind the seats on which one might carry any number of interesting things.

27

THE fog was the color of lard. It seemed to Knight that it actually had the feel of grease to it as he pedaled out of the coal yard and onto the frontage road that paralleled the freeway, the bicycle sliding crazily on the wet asphalt as he tried to spare his injured foot from sharing in the work. Twice he had come down hard on the left pedal and the pain, that was a pulsating throb, shot a dagger of fire up into his groin. He moaned and thought of Hugo and the corrupting flesh of his brother's foot inside the bandage that had turned green the day he died.

For years now Nicholas had cringed at the memory of Hugo's slow dying, at the pain he knew his brother had suffered in the long nights of that spring twenty-three years before. He fought the remembering, barraging it with other thoughts, averting his mind from Hugo's dying face that always loomed up in front of him, large, white, feverish, talking in a whispering way, "...when I'm finished

241

here. . . ." And always, always, he lost, the other thoughts falling away into the darkness in which Hugo's wasted face alone remained to talk to him, "I'll try to get to wherever you are. . . ."

I don't know if this is going to work, Hugo, you see these guys might be decent, and the only hope I've got is that they're going to be bastards. It all depends on who's on duty and how good I am at bullshitting them. At that base outside Munich this would have no chance of working. You see, there they'd look at my papers just so they could chew the fat. Nothing more boring than gate duty, and getting a chance to talk to someone breaks the monotony. Also, they like Americans there so they'd hold me up with a lot of pointless questions, phone ahead to wherever I say I'm going and get clearance, just to pass the time. They'd drag out pictures of their girl friends, their kids, their dogs, anything to keep you there. And they go crazy with amazement and good cheer if you speak to them in German, as though you did them some kind of honor. They're a panic. It's a great place to go through the gate.

But you see, I've got to get these guys here to hate my guts right away so they just want to get rid of me. Well, there's no other way. It's through that front gate or not at all. If I try climbing the fence, they'll shoot me down with impunity since I'm supposed to know the one-kilometer rule so wouldn't be climbing the fence, and dressed like this it would be a perfect accident.

There's a good chance I can rile them. Aachen was very hard to take in forty-four; they held on to it like tigers. It's the history, you see: thirty-two German emperors crowned here . . . Charlemagne's bones hidden away in the cathedral. And it's been Prussian since the beginning of the nineteenth century; lots of pride and crap like that. Then, too, it was an elite panzer base. Took eight days of street fighting to capture the city. I've got to count on old pride and all that aristocratic bull and that elitist attitude. It all depends on the guys on duty. Nothing to do but play it by ear.

On the freeway, a hundred feet to his left, the trucks crawled with laboring engines and the agonized shifting of gears in the slow traffic. He saw their headlights, moonstone eyes peering into the dull wet dawn, come toward him and vanish, new ones coming behind them and vanishing, too, like rows of giant sluggish insects migrating across the landscape of a dying planet whose feeble sun was turning cold.

The frontage road on which he pedaled toward the base angled away from the freeway, and Knight moved more slowly. He still had to find a shop, and in a hurry, before everyone got up and started stirring around. There was a small business district a couple of kilometers from the base, a few food stores, a couple of small hotels where rooms could be rented by the hour or the afternoon, some third-rate restaurants, the kinds of businesses clustered near every army camp in the world. If the military ever established a base on the moon, a few cocky merchants would set up shop two kilometers from the front gate.

The stores loomed out of the fog suddenly, a clump of wet buildings hunching along a street of dirty snow. The whole town was encompassed along the one main road, having neither secondary nor intersecting roads to it. Knight pedaled into a narrow alley between a restaurant and a tobacco shop and stopped in back of the eating house. But there were no cartons in the refuse bins; the garbage from the night before had already been collected. He moved painfully from store to store, searching all the sheds and awnings behind the establishments, where boxes might be kept. In back of one of the hotels he found a large square covered basket in an unlocked snow porch. It smelled of fish.

He tied the basket to the bicycle rack with the last piece of thong from his supply pocket and returned to the street. He began to whistle "Old Man River."

243

Is that necessary?
Mood music.
Shut up and have the sense to be scared.
I'm plenty scared.
Then quit being a comedian.
But try as he would, Knight could not stop whistling.

There had been some feeble lamps in the single-streeted town, but now revolving searchlights came into view whirling through the fog until the very air seemed to be the myriad churning of insects, sickly white and small as dust motes. A hundred yards beyond the town, two Army trucks were parked directly opposite each other on both sides of the road. Between them a bakery van was being searched. Knight stopped behind it, letting both feet touch the street, bracing his arms against the handlebars. "Whoa deah."

A flashlight shone toward him from the back of the van.

"Hey, mista, you tyin' up de traffic."

The German soldier ran his flashlight over the bicycle, stopping briefly at the basket, which could not possibly have held a man, and turned it back on Knight. Another soldier came around the side of the van and told the first that he had cleared the driver. He saw Knight and for a moment looked startled. "Who's this?"

"A black." The men spoke in German.

"Tell him to move on; he's in the way."

The first soldier lowered his flashlight. "Go ahead. Go ahead. Army business here. Go ahead," he said impatiently in English.

"Yassah, suh." Knight continued whistling and pedaled around the van. Behind him he heard one of the men say, "Check the roof, and tell that fool to stop the engine."

Knight pedaled into the one-kilometer safety perimeter of the base, fear clutching his heart: he was convinced that rifles were aimed at his head. He used both feet on the pedals now, the pain in his ankle and leg bringing out flashing red spots before his face.

At the gate, the bar was down and the sentry stood beside the hut, his rifle in his hands.

"Look out fo de lobsta express," said Knight cheerily, stopping near the man.

The guard craned his neck forward and pulled it back as if he were slightly farsighted. "You are an American."

"Fum de great state of Alabama, which gots de mos' beeootiful ladies in de whole worl', exceptin' maybe heah in de lan' of de froilines."

The guard muttered something and put down the gun. "What do you want? This is a military base."

"Doan I know dat? I know whar I is at."

The second sentry on the exit side of the gate turned at Knight's voice. "What do you want here?"

"I gots to dee-liver dis mess a lobstas to de kitchen at de club. Dey is fo de gen'l what's comin' fo de special doin's."

"Can't you speak English?"

"Suh, I is speakin' English."

The two guards spoke in German. "Can you understand him?"

"Yeah, they all talk like that. He's got something to deliver to the club. Fish, I think."

"Well, check his ID."

"Not me. Touching their stuff always leaves a smell on you, and this one stinks worse than most." He turned back to Knight. "Are you in Germany with the military?"

"No mo. I was, suh, but I done ma time and wen' home and come back 'cause dey is a purty gal heah what kain't do wifout me. And I's a gwyne to learn to talk German. Lissen heah to dis: *Goot Mogan. Vee Gates. Goot Dahnka.*" He laughed raucously as the two sentries watched him with sullen hatred. "I's em-ployed now wid de big fish place in de city. You know de one? Hit's got a whole tank a live fish in de winda. Day impote dis heah lobsta fo de gen'l, special whea evah he goes."

Knight waited, grinning broadly as one sentry translated

for the other, who turned away in disgust. "Christ, he stinks. How can a German girl . . . ? A slut, no doubt. Tell him to go. It's too repulsive."

The first sentry motioned Knight through. "Be quick about it and don't piss around."

"Yassah, suh. I sholy will do dat." He moved away slowly and commenced whistling again.

The fog swallowed him quickly as he pedaled toward the nearest building, feeling physical illness from the pain in his leg. A sardine taste rose in his throat as he leaned against a wall and relaxed his taut muscles, his tongue swollen and his damaged eye watering badly as it burned from the coal dust. The fog was more dense, a mucous substance that smelled of gas and garbage.

You'd never have made it into an American base, you know, not with that collection of mismatched dialects. Any good Southern white boy would have laughed himself silly listening to you. And when Dietrich finds out they let through a bicycle rider—no matter what his color—delivering a basket of fish that nobody bothered to check, at six in the morning, on this particular day, all hell is going to break loose.

He heard a truck and saw the blur of lights as it passed near him; it was the bakery van. He moved back onto the road behind it and followed it, pulling away when it stopped at the side of a building where lights marked some stairs. Knight circled the building and at once found the telephone stalls with the directories chained to them under a metal awning over another entrance.

28

Dietrich's quarters were south of the main gate, one-half of a duplex resting in an expanse of undisturbed snow. Only the walks to the two front doors under an enclosed weather porch were shoveled clean. A metal sign reading "Col. A. Dietrich" was attached to the frame over one of the doors. *A.? Alfred? Albert? Adolf?* He had never considered Dietrich's first name, but then, knowing it made no difference in the scheme of things.

He tried the door; it was open. He slipped the bicycle inside silently, his stealth in entering not coming from any belief that Dietrich would be there; but he prudently had no wish to awaken whoever lived next door—only a wall away. Dietrich was probably with the group that had the dogs, or if the man had any brains at all he would be at the front gate during these last hours, since he would be the first finally to realize that Knight would come through the gate and not over the fence. Well, he should have thought of that before.

Inside Dietrich's quarters, he waited for his eye to adjust to the dim outlines of the objects in the room. It did not take long; he had been in a hundred rooms like it. Military quarters were assembly-line stuff, rows of identical houses or barracks as symmetrical as prison cells and about as interesting. The variations usually amounted to a mirror reversal of floor plans next door. He was amused when he realized that he could as well be standing in his own quarters at Wiesbaden or those he'd had in Texas, Japan, England, or a dozen other places where, even totally blind, he could have found his way around with ease.

He wheeled the bicycle into an entry hall, diagonally across a living room, through a kitchen, and out the back door, leaving it standing under a piece of extended roof against the back of the house.

As he looked around for something to use as a cane, he considered his priorities. The first order of business was to wash out his eye and get rid of the blackface, then clean up in general so he'd be reasonably ready for the moment when he finally met his unreasonable enemy face to face. He ended up walking on his foot without a crutch, resting it whenever possible.

His damaged eye looked worse once his skin was clean; and in washing the coal dust out of the gash along the side of his head he disturbed the scab so that the wound oozed blood steadily for a time, even after he was through cleaning up and was sitting on the sofa in Dietrich's living room, a bottle of the German Colonel's brandy and a kitchen glass beside him, his leg propped up on the coffee table in front of him, and his old overcoat and rain cape folded on the floor nearby.

Knight had not turned on any lamps since he arrived, using his flashlight when necessary. He had searched the man's quarters thoroughly and discovered almost at once that Dietrich lived as though he had no past: there was nothing to link his life to family or friends. Nicholas felt a vast disappointment. He had expected clues to Dietrich's identity, something that would make him show up sharp and clear on the receding road of his own memory. He wanted to look into the man's soul, see what passages he underlined in books, what beloved framed face he looked upon on nightstand or mantel, what letters he deemed worth keeping, what souvenirs he had saved from his childhood, what relics of his superstitions he enshrined in some locked cabinet or dresser drawer, what kinds of notes he made on a calendar, his doodles on a phone pad. But there were no books, no photographs, no letters, no keepsakes, no marked days, not even the idle filling in of O's in a newspaper headline. In fact, no newspaper.

The furniture was obviously military issue and came with the apartment. In the bedroom closet Knight found only one suit of clothing that was not a uniform, a conservative, dated, three-piece affair that still had the price tag in the pocket. Except for a few mundane, useful objects—a radio, a razor, a bottle of brandy—Dietrich owned nothing.

The man's kitchen told him that he ate out. His bathroom cabinet held a toothbrush, razor, and shaving soap. Knight felt that he had entered the hotel room of a stranger who was staying only one night.

Dietrich appeared to be his uniform and nothing else, but that was an identity that Knight understood. There was another practical object that he found in Dietrich's quarters, and this he now placed beside the bottle of brandy as he waited: it was a 9-mm Walther P-38, loaded and ready for use.

Knight heard Dietrich before he saw him. At least he heard the car skid to a halt and then quickly the running footsteps on the snow-free pavement and the slamming of the outer door. It was ten in the morning and the density of the fog kept the interior of the house obscured and shadowy. It was into this duskiness that Dietrich came running, already pulling at his tie, and without even glancing into the room where Knight waited in the semidarkness. The man ran directly to the hall opposite the entryway and to the bedroom, where Knight listened to him undress hurriedly and a minute later enter the bathroom. There was a moment when water ran into the hand basin, then that stopped and there was absolute silence. Knight began to count the seconds.

Dietrich was stripped to the waist when he came slowly into the living room and snapped on the lamp. He was carrying a bloodstained towel, filthy with coal dust. Knight held the gun steady in his left hand, his right too stiff to be of serious use to him now.

"Of course. The black man delivering fish. Someone mentioned it and I ignored it. And then, when I came in . . . that faint odor. . . . I thought I detected. . . ." He smiled rigidly. "I take it you brought the bicycle through the house." He threw the towel toward the open bathroom door.

For three hours Knight had rehearsed a number of witty openings for his meeting with Dietrich, but now his mouth clamped tightly shut and he blinked in dumb shock at the man's body: a grotesque scar ran from the right side of his neck over his collarbone and down the middle of his chest to his waist, where it disappeared under his belt. It was a thick white growth of tissue that had dozens of smaller scars running off of it at all angles along its whole length. Knight's hand shook. The ugly facial scar was only a nick compared to this ridge of flesh that cut the man's body lengthwise as though he had actually been severed vertically and sewn back together again, badly.

Dietrich walked toward him. "You may shoot whenever you want, Boy Scout." He laughed low in his throat. "No? Not ready yet? Well, in that case I'll have a drink." He walked across the room and took a glass from a cabinet. The back of his white torso bore no scars except on one shoulder, where an eruption of keloids spread down the whole length of his right arm. "You look like you've had quite a time of it."

Knight followed the man's movements with the gun. Dietrich picked up the brandy bottle and held it up to the light. "To an American this is half-full; to a German it is half-empty. An old joke; I'm sure you've heard it. Which of those is it to you?"

Knight remained silent.

Dietrich poured from the bottle and looked away from the glass with raised eyebrows. "Not ready for that either?" He placed the bottle on the table and sat in a chair opposite Knight. "I was just going out to chase down another rumor that you'd been caught. You've been caught all over the country, and in several other countries, too." He laughed and shook his head. "I should have reconsidered that idiotic story of a black man delivering fish, but someone said they saw a cyclist leave the club's delivery entrance a short time later, so I let it go. I realize now that in this fog, that could have been any number of individuals."

He leaned back in the chair. "You know, Knecht, I always knew I would find you. Naturally, I assumed I would be holding the gun." He raised his glass in a silent salute and drank.

All of Knight's fancy plans for this moment vanished. "Listen, you son of a black-hearted bitch, why are you after me?"

"Come now, Knecht, please, no games. You have the gun. Use it. If I had it, I assure you I would use it."

Knight's whole body shook in exasperated rage. "Dietrich, what the hell did I ever do to you?" He waited, but the German Colonel said nothing. "Now, goddamn it; I want some answers."

Dietrich gazed at him in a long silence, his eyes piercing, unblinking. Knight felt the man's hatred like a physical touch, a murderous embrace meant to crush his chest, explode heart and lungs, snap his spine. Knight spoke again, more quietly this time. "Look, Dietrich, I'd like to say something funny, like 'This game's gone far enough,' but I guess it hasn't, because you know me . . . and I don't know you."

"Liar."

"Dietrich, until that NATO briefing, I never saw you before in my life, but you obviously know something about me, as, for example, my German name. I haven't been called Knecht since I was a small kid. . . ."

"Did you think changing your name would make me stop looking for you all these years?"

"Changing . . . ? I didn't change it. Americans can't pronounce that rough 'ch.' To them it sounds like someone's clearing his throat or getting ready to spit. A teacher in school said it looked like Knight and spelled it that way. It stuck. Hell, I was only a kid; it made no difference to me. It's been this way for thirty years." He hesitated. "What do you mean 'looking for me'? Why were you looking for me? What years?"

Dietrich drank without taking his eyes off Knight. "When you were in Germany, you set a trap for me. Oh, it worked, all right, but you thought I was dead."

"You're crazy. I have never seen you before. We fought on different fronts. The guys quartered in the hotel in France all died. There were no wounded. Not even the civilians . . . that French family, they were all burned . . . or something else. Anyway, they all died. I found out later."

"That's nothing to me. That was the war. That was necessary."

"Then what the hell are you talking about?" Knight roared at him, the image of the dead child lying in the mud in front of his face as vividly unbearable as it was eighteen years ago.

"I'm talking about the hole in the wall. You knew about the pit on the other side. You set the trap."

Knight's mind whirled. "What pit?"

"The pit beside the Lahn. Oh, Boy Scout, you have the gun, you don't have to lie anymore."

252

Knight lowered the gun slowly, resting it on his thigh. Dietrich and his road map of scars dissolved. Nicholas faced the teacher who was announcing that the Knecht family was moving to America. She hoped that Hugo and Nicholas would not forget their old school chums, that friendships made in childhood were the sweetest of all, the most enduring, the most generous.

But Hugo was not at school that day: there was something about his having to help with the packing. So after school Nicholas walked home alone. When he reached the tobacco shop, the first of the boys came running out of the side streets, screaming. Long shadows cut across the cobbles as he ran from them, terror giving him great strength, great speed. The boys were older than he, bigger, and they shouted a name at him, all of them chanting in unison. He ran past the confectioner's, the clock shop, where the angel was trumpeting the hour. There, more boys came running out of the dark places. They carried stones, knives, pieces of chain. Nicholas ran for his life.

They were almost upon him when he came to the chemical factory's hole in the wall. He darted into it, ran again a short distance, and with a mighty leap bounded over the pit of glass, ran on, through some marshy land, and flung himself into the Lahn. He came up snorting and spitting, hearing for a brief moment a great anguished cry, and then confused shrieks and screams. He let the river carry him away peacefully from the mindless, wailing clamor.

He and Hugo had been warned about the gangs of boys as wild as wolves who roamed the streets in those days. They had managed to stay out of their way, to keep to themselves and get home before dark. It was a terrible time, and stories were told about the wild boys throwing rocks through windows and tearing gates from their hinges. They grew braver and beat up children and old men, raped lone girls on their way home from work.

Then suddenly they belonged to organized clubs and wore

uniforms: short pants, knee socks, and identical shirts with black-and-red armbands. It was from a bunch of these that Nicholas had escaped. He never returned to the school; a few days later his family got on the train at Lahnstein and left for America.

Knight breathed deeply, letting his eye wander over the geography of Dietrich's scars. "So that was you running after me." He paused a moment. "You know, you are way off on this; I didn't trap you. I didn't know what happened that day."

"Liar."

"How could I have known? I was in the river. When you guys started chasing me, calling me . . ." He laughed. "Boy Scout! Yes, Boy Scout! For years I tried to remember what name you were calling me. Hell, I thought you were going to kill me."

"No, Boy Scout, you thought you could kill *me*, leading me into a trap. You knew about the glass pit. You lived near there; you knew the place."

That was true: he knew the place, knew the pit had to be jumped if he wanted to reach the river, knew the twenty-foot-deep pit was half-filled with broken glass. Knight felt sick: he saw the shattered acid-wet bottles and test tubes with the rats gnawing on the stoppers. "You fell into that pit."

"You pushed me into that pit." Dietrich spoke quietly.

"I was in the river: you fell into the pit all by yourself."

"You knew of it; you led me to it. It's the same thing."

"Bullshit."

He searched Dietrich's face for recognition, for some lost moment in which he had looked into his face before. Except for the scar, he was a good-looking man. He had a delicate, almost fragile-looking nose, high cheekbones, clear corn-flower-blue eyes, a thin even mouth. It was one of those faces that for some obscure reason people called aristocratic. But, no; he had never seen him before. The man was older than

he; those boys had been twelve, thirteen. There must be four
or five years between them.

"Dietrich, there is something I never understood. Tell me,
why were you running after me?"

"Because you were a traitor."

"You're nuts. I was eight years old."

"You were leaving Germany."

"I was eight years old; I had no say in the matter."

"Anyone who abandons his country in time of need is a
traitor. We needed everyone—your father, your brother, you.
All of you should have been part of that manpower that was
essential to raise Germany up again to her rightful place as
the leader of Europe."

"Dietrich, you're not listening; I was barely eight years
old!"

"At eight I already knew Germany was my country. I
loved her even then, and I knew my duty to her as I understood her destiny."

Knight snorted. "Yeah? Well, I didn't have your advantages. All your kind lived in town, and that meant you had
time to belong to those marching clubs you were all in. I was
just a farmboy that never got to play your games. I didn't
know anything about destiny."

"No, you went to America to become a Boy Scout," he
sneered.

Knight laughed. "Oh, yeah? Is that what I did? Tell me,
Dietrich, what did you do?"

The other's eyes seemed to fade visibly, as though heat
were burning out the blue from within. "I survived your
murderous attempt on my life. It is true, I should have died.
No one understood why I did not die.

"Of course, I could never return to the Youth Group; they
took only perfect specimens. But in time, I could join the
Army, and that brought opportunities. Can you imagine how
far I might have gone if I were not cut up like this?" He ran
his hand over his pale thick crew-cut hair.

"Dietrich, Germany still would have lost the war—even if you had been Rommel's buddy. Even if they had let you run the whole show."

"But I would have had the glory of—"

"Shit."

"To you, perhaps, but if you had known Germany in those first years of the war, your blood would have been on fire. The panzer victories, the U-boat successes.... Ah, Knecht, the armies were glorious, not like this comic-opera army Germany has now ... conducted and controlled by other nations.

"*You* know what real soldiering is; you were in it."

"It was not glorious, Dietrich, not glorious!"

"Of course it was. Have you experienced anything as interesting as the war?" He leaned forward, his eyes bright, happy, mad. "Go talk to any ten men on the street who fought in World War II and ask them what was the high moment in their lives; all ten of them will tell you that it was the war!

"Haven't the last ten days been thrilling ... when you knew that you had outmaneuvered, outthought your enemy ... when you discovered you were still alive? Have you done, anything this exciting since nineteen-forty-five? No! You haven't. I see by your expression that I'm right. You have enjoyed it; it brought you face to face with your own life. Peace can never do that. War is progress; peace is decay. War makes you live your life, not piss it away buying insurance for when you're dead!" He poured another drink and leaned back again.

Knight thought of Tyler grasping the stake driven into his belly. "The young Captain who was with me died in the jump, and not very gloriously, either."

"Yes. Some children found him, stumbled over him in the snow."

Knight raged inwardly. *I really should kill this bastard.* He remained calm. "What about the dead men in Mechernich, the civilians?" He lowered his voice, aiming for dramatic effect.

"That turned out quite well, actually. They were poachers, and you know how we feel about our National Parks. They had already killed a half-dozen deer. Unforgivable! There were photographs on the front pages of all the papers showing the poor dead animals so brutally slaughtered. It really incensed the public. We feel very strongly about innocent animals."

"Yes, I remember reading that Hitler wept when his canary died, or was it his pet rat?"

"His dog."

Knight's fury erupted. "I didn't know that execution was the sentence for poaching. But then, out in the woods I suppose there was no time for a leisurely trial."

Dietrich smiled again. "They fired on the Army. Hardly an acceptable action in time of peace."

"So you came out of it all without any problems. Five men are dead and everything turned out just fine."

"Seven."

"Seven?"

"Yes, there were seven casualties: a survival team of Italians drowned. Their skiff was rammed on the Rhine by a police boat. And there were the usual broken bones. These accidents are all perfectly normal and expected."

Knight groaned inwardly. "They are all perfectly pointless and stupid, too."

"Come now, Knecht, we have to keep the sword of war sharpened."

"Do we?"

"Of course we do, and you know it. You wouldn't be here otherwise; you'd be out selling shoes or driving a trolley car. Can you see yourself driving a trolley car, Knecht?"

"Actually, I was thinking of becoming a farmer."

"That's very amusing."

"I thought you might think so."

"You will have to solve this little problem here before you go out and buy a cow." Dietrich laughed.

"I have no problem here. I don't have to shoot you, not that it hasn't crossed my mind a time or two, but I don't have to. And you can't shoot me. Until now I believed you were in serious trouble with the death of the civilians and had nothing left to lose by killing me. But I see that you are still in good standing, so it would not be at all acceptable for my body to be found in your quarters full of bullet holes from your gun.

"However, you could bore me to death. No, the game is over. I think I'll just cycle over to headquarters and check in. I reached Aachen—and with a day to spare—so *you'll* have to buy the champagne for your boys."

"Do you really believe, Knecht, that I can let you walk out of here, that after waiting for you all these years . . ."

"Dietrich, have you considered the possibility that you are mad?"

"Frequently. But I always manage to hold it at bay—that madness—by simply thinking about killing you. I have shot you, stabbed you; I have even pushed you into a pit of broken glass. In more lucid moments, I have devised the most exquisite methods of executing you. You cannot imagine the hours I spent dreaming of this day, the years I spent looking for you, the lists I searched for German-born Americans in the military. I knew you would return. Every scar on this body assured me you would return."

Looking at the man's largest scar as it widened at the belt, Knight, with a violent shock, suddenly knew how far the scar went and felt sick; a sympathetic pain in his groin writhed obscenely. He listened numbly as Dietrich went on.

"You may think that I am only being dramatic, but I was absolutely certain that one day you and I would meet. Can you imagine what I felt when I saw you on that stage ten days ago, knowing with absolute certainty that I had found the right man at last?"

258

"I can now," answered Knight hoarsely. After a short silence he went on. "Listen, Dietrich, you were twelve or thirteen back there on the Lahn when I was eight. I didn't know you from the others you ran with. I only heard things about all of you. We were in different levels in school. To an eight-year-old, thirteen is almost grown up. You—not just you, but all those bigger kids like you—already wore the uniforms of the Youth Groups with all the fancy emblems and paramilitary gear. I was a little kid with bad trouble at home, and you were already the boy-soldier ready to kill for the Fatherland. You had a view I never had: how dare anyone, except maybe a Jew, immigrate to America when the whole country was waiting to be saved.

"You called me 'Boy Scout.' That's funny, Dietrich; I didn't even know what a Boy Scout was. By the way, I never became a Boy Scout in America. No good deeds. No merit badges. No knots tied.

"Ah, Dietrich, you were cheated—even out of that. You would have liked to think I spent my time helping little old ladies to cross the street. But you see, there was no time for that; it was a time for survival. From the day you ran me down to the Lahn, it was a matter of survival. If it's any comfort to you, I've been at this game since I was eight years old, so I always had the advantage. I've had more experience than you, more than all your seven hundred hunter-capture team members put together.

"That day you asked after my credentials, I lied to you. A little experience with SAC in the Sierra Nevada foothills, I said to you, but that wasn't true. No, no, Dietrich, I admit that was unfair of me; I had all those important early years of practice. First you, then The Old Man. Ah, Dietrich, you should have known The Old Man. . . ."

"When you are through sentimentalizing, Knecht, you had better shoot. I will kill *you* if you don't kill *me*."

Knight tightened his grip on the gun and knew at once that Dietrich saw the faint movement. "As you said before, you are not holding the gun," began Knight, "and if you were—let us say for the moment that you were—and you shot me now, I'm afraid the Army would consider it murder. You would be sacrificing your own life. It's stupid to die, Dietrich, if you don't have to. One is dead so long."

"It's not necessary for either one of us to die." He knew that this was no longer true, but he went on anyway, speaking rather casually, while a dark fear crept into his soul. "This whole bloody business makes no sense anymore. If it means that much to you ... what the hell ... you can bring me in; then you can be the jolly good fellow—even a hero— and I can look like a dope." He smiled and waited for the man to lunge at him, but Dietrich never moved; even his facial expression remained the same—bland, assured, reasonable.

"You're being a Boy Scout, Knecht. You think I need help from a Boy Scout? No, no, I have no intention of bringing you in; I'll win that one because you won't show up. And it won't look like murder at all. You think I would jeopardize my career because of you?"

"You're overlooking something, Colonel: I *have* shown up."

Dietrich rose. Knight kept the gun aimed at him. "Well, Boy Scout, you better shoot. It's your last chance."

Knight stared at the smiling Dietrich, who looked all the world as though he had a mouthful of the devil's gizzard and loved it. The man had no weapon in his hands; he was stripped to the waist, and a gun was aimed at him. He laughed and started to turn away, but he never completed the pivot; in midstride he brought the full force of his boot down on Knight's broken ankle.

Knight screamed and for a few seconds he believed the gun, no longer in his hand, actually went off, but the loud noise was only the breaking of the low table on which his foot had rested. For a time the room was totally black. When the light returned, Dietrich was holding the gun by the barrel. Knight tried to get up off his knees, but nothing seemed to work. In a curious gray twilight, he saw the butt of the gun swing away from him, then come toward him again. He started to turn his face. The gun caught him on the side of the head. A long moment later he felt it hit him again, but there was no pain by then at all.

It seemed to Nicholas that he took a long time in falling: he saw Dietrich's wound disappear under a belt buckle, then the splintered edge of the table drifted past him, and finally the carpet tilted and rose to meet him.

29

WHEN Knight regained consciousness, he was in the trunk of a moving car. His head beat hideously and his damaged foot lay twisted under his own right boot. He shifted his legs and all the stars in the universe exploded in front of his face. The sound of the engine, the hiss of the tires on a wet surface, all vanished inside the roaring time bomb that was his head. He fought for consciousness.

I'm supposed to do something. What am I supposed to do? My hands. Where are my hands?

He breathed deeply and passed through the pain inside his head and leg to reach the rest of his body, which seemed to have vanished altogether. He concentrated on his hands: one arm was under him; one lay flung toward the back of the compartment. He moved it. *Ah, that's my right one. Good.* He flexed the fingers; they moved as one, like a lath bending under pressure. *The river at the walled city did that ... there was a snake, or something, that stung and whipped away.*

No. No. Not a snake. Someone was shooting from the ramparts.

When was that? Friday? Saturday? Sunday? Not Sunday. Sunday was Erda.

It was the day before Erda. Remember the market stalls in the walled town? It was raining.

Yes.

You're way past that. You're in Aachen. You came through the gate with a day to spare. That was Wednesday.

Ah, yes, Wednesday.... What day is it now?

What's the difference? It's all over, you moron. You knew you had to kill him. Why didn't you shoot him when he told you to? What the hell were you waiting for? You know ... you were better in blackface.

I know. I know.

He raised his hand and touched the lid, estimating six or seven inches of clearance. A big car. Gingerly he groped in the darkness around him: Erda's coat and the miner's rain cape were in the trunk with him. *Of course. Dietrich has to get rid of all the evidence. My flashlight and compass might be ...* The compass was there, but the knife and light were missing.

Did you think he would leave them for you?

No, no. But he might have forgot....

Ha ha. You really think so? Don't worry, you'll see the knife again.

He's not going to cut me up, if that's what you mean; and he can't afford to have my body found with his bullets in it, either.

Right. He's looking for an accident. And maybe he knows just where to make one and maybe he's just cruising around for inspiration.

Knight struggled to free his left arm, every move adding to the pain. When it was out from under him, he could not understand why the iridescent pointers of the watch refused to glow. He touched the face of it with his stiffened fingers and felt only a bit of jagged metal. His compass, too, was crushed.

Dietrich smashed them.

Why?

Why not? He's going to have to dump you somewhere, somewhere fatal. Why not mess you up first, so it will all look convincing when some hikers—probably children picking wildflowers—find your bones in the spring? You are going to be one of those perfectly normal and expected accidents.

For a time Knight entered into the pain in his leg, picked up its rhythm—the concentric circles that flowed outward from a tight hot center. Years ago, he had learned to deal with pain, learned not to fight it by struggling fiercely against it, but to join it, even as something weightless and unrigid lets itself be lifted and carried easily by the unceasing waves of the tide.

The road on which the car moved was smooth and without much traffic. Occasionally Knight heard another car pass, and several times he heard a laboring truck, which Dietrich passed. They had to be in the mountains, but where? To the north were the flatlands of Holland and the Cologne basin; to the west, Belgium lay mountainless to Liege; in the south, the Venn plateau stretched across the frontier between Germany and Belgium. So it had to be east—back across the Eifel toward the Rhine. Dietrich had no choice except to dump him in Germany. Knight considered the roads on the map in his memory: except for the freeway hemming in Aachen and one fine highway going southeast through the nature parks, there were only secondary roads across the hills back to the lakes, and considering their winding nature, that could mean forty or fifty kilometers before he found a good place for an accident—and it would have to be in line with the direction the survival teams would have taken to get to Aachen.

The survival teams! He thought now of the whole absurd operation. It was all idiocy to him. Tyler's snow-shrouded body found by children running to the woods on a happy holiday morning before Christmas. Two men drowned in the Rhine. Would their ghosts climb out of the dark water on some demon-hunting night and slosh to the towers to pull the bell ropes with their blue, fish-smelling hands?

Ah, Hugo, Hugo, it's all such madness. Remember the children shooting at the animals? My God, Hugo, the children have guns! Do you suppose they hit the dolphin?

He blinked into the darkness. *Hugo, back there when we lived near the Lahn, do you think I led him to that glass? Think of it . . . running with great strides into that pit.*

The darkness looked back at him. *You should have shot him.*

I couldn't.

Why not?

I don't know.

What if you did lead him to the pit beside the Lahn? What do you think they would have done to you if they had caught you? There must have been ten or fifteen of them, and all of them armed with knives and pieces of chain. Remember the story that got around about a boy in another town who made fun of one of those Youth Clubs, who laughed at their comical marching? They ran him down one night and cut off his pecker.

Knight groaned.

You better think up something in a hurry, no telling how long he's been driving. He may be stopping soon. Look for tire tools or start considering lupines growing up through your eyepits around April.

Knight groped around in the trunk. Nothing.

Play possum. Be deadweight when he opens that lid. Give yourself time to size up the opportunities. If there aren't any, at least take the bastard with you—if you can. Why didn't you shoot him?

For the hundredth time—I don't know!

I'll never understand that. And he knew you weren't going

*to shoot him. He counted on it. That insulting offer to let him
bring you in—that really gave you away.*

*Look, I know it was dumb, but I was ready to try anything
except kill him. I thought if he came for me I could hit him
with the gun, but he didn't.*

*So why didn't you shoot him in the leg? Even things up a
little.*

*Even things up! My God, the scars! How the hell could I
shoot at all those scars ... and I know damn well from the
size and shape of those gashes spreading below his belt that
he can't have much of a cock left. No lack of balls, I expect.
But can't you see what a crummy life he's had? Look at his
quarters! There's nobody living there. And I expected to find
pictures of a woman ... a family ... someone ... anyone ...
anyone that he loved. And what about that dumb-looking
suit? It's amazing to me that he bought that suit at all. ...
Why did he? A blind moment of hope? What the hell does he
say to his face every morning when he's holding that razor in
his hand?*

You didn't do it to him.

*I don't even know that. He believes I did. For thirty years
he has believed it. Poor bastard ... hating that much all those
years. He really wanted me to kill him. And I knew it! That
was the strange part. Ten days ago when I first saw him at
the briefing, I had the damnedest feeling that one day we'd
be looking at each other across a distance that had nothing to
do with space or time. When he started to turn away I think I
even knew he was going to get something to kill me with. Oh,
I didn't expect him to mash my foot. I thought he probably
had another gun. He has to kill me. He can't go on living
without killing me first. Maybe he even believed me that I
didn't trap him, but he can't stop now ... too many years of
fighting a phantom that's so close to him it's part of him.*

So what are you going to do, lie down and die for him?

The car slowed, turned off one surface and onto another.
Knight listened: snow. Dietrich was driving on snow. Still

fairly smooth, but a road not used much, or it would have been cleared. He began to count in his head, lost the count when the car bounced over something, and started again.

Three minutes later, more or less, the car slowed again and stopped. Knight heard the door open and close. He counted again—much longer than Dietrich needed to get to the trunk. *Reconnaissance. That would be Dietrich, the perfectionist, checking out the terrain for the perfect accident.*

The trunk opened slowly. Even with his face turned away from the outside, Knight knew at once that it was nearing twilight. The air was cold, thin, and he caught the scent of pines. He heard the muffled sound of cascading water, but it seemed a long way off to him.

Dietrich took Erda's coat and stretched it out on the ground behind the car. Straining and swearing, he dragged Knight over the bumper and let him drop onto the garment. Knight lay still in apparent crumpled unconsciousness, his face partially in the snow.

A moment later Dietrich dragged the coat with its unwieldy burden away from the car. There was almost no fog, only some light drifting mists through which Knight caught a glimpse of some kind of wooden construction, then the coat slid out from under him.

Dietrich, swearing steadily, rolled Knight's body back onto the Army coat and dragged it across an obstruction that was sharp and metallic. He pulled the coat viciously over something that felt to Knight like wood: evenly spaced squared-off pieces of wood. It was a railroad track; and the construction Knight had seen was a trestle spanning a gorge. Abruptly the sound of the water was louder, clearer, coming from below him in a lusty, deep-echoing rumble.

Dietrich pulled him steadily for some distance as Knight carefully inched off the coat, finally rolling off entirely and lying inert between the rails.

The German Colonel wiped his forehead with his sleeve,

swore, and started to walk back across Erda's coat. Knight rose to one knee, grasped the shoulder of the coat, and violently jerked the garment out from under the man's feet. Dietrich made no sound at all as he did an odd little dance in the air, coming down with both feet on one slippery rail, teetering wildly, his body swinging out of control. Knight, on his knees, reached out for him with his right arm, which Dietrich actually tried to grasp, his mouth making large, soundless words into the air, his eyes locked for a split second into Nicholas' horrified stare, before he slipped off the outer edge of the rail and sailed backward into space.

Knight, his right hand still extended while his left held the coat, gaped at the spot where Dietrich had done his gravity-defying jig before he vanished. Into that vacancy there now entered a ratty-coated magician, holding one arm up in exaltation to the cheering crowd while the other still clutched the white tablecloth pulled from beneath the china and crystal that sparkled on a carnival stage.

Knight collapsed on the ties with a moaning cry. Slowly his streaming eyes focused on the wild river seventy feet below, where green and white water churned around massive boulders. Dietrich lay caught in the wedge formed by two large gray stones, his head twisted over his shoulder so that he gazed upstream. He appeared to be hiding between the rocks, waiting for someone, his left hand braced against the edge of one of the stones as if to keep himself from slipping.

Knight shivered at the cold and the pain and a sorrow that seemed older than his life. It was twilight and he was a child lost in The Bad Time, trapped out in the layers of gray after sundown. He was crying, running down dim deserted roads, across barren fields, searching for warmth and light, for home.

After a time he crawled back to Dietrich's car. Half-mad with pain, he slowly drove the forty kilometers back to Aachen and the base, where the sentries saluted the German

Colonel's car smartly as Knight sailed through the gate without stopping.

In the stunned presence of several NATO officers, including the Commanding General, who was irritable at having to leave his bridge game, Knight made his report. Except for a shot of morphine, he refused medical aid until he was finished. A detail was sent to retrieve the German Colonel's body.

Everyone was unwittingly eager to verify his story: Dietrich had left the base at noon, they told him, saying he had a lead on where Knight was holed up. Knight admitted that he had hitched a ride near the lakes and that the driver did look him over suspiciously, so at a crossroad he left the car and headed for the railroad, where he hoped to catch a slow-moving train near the trestle. He was waiting under a signal shed on the other side of the crossing when he heard Dietrich cry out. He looked up just in time to see the man slip and fall.

It was twenty-one hundred hours when Knight, a little light-headed from the drug, but not enough to make him careless, was still setting everything straight for the record. He was convinced that the three German officers listening did not believe any of it—not that that made any difference. As far as he was concerned, they could sit there looking at him through steadily narrowing eyes until they shut them altogether and commenced to snore.

"He would never have come after me if I hadn't hitched that ride, and I wouldn't have a busted ankle. . . ."

"Yes, well, we expect those things to happen," snapped the General, glowering at Knight, whose ripe odor had caused the four men present to keep a polite distance. "Can't cry about a broken ankle when a man is dead."

"Two," said Nicholas.

"Two what?" asked the General, as the Germans shuffled their feet and gave each other uncomfortable glances.

"Two are dead. Tyler died in the jump. I assumed he'd been found."

"Yes, Colonel," said one of the Germans after a little silence. "Captain Tyler was found. By some civilians, I believe." The officer resumed his tight-lipped expression.

The General cleared his throat and looked into the pipe bowl he'd been scraping with a penknife for the previous ten minutes. "Yes, yes. There *were* two casualties. Of course, Tyler's already been taken care of, family notified and all that, so no problems there." He paused and sucked on the pipe, making a gurgling sound. "These kinds of things are all perfectly normal and expected. We must remember, gentlemen, that we can gear these operations for total safety only on paper. In the field, there is always the unexpected."

Knight's head, already a little cloudy, worked around with the "expected/unexpected" and came up with the vision of Tyler impaled on the grape stake.

He listened to the General drone on. "Still, all in all, two casualties is within the reasonable range, so I think we can consider the operation a success. There are some valuable lessons to be learned here, and when the reports are in, we'll have some good material on file."

Knight looked from one man to the next, but nobody mentioned the other six dead men. The senior German officer commented that from his point of view, he, too, felt that the exercise had been highly successful. The other two also added comments of polite agreement, and a discussion on the merits of more maneuvers to keep the troops from getting soft was well under way when Knight, who had eaten nothing but snow since he'd had the can of sardines in the coal yard, vomited without warning.

Three days later, he hobbled out of the hospital on crutches to attend Dietrich's funeral. It was raining. A dozen men in uniform stood in two uneven rows in the drizzle. There were no civilians. Knight, who irritably told his driver to take away the umbrella and stay in the staff car, approached one of the mourners. "Were you a close friend of his?"

The man looked embarrassed, shrugged, and gave an evasive answer. Knight asked him again. Another soldier next to the first spoke up. "American, we are here because the Commandant insisted. None of us knew him well. He wouldn't allow it. If you want to know the truth, he was ruthless, cold-blooded, held his hand open to no man. We are here for duty."

Minutes after the service, Knight stood alone in the soldiers' cemetery, the rain falling more heavily, and the driver of the staff car standing ten feet away holding the open umbrella.

The next day, he was flown back to Wiesbaden.

For two months Knight convalesced in Wiesbaden, his ankle bones realigned with pins, and eighty percent of his vision returned to his right eye. Every night he dreamed, usually of Erda, but occasionally of Hugo.

One night he dreamed about Dietrich. They were fighting on the railroad bridge that spanned the snowdrifted gorge. Locked in a fatal embrace from which he could not disentangle himself, Nicholas went over the side with his deadly enemy. In all prior dreams of falling, his terror usually awakened him before the impact, but in this fall, he hit the bladelike rocks seventy feet below without injury, got up, and walked away along the river, passing a cluster of sun-laced willows and sugar sand, old, familiar, as sweet as summer. He believed a voice awakened him, but when he turned on the light, he was alone. He lay awake until morning, making no effort to sleep. He tried to remember the years since he left Hugo beside the river, but all the events seemed to grow out of his past as wild grasses in a meadow, their roots commingling and inseparable. Only the ten days of his journey in December came to him clearly and without confusion, their minutest details sharp in his memory: the unfaded blue eyes of the Abbess; the oblique circling of the ravens above the dead castle where he slept in the oven; the smooth blunt noses of the cows which sniffed him as he crossed the Rhine; the farmer cupping his wife's breasts with his hands as the two made love in the barn.

He felt great joy at the memory of Erda's silver horse quivering under his touch, the shape of Erda's wrist as she worked on his wounded eye, Erda drying her hips and thighs as she stepped from her bath, Erda filling his glass with apple juice at dinner, Erda saying good-bye: "We wish you well and hope for your safety." How desperately and hopelessly he had wanted to tell her the truth, only to discover that lies alone could have been believable.

He thought of Mechernich, where someone died in his place; of the old night-watchman/soldier from another war weeping over his tarnished trinkets; the rat eyes glinting in the garbage heap; the horrified faces of the demon-hunters before they sprang upon him; the hunched, animal shapes of the Army trucks in the fog under the freeway lights at Aachen.

Of Dietrich he remembered everything: the man's barren cupboard save for a single bottle of brandy, his razor and soap, the expensive never-worn suit in the closet, his scars—those seen, those surmised. But most clearly, Nicholas remembered his first and last wild look into the man's soul as their hands, almost touching, reached for each other on the trestle.

He did not know by morning what he was going to do about his life, but he knew where he was going to begin. On a fine spring day, when he was able to drive again, he crossed the Rhine and headed back into the Eifel uplands to return the borrowed overcoat.